THE Lighthouse INN

A. M. KUSI

Published by A. M. Kusi 2020

amkusinovels@gmail.com

Visit our website at www.amkusi.com

Editor: Anna Bishop of CREATING ink

Sensitivity Edit: Renita McKinney of A Book A Day

Proofreader: Judy's Proofreading

Cover Design: Regina Wamba of ReginaWamba.com

ISBN: 978-1949781182

OTHER BOOKS BY A. M. KUSI

A Fallen Star (eBook FREE on all retailers)

(Shattered Cove Series Book 1)

Glass Secrets

(Shattered Cove Series Book 2)

Defying Gravity

(Shattered Cove Series Book 3)

His True North

(Shattered Cove Series Book 5)

The Orchard Inn (eBook FREE on all retailers)

(Book 1 in The Orchard Inn Romance Series)

Conflict of Interest

(Book 2 in The Orchard Inn Romance Series)

Her Perfect Storm

(Book 3 in The Orchard Inn Romance Series)

For a complete list of all our books, visit:

WWW.AMKUSI.COM/BOOKS

"I can talk to you about broken families, addiction, depression, loss, survival, grief, heartache, death, abuse, neglect, abandonment, suicide and betrayal.
I can also talk to you about empathy, kindness, compassion, love, energy, forgiveness, self-love, self-care, strength, peace, healing, recovery, unity, gratitude, grace, hope and the power of positivity.
All these experiences have taken part in creating the woman I am today. I am a combination of both the light and the darkness. I may be flawed but even with rough edges I'm still worth loving. I am not ashamed of my story.
I am a survivor."

- Donna, daughter, sister, survivor.

"There is nothing stronger than a broken woman that has rebuilt herself."

– Hannah Gadsby

DEDICATION

This series is dedicated to all those out there who've been through trauma and decided to not let it define you. To those who do the hard work to break the patterns. To the cycle breakers, we see you.

A note to readers: *This book has sensitive subject matter that deals with abuse, both physical and sexual, that may be triggering for some.*

GET A FREE SHORT NOVEL

Join our newsletter to get a FREE short novel that's not available on any retailer. Plus updates about new releases, giveaways, pre-orders, sneak peeks, and more.

Visit the website below to join now.

WWW.AMKUSI.COM/NEWSLETTER

TABLE OF CONTENTS

1.	Jasmine	1
2.	Atlas	10
3.	Jasmine	18
4.	Atlas	26
5.	Jasmine	34
6.	Atlas	41
7.	Jasmine	51
8.	Atlas	62
9.	Jasmine	67
10.	Atlas	72
11.	Jasmine	78
12.	Jasmine	86
13.	Atlas	96
14.	Jasmine	103
15.	Atlas	113
16.	Jasmine	120
17.	Jasmine	131
18.	Atlas	137
19.	Atlas	145
20.	Jasmine	151
21.	Atlas	157
22.	Jasmine	166
23.	Atlas	175
24.	Jasmine	185
25.	Atlas	195
26.	Jasmine	203
27.	Jasmine	209
28.	Atlas	213
29.	Jasmine	219
30.	Atlas	228
31.	Jasmine	233
32.	Atlas	239
33.	Atlas	248

34.	Jasmine	255
35.	Jasmine	258
36.	Jasmine	263
37.	Atlas	273
38.	Jasmine	278
	Epilogue - Jasmine	282
	Sneak Peek of His True North	291
	Join Our Newsletter	299
	Thank You	301
	About A. M Kusi	303
	Also by A. M. Kusi	305

1

JASMINE

Jasmine pulled the sheet over the two fluffy pillows, smoothing out the wrinkles before reaching for the soft, pink comforter. A paper card fell off the night-stand. Picking it up, she smiled. *Happy Mother's Day, Mommy!* The script no doubt belonged to one of her sisters-in-law, but the shakily scribbled Z's all over the card were from her favorite person in the world. Zoey had drawn two smiling faces: one for Jasmine and one for herself. Jasmine set the card back on the nightstand before running her hand over the bedspread once more. Never in a million years would she have imagined having such a feminine color in her space. Mother-hood had changed more than just her body.

After tucking the edge of the comforter under the pillow, she moved across the small room she shared with her three-year-old daughter. She pulled open the old and worn dresser, wiggling it side to side at the same time so it wouldn't stick. Like everything in her life, it had been used almost beyond its limit. She placed Zoey's carefully folded clothes inside before wriggling it closed again. She scanned the room, catching the few dolls scattered across the floor. Jasmine bent and picked them up, opening the wooden dollhouse that Mikel, her brother, had made especially for Zoey. He'd painted it bright pink at her request. Jasmine bit back her smile. Only she would end up with such a girly girl for a daughter and be terrified.

She sighed, tracing the edge of the doll's expression. The two smiling faces on Zoey's Mother's Day card flashed in her mind. Her chest tightened. *Would Zoey have had a better life if I'd let someone adopt her? Would she have two parents who loved her, rather than just me? I can barely keep a roof over her head and used clothes on her quickly growing body.*

Maybe it had been selfish to keep Zoey, but the moment she'd seen that little heart beating on the ultrasound, she'd known: she'd never be able to give her up. *But will I be good enough? Will I be able to protect her? Will she resent me when she knows what I've done? Who I was?* Life would be so much easier if Jasmine was someone else with a different past.

The walls seemed to be closing in. Her ribs squeezed and the backs of her eyes burned. She gently placed the doll inside the wooden house and straightened. Taking a deep breath, she steadied herself. *I just need to keep doing better. For Zoey.* Her phone chirped, jarring her out of her thoughts. She had one guest checking in today, and that was what she should have been focusing on. She needed guests to keep her inn—her livelihood—afloat.

She wiped her hands on her ripped jean shorts that had seen better days and opened her door. As she walked down the stairs to the desk, a tall figure caught her eye. His back was to her, all attention focused on the painting of the crashing ocean waves on the wall.

"Good morning. You must be Mr. Remington."

A low chuckle sent a shiver through her. "My father is Mr.

Remington. I'm just Atlas."

She smiled politely as her eyes darted to his face, and she froze. Time stopped. The air evaporated as terror gripped her heart and squeezed it like a vise. His tall frame filled out an expensive-looking suit. His black hair was long at the top and flecked with grey at the shorter sides. Dark scruff peppered his perfectly chiseled jaw. She shivered, remembering the way it had felt brushing across her shoulder. And those eyes. Grey and bright. She only knew one other person with the same cloudy orbs. *Zoey.*

He'd changed some in the last four years since she'd seen him. Not that she'd had much time to really look at him before she'd nodded towards the dingy bathroom in the bar where he'd followed her and bent her over the sink. Flames of embarrassment lapped at her skin. She'd been looking for an escape that night, and the stranger had been more than willing to help.

Atlas. Atlas Remington. She finally had a name for Zoey's biological father.

"What are you doing here?" She gasped. Was he here to take Zoey from her? Had he known all this time? *No.* That wasn't possible. No one knew what had happened in that bathroom except them.

His eyebrows furrowed. "Uh, checking in. I should have a reservation for two weeks."

Did he not recognize her? Was it possible? He'd smelled strongly of whiskey that night. Maybe he had no idea who she was.

"Right. Sorry. We don't know each other, do we?" She held her breath.

"I think I'd remember if we did." He smiled. Was he flirting with her?

"What are you in town for?" she asked carefully, finding

his paperwork.

He looked around the room at the high, white patched ceiling and then over to the paint-chipped furniture, rather than at her before he answered. "Just needed a little vacation."

"And you chose my inn? Was it my two Yelp reviews that convinced you?" She couldn't hold back her smile.

He chuckled again. Those grey eyes flashing as they focused on her. "I like the location and wanted to see it for myself. The pictures didn't do it justice though."

Her eyes flicked down momentarily. "Well, someday I'll hire a professional photographer."

"Oh, no. The pictures were great. I just meant it's even better in person." He smiled, showing off his perfect, white teeth. Good God. Was he a toothpaste model?

"Do you need my credit card?" he asked.

Shit. She'd been staring. "Uh, no. It's all on file. Just sign here." She pointed to the space on the form ready and waiting on the counter. "You have the Lighthouse suite like you requested. There are extra towels in the closet in the bathroom. I'll come in to clean every three days unless you need it done sooner—just let me know."

He nodded and scribbled his signature on the paper. Jasmine held out the lone key ring with a lighthouse chain and his receipt. "I'll charge the card you provided when booking with any incidentals. Your room is just up the stairs to the left." *Across from mine.* "There's a sign on the door. The silver key works for the front door, and the brass key is for your room. Did you need more than one set, or will it just be you staying with us?"

"Just me. The one is fine." He took it from her and reached to grab a duffel bag she hadn't noticed in the shock of seeing her baby daddy from a one-night stand—if you could even call it that. Were ten-minute stands a thing?

"Enjoy your stay. I leave my number at the desk here." She pointed to the folded card stock sign right next to the one stating *No cash kept on premises*. "And it's also on the copy of your receipt. Just text me if you need anything and I'm not at the front desk."

"You run the inn by yourself?"

She smiled with pride. "Yes, I do."

He nodded and grabbed the papers before walking towards the stairs. She waited until the click of his door closing sounded to let out the breath she'd been holding.

"Holy fucking shit." She placed a shaky hand over her racing heart as if it would help to calm the panic.

She whipped out her phone and stepped into the large kitchen, dialing her big brother Bently's number.

He picked up on the second ring. "Hey, Jas. You on your way?"

She swallowed hard before answering. Jasmine didn't need her brother freaking out and showing up here to make things worse. Even she didn't know what the hell was going on yet. "Uh, no. Actually, I need you to keep Zoey overnight."

"Is everything okay?" The concern in his voice brought a rush of guilt crashing over her.

Not even close to okay. Of all the people in her life, Bently had been the one constant—the only person she could count on. She hated to lie, but she'd brought enough trouble to their family. No. She'd handle this on her own.

"I have everything under control, Bent. I just need you to do this and not ask me any questions. Okay? I'll owe you one." More like a million, but who was counting?

"Okay. Fine. Anything you need," Bently said.

"Thank you. I'll call before bed to say goodnight to her."

"Sounds good." Bently ended the call.

Jasmine opened her contacts. She needed to talk to

someone about this. But her best friend, Remy, was married to Mikel, and she was shit at keeping secrets from him. The last thing Jasmine wanted was her two overprotective brothers jumping in to save her. *Again.* She'd caused them all enough pain. This was her doing and she would fix this. *Somehow.*

She scrolled through her contacts until Emma's name popped up and hit call before she could back out. It rang and rang until her friend picked up.

"Jazzy! Hey, mama. I got a quick break from the studio. How are you?" Emma asked as background music filtered through the phone.

Jasmine covered her mouth with her hand, trying to quiet the sob that surprised even her.

"Jas? What's wrong? Are you okay?" Emma asked. The noise grew quieter, as if she'd moved away.

"He's here," she managed.

"Who's there?"

"Zoey's father. He's staying at my inn."

Emma was silent for a few beats. "Is this a good thing or a bad thing?"

She couldn't blame her friend for not knowing. There were several things Jasmine kept locked away in a vault of topics she wouldn't talk about. Zoey's biological father was one of them. She was too ashamed.

"I don't know, honestly." Jasmine wiped the tears from her eyes and walked out to the back deck. Salty sea air blew gently over her skin as waves crashed in the distance.

"Okay. Does he know about Zoey?"

"I don't even think he remembers me."

"Oh, sweetie."

"I—I don't know what to do." Jasmine shook her head.

"I wish I could offer advice, but you have never said anything about this guy."

Jasmine sighed. "I know. It's a part of my past that I'd like to omit. I did a lot of fucked-up things, and I'd just rather forget the girl I used to be."

"I get it . . . So, can you explain how you made a baby with him, but he somehow can't recognize you?" Emma asked carefully.

Flashes came back of that dark bar. Those grey eyes had burned her skin with awareness, making it clear exactly what he'd wanted from her before he'd ever even offered to buy her a drink.

"He was just a guy from a bar. We never exchanged names, just . . . body fluids."

"Thanks for the mental image," Emma said and laughed. "Is he hot?"

Jasmine rolled her eyes. "On a one-to-ten scale, he's an eleven."

"Damn, girl. So, how can this godlike man not recognize you? Tell me it was something kinky like a sex party with masks."

Jasmine laughed. Only Emma could take a subject like this and turn it into something to laugh about. "It was less than ten minutes in a bathroom and I never saw him again . . . until today."

"Was it a good ten minutes?" Emma asked.

Jasmine blew out through her nose. "It was . . . okay." Achieving orgasm with a partner was pretty rare for her. Zoey's father hadn't been one of those unicorn moments.

"Hot but not great in the sack. Got it. Well, we can't all be perfect. Maybe you should try sleeping with a woman; I've never not had an orgasm with a woman. With guys, it's fifty-fifty."

"I wish I could be sexually attracted to a woman." They seemed safer.

"Okay, so maybe it is a good thing your baby daddy is back in your life," Emma suggested.

Jasmine paced back and forth over the long porch. "How exactly?"

"You can get to know him and see if he's a decent guy. Maybe Zoey can have her dad in her life after all."

Jasmine stopped, a rush of dizziness spinning though her head. She sat on the ground with her head lowered to her knees. "I'm scared. What if he tries to take her from me? What if he says I'm a bad mom? What if—"

"What if he's a great father? What if Zoey could have two parents in her life? What if he can help provide for her and take some of that stress off you?"

Jasmine blinked back more tears. She hated showing her emotions like this, but that was something else that motherhood had changed. She couldn't hide anymore.

Emma had a point. Jasmine wouldn't let fear stand in the way of Zoey's chances of happiness. If Atlas was a good father, and she didn't try, then she'd be robbing Zoey of something Jasmine herself had never had but always wanted. She couldn't hold the man's sexual history against him. After all, she'd done the same thing—more than once.

"You're right. I'll get to know him. I'll see if he's a safe person, observe how good he is with Zoey. Then I'll tell him."

"I'm here for you. Whatever you need," Emma offered.

"Thank you. I appreciate it. Can you keep this between us for now? I don't want Remy to find out just yet. She'll tell Mikel and then—"

"And then you'll have two big brothers and their best friend knocking on your door and getting into the middle of your business. I got you."

Jasmine laughed. "They probably wouldn't even knock. They'd bust the thing down."

Emma giggled. "True. Well, I know they have your back, but I also respect your right as Zoey's mother to do what you think is right."

"You're the best, Em."

"Tell that to my stepbrother the next time you see him." Emma laughed again, but this time it sounded forced.

"I'll mention it to Link," Jasmine promised. It was a hopeless cause, much to her friend's dismay.

"Okay, well, I gotta get back. Almost done with this album and then I start my tour next week," Emma said.

"I'm so happy that your dream is becoming a reality. Soon you'll be too famous to be my friend."

"Never!"

"Talk to you later." Jasmine smiled.

"Love you, bitch."

"You too." Jasmine slipped the phone in her back pocket and got to her feet once more.

Taking a deep breath, she stared past the tall beach grass and rose hip bushes towards the expanse of green-blue waves. They crashed against the rocks to her left and licked the sandy coast to her right as the ocean tide worked its way in. She could do this. For Zoey, she'd do anything. If that meant giving her father a chance, she'd do it. And if it meant keeping who he was a secret for the rest of her time on earth, she'd do that too.

Because Zoey would not go through the shit she'd been through. Jasmine would work through the pain of the past so that her daughter didn't have to have one-tenth of the trauma in her life that Jasmine had had. She'd protect her daughter, no matter what it took. Jasmine knew better than anyone that of all the people in a child's life, the father figure could be the most dangerous.

2

ATLAS

tlas placed his bag on the navy-blue comforter and stretched his neck from side to side. He walked over to the window and opened it. Salty sea air rushed into the room, the white curtains billowing. Seagulls cawed and sage-green waves crashed before they lapped at the sandy beach.

"Definitely not New York City," he said to himself.

Turning, he took in the simple room. One large dresser swallowed up most of the space next to the door. It was white with the weathered look that seemed to be in style. To his left was a giant wrought-iron king bed covered with grey linen sheets with several over-stuffed pillows on top. Two bedside tables were tucked against the headboard on each side and topped with white honeycomb ceramic lamps. Each thoughtful piece added to the character of the inn.

He opened the white door to his right with the lighthouse painted on it. It was a small bathroom but included a large tub with jets. Atlas went back to the bed and lay on the mattress. He kicked off his dress shoes and folded his arms under his head to look out the large bay window. The real treasure of the bedroom was the view to the beach.

Bzzz. Bzzzz. Bzzzz.

He pulled his phone out of his pocket and glanced at Oliver's name flashing on the screen, and smiled before answering. "Calling to congratulate me, big brother?"

"On what?" Oliver asked.

"Me closing the deal on this inn."

His brother scoffed. "Didn't you just get there?"

"Ah, it's only a matter of time. It'll be a done deal in two weeks. Then you can kiss that CEO spot goodbye." The innkeeper had been beautiful, but she was young—surely a large sum of money would convince her to be on her way soon enough.

"Your arrogance never ceases to amaze me." Oliver chuckled. "You know as well as I do this is a lost cause."

Atlas sat, his jaw ticcing. "Just because you couldn't get it done doesn't mean I can't."

"Look, bro. You wanna waste your time in Nowheresville, that's your mistake. I called because I have some news," Oliver said, his voice dipping.

Atlas's brows furrowed. *Did Mother and Father already name him the new CEO of the Remington empire?* His stomach clenched. "What is it?" he asked cautiously.

"I thought you should know—you're gonna be an uncle."

Atlas sucked in a breath. "Wow. Christina must be ecstatic. The in vitro worked?"

"Third time's the charm. She's eighteen weeks."

There was no need to ask why they'd waited so long to tell him. Her last two pregnancies hadn't lasted more than 3 months. "I'm happy for you, Olli. Tell Christina I said congrats."

"I will."

Olli really had it all now. He had his parents' approval, a wife who seemed to fit perfectly into his life, and a child on the way.

"Well, I've gotta go. Just wanted to let you know," Oliver said.

"Thanks, man. Talk to you later." Atlas tapped his screen and ended the call before he ran a hand over his face and let out a long breath.

The joy for his brother was quickly diminished by a sinking pressure building within him. His mother was sure to be on his case even more now that Oliver had checked all the boxes of perfect son. It was hard not to compare himself to his brother; people had done it all his life. *Damn.* He really needed to get his shit together. Not that he hadn't been giving his all. Recognition wasn't too much to ask for—especially after his hard work and sacrifice for the company. The inn owner was the only thing standing between this life of second-best purgatory and his happiness.

That green gaze of hers flashed in his mind. He'd nearly forgotten how to speak once he'd laid his eyes on her. Sure, he'd seen pictures of her on the website, but in person she was . . . stunning. She wasn't the typical model type he normally found himself attracted to. Ms. Evans was a category all of her own in an alluring-beauty-meets-girl-next-door kind of way. She was a little rough around the edges—and jumpy— but their verbal exchange had proved she wasn't immune to his charm.

His phone vibrated in his pocket again. *Who is calling me now?* Atlas pulled up his device, taking a deep breath and standing as he answered. "Mother."

"Atlas, where are you?" she asked, managing to sound distracted and annoyed at the same time.

"I'm in Shattered Cove, New Hampshire, like we talked

about." He tried to hide the resentment in his voice with an even tone. *Not that you ever listen to me anyways.*

"I didn't think you were serious. You know your brother couldn't make any progress on that deal with the last owner. Why waste your time?"

Because I'll get this inn and prove to you I'm the one you should pick to run the company. Because I can't be overlooked as your second choice —again.

"This plot of land is too good to pass on. You know the money we could make with a prime piece of real estate like this. It's worth giving it a shot. And once I do this, you're going to see I'm the right fit for CEO," Atlas said, his stomach twisting into knots.

"Did you hear Christina is pregnant?" His mother didn't even bother to acknowledge his response.

He walked over to the window, staring out at the beach. "Yeah. I heard."

"Your brother is married, and now we have a grandchild on the way. I think it's about time you settled down too."

Here we go again. He gritted his teeth as she went on.

"When you come back, we should have dinner with Veronica and her parents. Maybe talk about an engagement party."

Right. The other reason closing this deal was so important: Veronica. "I don't think that's a good idea."

She clicked her tongue. "Nonsense."

"There has to actually be an engagement first," he argued.

"We all need to eat dinner. It's been ages since I've seen Bill and Kathy."

He sighed. If he landed this deal, it would soften the blow when he told his parents he wouldn't be marrying the woman they'd chosen for him when he was in diapers—political family connections or not.

"Atlas? You there?" his mother asked impatiently.

"Yes, Mother. I'm here. I don't know exactly when I'll be back. Depends how soon I can close this deal. Then we can talk about Veronica." *And how it will never happen.*

"Alright. Well, I have to run. Your father and I are meeting for lunch at the club," she said.

"Okay. Bye."

"Ciao."

He shook his head and tossed his phone onto the bed. He threaded his fingers through his hair and groaned in frustration. He just needed to get Ms. Evans to sell him the inn and then all his problems would be solved. He'd prove he was as good as his brother, and his parents and all their expectations would get off his back.

"You can do this. Just got to stay focused and find her weakness. Find out what she wants and give it to her." Everyone had a price; Atlas just had to find Ms. Evans's.

Atlas walked into the bathroom and checked his reflection in the mirror. He smoothed over his dark hair. He unbuttoned the top of his shirt. He'd need all the tools in his gear belt to accomplish his goal, and harnessing his sex appeal wasn't beneath him. Not when his entire future was riding on this deal.

He left his room, tucking the key in his pocket. *Who even uses actual keys anymore?*

Right across from his door was another marked "Private." He turned left and glanced down the hall towards three more doors, each marked with a sign like the one on his, only they read "Sea Breeze suite," "Starfish suite," and the "Anchor suite." *Cute.*

Atlas continued his self-guided tour down the white and grey wooden staircase that matched the rest of the inn. A large common area was to his left with a simple grey L-shaped couch and a couple of matching over-stuffed chairs. Turquoise accent pillows were spaced along the sofa. Several ocean-themed knickknacks decorated the shelves. A rope net lay over the coffee table. The style seemed to be minimalist farmhouse with a nautical twist. The inn had character. It would be a shame to see it demolished.

What? He stopped in his tracks. Since when did he care about a property being knocked down to build something grander? Something more commercial?

Shaking his head to rid it of the thoughts, he walked into the lobby where he'd checked in. He searched the C-shaped desk, finding the card stock sign front and center with Jasmine's contact information. *Where is she?*

He turned down another hall, focusing on the painting of the stormy sea that had caught his attention when he'd arrived. Dark, dangerous waves rose taller than the ship alone in the chaotic expanse. A tiny light shone in the distance—a lighthouse. The splash of lightning lit the grey-black clouds, showing the peril the vessel was in. It seemed depressing; the ship would surely sink with everything against it. The tiny lighthouse of hope seemed sent to tease the sailor in danger. But something about the painting was hauntingly beautiful.

He forced himself to look away and walk down the hall into a giant dining room with high-vaulted ceilings. One end was a large kitchen with mostly updated appliances. Past that was a screen door with a view of the ocean. He stepped towards it, some invisible force drawing him out there.

Atlas pushed it open with a creak and exiting the back porch before it shut behind him. He glanced at his feet. He'd forgotten to put his shoes back on. He bent and removed his socks, sticking them in his pocket and then continued over the steps to the warm sand. He searched the beach. A flick of black hair past the beach grass caught his attention. His legs moved of their own accord along the sand path. The floral scent of the pink and white flowers was intoxicatingly sweet in the warm breeze.

Jasmine's arms reached towards the sun before she folded herself in half, fingers drifting to her toes on the purple yoga mat. His cock twitched. The tight leggings she wore showed off her *very* fine ass. *Down, boy. This is just business.* She hooked her arms behind her knees, slowly rising again. Jasmine stretched her hands out to the sides before bringing her palms upwards to face the sun. Drawing her prayer hands to her chest, she bowed her head.

"Namaste," he said.

Jasmine jumped and swiveled around.

Atlas held up his hands. "Sorry. I didn't mean to scare you."

Her cheeks reddened as she lifted her chin. Jasmine's green eyes glinted in the sunlight and narrowed. "Did you need something?"

Wasn't that a loaded question? If he wasn't here for business, he might have given in to the dirty fantasies playing in his head. But he had a job to do. *Sell me your inn* probably wasn't the best answer right now. Atlas cleared his throat. "Just going for a walk."

Her gaze traveled down his dress pants to his bare feet. A triangle formed between her brows before one lifted higher than the other, as if she could see straight through his lie.

"Might want to roll your pants up at least. If you head to your left, you'll find tide pools and rocks. If you just want sand, then right is your best option." She picked up her mat.

"Thanks." His throat was as dry as if he'd swallowed a bucket of sand.

Her loose-fitting T-shirt was so worn it was see-through. The pink bralette underneath did nothing to hide the stiff peaks of her breasts. He gritted his teeth and shifted, hoping she wouldn't look at his crotch to spot his arousal.

Jasmine stood and walked towards him. "Have fun."

He nodded, unable to take his eyes off her. There was something about her that was mesmerizing, like a siren from the sea. She licked her lips, making them glossy. Jasmine's blush only grew deeper on her white skin as he stared. His eyes flicked to hers, green spheres flashing with the attraction he recognized from experience, but it was tinged with something else. Fear?

He forced himself to move to the side so she could pass. The last thing he wanted was to scare her.

He didn't allow his gaze to follow her ass as she walked inside. Instead, he pushed one foot in front of the other, turning right down the beach. The owner was *hot* and seemed like more of a challenge than he was used to. But he couldn't afford to fuck this acquisition up over his inconvenient libido. But damn, this job had just gotten a little harder. She was gorgeous—there was no doubt about that. But there was more there beyond usual attraction. Why did he feel like a horny teenager again?

He shifted his cock in his pants. Once she found out why he was really here, she'd probably not want anything to do with him. He was using her, and eventually she'd use him for his money. *Just like everyone else does.*

Time to clear his head and come up with the next steps of his game plan. The Lighthouse Inn was as good as his, and then everything else would fall into place. His life would finally be perfect.

3

JASMINE

Sprinkling mozzarella over the lasagna dish, Jasmine bobbed her head to the smooth music bleeding into the kitchen. She needed all the help she could get to stay focused while Zoey's father was staying at her inn, and music was her lifeline. How was she supposed to tell a perfect stranger who didn't even remember her, "Hey, by the way, you have a kid"? And what did it say about her, to not even have known the name of her daughter's father? She shook her head. Shame blanketed her shoulders with leaden weight.

"You're such a dirty whore. Just like your mother. A little slut like you is only good for one thing."

Jasmine pinched her eyes closed tightly, fighting the vomit that crawled up her throat every time her stepfather's voice poisoned her mind.

"Oh, here she is. Miss Evans?" A woman's gentle voice pulled her from her dark memories.

Jasmine turned, plastering a fake smile on her face. "Yes? How can I help you?"

An older couple who had checked in the day before

entered the open kitchen and dining area. Annie Hobbs was a bit eccentric by Shattered Cove standards with her silver hair, highlighted by streaks of blue and pink. She waved her hand, her dozen bracelets clanking together. Jasmine hadn't yet seen the woman in a pair of shoes, but her long tunic-style dress in muted brown and indigo looked like one of the ensembles from the organic hemp clothing magazine that her friend Mia had in her yoga studio.

"Steve and I would like to find a place with local fare and wondered if you had any recommendations?" Annie asked.

"I wanted to take my girl somewhere special. We're celebrating our anniversary tonight." Steve smiled. He seemed to be the polar opposite of his wife, in dress pants and a button-up shirt. The grey hair on his half-bald head was neatly combed.

"There aren't many fancy places around here; you'll have to go into the city. I can get you the directions if you need—"

"Oh, no. We want to stay local." Annie waved her hand.

"I have a list of all our local restaurants. The closest to fine dining would be the top two." Jasmine wiped her hands on a towel before leading them out to the front desk. She rustled through her stacks of paperwork and pulled out the printed list she kept on hand for all her customers. "There you go."

Steve took the paper. "Thank you."

Annie spun around in a circle. "This place is just beautiful. Wouldn't Ella and Maggie get a kick out of it?"

Steve nodded. "Yes, dear."

"How long have you been married?" Jasmine asked.

"We're not married," Annie corrected her.

"Oh, I'm sorry."

"Can't get this one to commit." Steve smiled, looking at the woman next to him with nothing but pure adoration.

Annie laughed. "Steve has been my boyfriend for fifty years."

"Wow."

"Marriage isn't for everyone. I like my space. Then, when we get together, it helps me enjoy our time that much more. That's the secret to lasting this long." She winked. "Don't let the patriarchy tell you that you have to play by anyone's rules but your own."

Jasmine's chest tightened. *Play by my own rules.* Yes, that was exactly what she'd do.

"Alright, dear. We'd better get going," Steve said, wrapping an arm lovingly around her.

They walked towards the front door together, both of them leaning on the other as they exited the inn.

Beep. The oven was ready. Jasmine went back to the kitchen and opened the stove. Next, she plucked the lasagna from the counter and bent over to slide it into the hot oven. The hair on the back of her neck prickled with awareness. She turned her face towards the doorway.

Atlas leaned against the frame, his eyes darting from her backside to her face. Fire erupted in her finger. She jerked her hand away from the heat source. The casserole shattered on the floor.

"Motherfucker!" Jasmine slammed the oven closed and focused on her throbbing finger.

Warm hands enveloped hers as another kind of heat pulsed through her body. Every nerve ending hummed like she'd been electrocuted. Atlas winced. Could he feel it too? That hadn't been there last time they'd touched. Maybe it was just the burn on her finger.

"Shit, I'm sorry. Run it under the cold water." Atlas guided her over to the sink, carefully stepping around her ruined lasagna.

He turned on the tap and held her hand under the steady stream of cool water.

She hissed, flinching in pain. His grip tightened on her wrist. "It will help."

Jasmine had lost her ability to communicate. Her body hummed with warmth like she'd had one too many glasses of wine. Her heart raced both from the shock of the burn and from his closeness. God, he smelled good. Like icy water, and the earthy musk of man.

"Do you have a Band-Aid?" Atlas asked, pulling her red finger from the water.

"Uh, yeah. Over there." She pointed to the cabinet next to him.

He pulled a paper towel from the roll above the sink and gently dried her finger before opening the cupboard door. Atlas's brows tugged together and then he smiled and picked out two boxes. "My Little Pony or Barbie?"

Heat flushed to her cheeks. Her eyes snapped to his, where only amusement was reflected. "Either or."

"My Little Pony it is." He picked one out and placed it carefully over her newly forming blister.

"Thank you."

"I'm sorry for startling you." Atlas backed up, sliding his hands into the dark-wash jeans pockets. Gone were the dress clothes, replaced with a T-shirt that clung to his sculpted muscles like it had been designed solely for him. Her mouth watered. He definitely had bulked up in the last four years.

"It's alright."

"Your dinner is ruined. Let me make it up to you and take you out," Atlas said.

Jasmine tensed. "No, that won't be necessary."

His eyes flicked around the room. "How about I cook dinner for you, then?"

She rolled her eyes, a habit she hadn't yet been able to break. "*You* know how to cook?" His clothes looked like they cost more than her car. Someone like Atlas probably had maids and chefs who did everything for him.

He smiled, showing off those perfect white teeth again. "I guess you'll have to wait and see."

Atlas was definitely flirting with her. She'd still needed some space when she saw him at the beach, but he was here for two weeks—she couldn't hide forever. And what better way to get to know him than a conversation over a meal? She wanted to find out what kind of man he was and if Zoey would be safe with him in her life. Not to mention figure out how exactly she was going to broach the subject of her—*their*—daughter.

"You're my guest. You shouldn't be cooking me dinner."

"I'm cooking *us* dinner, so really, I'm helping myself to your hospitality." Atlas licked his lips.

Get to know him. "Alright."

He clapped his hands together and smiled. "Do you have any of the sauce left?"

"In the pot." She grabbed the broom and dustpan before bending to clean the mess on the floor.

"I can do that," Atlas offered.

She shook her head. "No way. You focus on dinner. Let's see what ya got, city boy." The taunt left her mouth too quickly to think it through. Maybe she was being a little too comfortable with Atlas. After all, he was still her guest.

He chuckled, settling her unease. "Challenge accepted."

* * *

Forty minutes later, they both sat at the table with plates of spaghetti and shrimp she'd had in the fridge. It wasn't the lasagna she'd wanted for Mother's Day, but it was delicious. Her gaze flicked over to the chair where Zoey usually sat, now occupied by Atlas. Her present company was the other blaring discrepancy in her plans.

"I never would have thought to use shrimp with spaghetti." She twisted the pasta around her fork and took another bite.

He swallowed a sip of the beer she'd found for him. "Good though, right?"

"I guess you do know how to cook," she conceded.

"Glad I passed the test." He smirked. "You seem pretty young to own an inn by yourself."

"Is that your subtle way of asking me how old I am?"

He shrugged. "Maybe."

"Twenty-four. I've been saving up for this inn since I was fifteen."

His eyebrows rose. "You knew what you wanted out of life so early?"

She focused on her plate. It was the only thing she'd done right until Zoey. "Mm-hmm. What is it that you do?"

He lifted the beer to his lips and took a drink before answering. "I'm in real estate."

"Did you always want to do that?"

His eyes bore into hers and he gave a slight shake of his head. "It's kind of a family tradition."

"What is your family like?" *Would they accept Zoey?*

He shoved another bite of pasta into his mouth, chewing and swallowing. "They're great. Do you like running an inn?"

He was too vague about his job and his family. Was he hiding something? Or was she reading too much into this? "I love it. How old are you?"

He chuckled. "Quid pro quo, huh?"

"It's only fair." She took another bite.

"Thirty-five."

Eleven years difference. That wasn't too bad. The man looked like sex on a stick. Whoever said you peaked in your twenties had clearly never met a man like Atlas. The flecks of grey in his dark hair only added to his masculine charm. She shifted in her seat, arousal pooling between her thighs. It had been way too long since she'd had anything more than a self-induced orgasm. But anything more wasn't worth the guilt that always drowned her afterwards. And she certainly couldn't have sex with the man who was the father of her child. That would add too many complications to an already chaotic mess.

She wanted to ask him more. Did he have other kids? But then he'd probably ask her, and she wasn't ready for that conversation yet, despite what he might have already assumed thanks to those Band-Aids. "You're from New York City?"

His gaze narrowed on her. "How do you know?"

"Your reservation paperwork."

He blinked, his shoulders dropping slightly. "Oh, right. Yes, I am. What about you? Is Shattered Cove where you grew up?"

"Born and raised. I haven't traveled farther than New England, honestly."

"Never wanted to see the world?" he asked.

She bit her lip. Of course she'd love to see it, but being able to afford such a pipe dream was another story, and it started with "Once upon a time." This was just another reminder of how different Atlas's life was. What little she knew of him couldn't be further from her reality. The only thing they had in common was a little girl named Zoey. "Someday," she answered.

"If you could do anything in the world and money was no object, would you still want to be an innkeeper?" Atlas asked before taking another swig from the glass bottle. He saw right through her. Between the patched ceilings and chipped paint, he must have known a woman like her was barely holding it together.

"I can't afford what-ifs and to live in a fantasy world. This is the home and life I've chosen. This place is a part of me. I couldn't imagine living anywhere else."

He nodded. "Well, it sure is beautiful." His gaze never left her as he spoke. She got the feeling that he was talking about more than the inn.

"It's also a lot of work."

"Looks like it's worth it."

A million butterflies fluttered in her belly. Was it too much to hope he'd think that when all was said and done? When he found out the secret she was keeping? She'd heard pretty words in the past, and not a single one had ever been more than bullshit. However, something about the way Atlas looked at her as he said it was like a flash of light in her dark existence. But then again, hope could be dangerous.

4

ATLAS

A tlas held the paper in front of his face, focusing on the lines of numbers. Jasmine Evans was mortgaged to her eyeballs. With the digging his lawyer had done, he had a small case file on the woman. Still, she was making payments on time—though barely, from what her bank records could tell him. This alone was incentive to sell. She could get out of the stress of debt and start over.

His stomach grumbled. Atlas tucked the page back into the folder and slid it into his bag. He opened the door and headed down to the dining room. As he drew closer, the scent of bacon grew stronger and light chatter drifted out.

"The Oyster is a local treasure. Pippa has the best book-store selection on the seacoast, and some pretty cool art," Jasmine said as he walked in. Her smile wavered a moment as her gaze met his.

"Good morning," he greeted her and the two older guests sitting around the table.

"Good morning," Jasmine said before she flipped the pancake in the pan. She nodded towards the opposite side of the room. "There is fresh coffee in the pot or hot water for tea."

"Coffee sounds great." He plucked one of the upside-down mugs laid out beside the coffee maker before filling it with the hot earthy brew.

He turned and leaned against the wooden edge of the counter, studying her as she filled a platter with sweet and savory breakfast foods.

"How long have you two been together?" the older woman sitting at the table asked.

Jasmine's head snapped to the guests before returning to him. Her cheeks flushed pink.

The lady was talking to him? Atlas furrowed his brow.

"Oh, we're not—" Jasmine started.

"I'm a guest."

The woman's mouth turned up in a knowing smile. "Careful, then. Might burn those pancakes with all that heat over there."

Jasmine grasped a platter and carried it over to the table. Atlas pulled out a chair across from the older couple.

"Leave them alone, Annie," the older man said with more humor than actual command.

"Help yourselves. I can make more if you need it," Jasmine said before returning to the kitchen sink.

"Thank you," they all said at once.

"You're welcome."

Atlas sipped his coffee while he waited for the couple to serve themselves. He winced, staring into the bitter java.

"It'll put some hair on your chest." The old man chuckled.

Atlas smiled and set his mug on the table before grabbing a plate and collecting three big pancakes for himself and a couple pieces of bacon. Hopefully Jasmine's cooking was better than her coffee-making skills.

"What are you in town for?" Annie asked, her eyes seemingly assessing him.

"Just seeing the sights." He poured maple syrup over his meal and then took a bite. Fluffy, sweet goodness exploded on his taste buds. The woman knew how to make hotcakes.

"And how are you liking these *sights*?" Annie nodded towards Jasmine, whose back was still turned to them as she did the dishes.

"Annie, stop bothering the man."

Atlas took another big bite rather than answering right away.

"Hush up, Steve. Don't you see the vibrations coming off these two?"

"Vibrations?" Atlas asked, unsure if he really wanted the answer or not.

"Your aura gets so much more vibrant the closer you are to her," Annie said, leaning forward.

He studied the woman, her silver hair tipped in bright colors. Her chunky wooden necklace and several silver and turquoise bracelets that clanked whenever she moved her arms. If there was an image under the definition of eccentric in the dictionary, Annie would be there.

"She might be pushy, but she's usually right," Steve said, offering a smile.

Atlas nodded and took another sip of the bitter coffee to wash down the pancakes stuck in his throat. He needed to run out of here and get some air.

He glanced back to Jasmine—her head tipped as she rinsed a dish in the running water. Her shoulders stiffened before she turned her face to the side as if she could sense his stare. *Sense me?*

Maybe he'd let too much of this woo-woo Annie get to him. He stood and brought his plate over to the counter, suddenly no longer in the mood for pancakes. He just needed fresh oxygen.

Jasmine spun around, frowning at his half-full plate and then him.

"It was delicious. I'm just not much of a breakfast person." *Lie.* He was an any-meal-whatever-time-of-day person.

She nodded and took the plate, giving him a polite smile.

"Have a good one." He waved to the older couple and Jasmine before escaping out the front door into the fresh salt-tinged air. He filled his lungs with untainted oxygen and pulled the keys out of his pocket. Clicking the button, he unlocked his Mercedes and climbed in. The scent of leather overpowered the lingering sea breeze.

He gripped the steering wheel and squeezed. Why was he so unsettled?

Because I can't fuck this up. His attraction to Jasmine was an outlier he hadn't counted on. If other people could pick up on it, it was time he got a handle on things. They couldn't happen. He needed to focus on his job. How could a young woman get the previous owner to sell her this inn at below market value and turn down his family's offer? Jasmine was hiding something; he just had to find out what. Time to do a little recon . . . and get some half-decent coffee.

Atlas started the car and drove into town. A few miles later, the sign for Stardust Café caught his attention. He pulled over to the side of the road and parallel parked. He clicked the fob and locked the car before he opened the door to the bakery. The smell of freshly baked pastries and the aroma of coffee saturated the small café.

There were a few customers on laptops at the tables around the establishment. He waited his turn and glanced at the chalkboard menu on the wall.

"Hi, how can I help you?" the woman behind the counter asked.

"A large black coffee, please. And one of your chocolate scones."

"Sure thing." She used a paper sheet to take a pastry from the display case and placed it in a bag for him. Then she poured a coffee and slid it carefully over. "Nine forty."

He handed her his credit card. This was as good a place as any to dig for dirt on the innkeeper. He sipped the hot java, peeking over his shoulder to find no one else waiting to be helped. The earthy, dark roast was just what he needed. "Damn that's good coffee."

She scanned his card through the reader and smiled. "Glad you like it."

"Are you the owner?"

She handed his card back to him and turned the screen so he could add a tip and sign. "Yes. I'm Remy."

He smiled. "Nice to meet you. I'm Atlas. I'm staying at The Lighthouse Inn."

Her brown eyes lit up. "Oh! That's the best spot in town. How do you like it there?"

"It is beautiful. The owner seems nice."

Her gaze focused more intently on him and her smile grew. "Jasmine is the best."

He nodded and tapped the button for no receipt before he grabbed the bag with the scone and took another sip of the dark brew. "She seems nice, but her coffee could use some work," he joked.

Remy laughed. "That's what you get when you have a non-coffee-drinker make you a pot."

He scrunched up his nose. "She doesn't drink coffee?" Who didn't like coffee?

"She's a chai latte kinda girl." She nodded towards the teas, insinuation in her eyes.

Damn. That's not what I meant. I don't want to bring Jasmine back a tea or try to flirt with her any more than I already accidentally have.

It was clear he wouldn't get much else from Remy. "Thanks for this."

"You're welcome. Tell Jasmine I said hello," Remy called after him as he left.

He nodded and climbed back into his car, setting his coffee in the cup holder before pulling out the chocolate scone and taking a bite. *Delicious.*

He steered the car onto the road and drove to the stoplight. A sign caught his eye. *Farmer's Market.* He smiled. He'd get some fresh produce and show Jasmine just how well he could cook from scratch, since she'd appreciated it so much the first time. He'd use the time together to find out how to get her to sell and prove he was still in control.

Atlas found another parking spot and made his way down the sidewalk through the park. A small crowd of venders and shoppers clustered off to one side. He took his time observing tents and tables. Local artists showed off their wares. He quickly found a fisherman with fresh crab, and paid him for a pound. All he needed now were some vegetables. He wove through the tables as a flash of jet-black hair drew his attention to the right.

Jasmine was wearing the same thing she had been in an hour ago when he'd seen her at the inn. Tiny cutoff shorts with Chucks and a loose-fitting T-shirt. She smiled and laughed at something the farmer across from her said. Atlas's stomach started to burn. *Must be that terrible coffee.*

Jasmine bent, tucking the hair behind her ear before she waved to the little girl clutching the leg of the man's pants. The little girl shyly waved back. Jasmine pointed to the child, her hands moving into different formations, signing to the child. The father looked at Jasmine with a gleam in his eye of appreciation, and maybe something more.

Atlas clenched his jaw tight. A moment later, Jasmine straightened and gave the father and daughter a wave before picking up a paper bag and walking away. Who was this woman? She bought an inn fresh out of high school, renovated it to look like something you'd see in one of those fancy restoration magazines, and she used sign language with little kids. Jasmine was a business mogul and a saint—could that be true?

His feet were moving before he could think twice. He followed her, observing her ass as it swayed side to side. She made her way past the vendors, greeting most of the people she passed, though the majority of women turned their noses up at her. That was curious.

He stopped when she paused to purchase some handmade soap, ducking behind a tent to watch her like a stalker. What the fuck had become of him? Desperation—that was what. Everything was riding on this deal. He'd do whatever was necessary to close it.

Jasmine set the paper bag she'd been carrying on the table for the local food shelf while chatting with the woman manning the stall. Was this woman Mother Teresa? He'd seen her financials. She barely had enough money to scrape by, and here she was giving food away. What was her motive?

She headed back through the tables, sharing more greetings. She stopped and spun around. He darted behind a display of woven hats. Peeking around the corner, he checked if the coast was clear. She bent to smell a bouquet of wildflowers before running her fingertips over the vase full of sunflowers.

She shook her head and walked out of the market. His

gaze followed her until she disappeared. He focused on the bright yellow flowers. His hands itched; the urge to buy them for her was strong.

She was so interesting. A woman like her would make an excellent partner.

What?

No.

He needed to get his mind out of the clouds and back to reality. He had absolutely no time to entertain such distracting thoughts.

He didn't know what he'd gotten himself into. But he was in way over his head. Atlas just had to keep his eye on the prize and off her luscious ass. Yet the more he saw of her, the more impossible keeping this strictly business seemed.

5

JASMINE

Jasmine pushed with all her weight to close the lid on the bucket of plaster. She wiped her hands on her mud-speckled jean shorts. She studied her handiwork and stretched her aching back. The second coat of plaster on the drywall would set by tonight, especially with the windows open.

A bead of sweat trickled down her temple. She lifted the bottom of her shirt and wiped her face and forehead.

Ding-ding. Ding-ding.

She pulled her phone from her pocket and silenced the alarm. Almost time to pick up Zoey from preschool. Jasmine made her way to the kitchen and grabbed a glass before filling it with tap water. She drank the cool liquid, quenching her thirst. She peeked out the window, beyond the back deck to the ocean in the distance. It had always been a source of calm for her. Never in her wildest dreams would she have thought she'd actually get to live here—to have her vision become a reality. Pride swelled in her chest. *Zoey will know that her own dreams can come true because of my example.* Jasmine had done something right.

She glanced at the clock on the stove. *Time to go.*

Jasmine grabbed her keys and purse, then threw in a juice box and bag of crackers. Zoey always got hungry on the drive home.

She headed out through the front of the inn, making sure the sign with her number was front and center for the guests, should they need anything from her. As she pushed through the door, the fresh spring air wrapped around her like a soft pillow. She inhaled, the sweet scent of rose hips melding together with the salty sea air in perfect harmony. She pulled hard to open her car door with a squeak. The rickety old Toyota Corolla was barely hanging on. But it ran. What more could she expect from a twenty-year-old car?

She slid into the hot vehicle, her legs sticking to the leather seat cover, the tears held together with tape. The heat was stifling. She cranked down the window manually. She just needed to get it started and then she could get a breeze going.

She pressed the key in and turned.

Click.

Please no.

She tried again.

Click. Click.

"For fuck's sake!" She slammed her hand on the steering wheel. This was the last thing she needed right now. She could barely afford groceries for her daughter and their guests. Now she'd need to call Lincoln and hope he could fix her car. *Again.* And pray it didn't cost too much. Not that she could even afford a hundred-dollar repair at this point. Tears pricked the back of her eyes. She inhaled long and deep through her nose and let it out.

"It won't always be like this."

She pulled out her phone and exited the car, dialing the one person she could always count on.

"What's up?" Bently answered.

"Can you do me a huge favor? My car won't start and I need to get Zoey from preschool."

"No problem. You need me to call Link?" Bently asked, the sound of jangling keys filtering through the phone.

She clamped her eyes shut, holding back her frustration. "No, I can handle that."

"Okay. We'll be over soon. Might stop for ice cream first. High Tide Diner just opened up the summer treat window." Her brother was truly the best. He'd do anything for her. He already had.

She swallowed and pushed away the dark cloud of memories that always seemed to hover around her. "Thank you, Bently."

"What are uncles for?"

"See you soon."

"Yup," he said before ending the connection.

Jasmine inhaled and looked towards the inn. An outsider might say the old white Victorian-style building looked like something from a postcard. But she saw every hour spent sanding down the surface for a fresh coat of paint. The palm prints she and Zoey had added to the sidewalk. The hours her brothers and their friends had toiled bringing this place to life. This was her home. The haven of safety she'd created for herself and her daughter. Their lighthouse in the storm. Nothing could hurt them here. She'd make sure of it.

Picking up her phone again, she dialed Link. He answered on the second ring. "Let me guess—that piece of shit finally kicked the can?" Link laughed.

Jasmine grabbed her purse as she spoke. "It won't start."

"That beater was on its last legs three breakdowns ago. I

think it might be time to get a new one. I can make a couple calls and find you something for your budget," Link said, the sound of metal clanking against metal in the background.

Just towing it isn't in my budget. "I'd rather you work your magic and fix it."

"Okay. I'll be over to pick it up in a bit," Link said.

"Thanks so much." She ended the call and slid the phone into her back pocket.

She turned around and pushed the door closed. It took more effort than it should have. Her gaze swept over the banged-up, rusted car. Zoey deserved better. More than Jasmine could give her. *More than me.*

A twinge of pain tightened her chest. She closed her eyes and imagined Zoey's smiling, laughing face. She painted a picture in her mind of her little girl with a room all of her own, and a car that was safe and always worked. A full fridge, and dinner on the back deck with the clap of the ocean waves in the distance. She'd have a mother who loved her, but she wouldn't be alone. She'd have her father there too. *Atlas.*

Nerves skittered up her spine. Her eyes snapped open, ending the fantasy. When Zoey came home, would he take one look at her and know? Would he try and keep Zoey from her?

The sound of a car door shutting jarred her out of her head.

"Jasmine?" Atlas called.

Fuck my life. Couldn't he have come back after she was showered and looked presentable? When she looked more like a great mother figure? Not covered in sweat and plaster?

She took a deep breath, summoning her courage, and turned to face him. "Hey."

His gaze slid over her body. His eyebrows bunched

together as if he was trying to figure her out. *You and me both, buddy.*

He lifted a bouquet of yellow sunflowers towards her. "Uh, these are for you."

She stared at the flowers, frozen. No one had ever bought her flowers before. He really must have no idea who she was if he thought she needed wooing. The reminder brought a sense of relief, but also a pang of shame. There wasn't much need for flowers when you were having a quick fuck to numb the deepest pain in a supply closet or a bar bathroom.

"You don't have to take them. I just saw them and thought of you." Atlas winced and dropped his hand to his side.

Damn that was corny, but oddly enough, it stirred something in her. A lone butterfly flipped and tumbled in her belly. She'd been staring at him like a deer in headlights. "Oh, no. I mean, they are beautiful. I've just never . . . had anyone get me flowers before."

He blinked as if in disbelief and handed her the bouquet. Just like the ones she'd looked at earlier today at the farmer's market.

He adjusted the paper bag in his other arm. "I got some supplies. I thought maybe I could show you more of what I'm made of in the kitchen."

She swallowed, her mouth going dry. Zoey would be home soon. "That really isn't necessary."

He shook his head. "You challenged me yesterday, and I still have yet to prove what I'm capable of."

"But you did cook last night."

He smirked. "Technically, I boiled pasta. You already had the sauce done. I promise my culinary skills are beyond boiling pre-made spaghetti."

Zoey's grey eyes flashed in her mind—the mirror image of

the man who stood in front of her. He was going to find out one way or the other. Might as well see how he was with her.

"I—"

"Hey, you were the one who doubted my abilities. Give me a chance to prove you wrong." Atlas's voice, mixed with his pleading look, stoked a different kind of challenge inside her.

Her eyes flicked to his mouth—so full. How soft would those lips be against hers? He'd never actually kissed her before. They'd been in too much of a rush. Would he take his time if they tried again?

She blinked twice. *No.* They couldn't. Zoey needed her father in her life and Jasmine wasn't going to ruin that for her. She had to get to know Atlas as a person, not in the biblical sense.

"Okay, dinner sounds great. I'm going to go put these in water and then shower. Help yourself to anything in the kitchen." Jasmine spun around and walked into the inn, escaping the building attraction between them—running away like she'd done so many times in the past. *Until Zoey.*

She grabbed a glass quart jar from the cupboard and filled it with water before unwrapping the flowers and setting them inside. Jasmine couldn't hold back the smile as she looked at the bright sunflowers. They were beautiful.

Her phone chirped, the security system alerting her that the front door had opened. She left the kitchen, passing Atlas with a nod before jogging up the stairs to her room. She shut the door and slipped off her shirt, throwing it into the hamper.

She pulled out her phone as her screen lit with a text.

Emma: *How is it going with your baby daddy?*

Jasmine chuckled. Emma was never one to mince words.

Jasmine: *It's going . . . 99 percent sure he doesn't remember me at all. But Zoey will be here in a few minutes, so I need to shower quickly. Do you think he'll take one look at her and know?*

She slid off her pants and underwear as she waited for her friend's response to come through.

Emma: *No. That shit only happens in romance novels. I mean, maybe if he remembered you, he'd be able to put two and two together. But if he truly doesn't know you except as the sexy-ass, inn-owning boss-bitch that he's renting a room from, then I'd say you're safe. Let me know how it goes!*

Jasmine: *Thanks. Will do.*

Emma: *You got this, mama.*

Jasmine smiled and tossed her phone on the bed before she went into the bathroom. Turning on the water, she climbed into the shower. She sucked in a sharp breath as ice-cold liquid rained over her naked skin. She needed the jolt to her system. She didn't have time to entertain fantasies of a man like Atlas falling for someone as damaged and broken as her.

A wounded mama bear was ten times more dangerous when you messed with her cub. Her role was Zoey's protector. Would Atlas rise to the occasion once he found out?

There was only one way to know for sure. The way a man treated a young girl said a lot about him. And in a few minutes, she'd discover just what kind of man Atlas was.

6

ATLAS

Atlas was in the zone—the place where sound around him muted and his other senses heightened. He only knew the feel of the pasta dough stretching underneath his fingertips, the scent of the crab mixed with ricotta and fresh herbs he'd expertly chopped. The white flour was bright against his tan skin as he kneaded it into the dough.

Cooking was the one thing he still did for him—when he had the opportunity. He'd never actually cooked for anyone else besides his parents' chef who'd taught him. So why did he feel comfortable enough to share this with Jasmine?

Maybe because she was still practically a stranger. And this gave him the opportunity to get closer to her. He needed to find out how he could buy this inn. Focusing on the task at hand also got his mind off the fact that Jasmine was upstairs right now, naked in the shower. His cock hardened, pressing against the edge of the dining table where he worked. Atlas shook his head, trying to rid himself of the intrusive thoughts —flashes of that dark hair slick against her skin, dripping fat water droplets down two perfect handfuls of breasts. Would her nipples be rosy? Or maybe light brown?

"Who the hell are you?" an authoritative voice boomed from behind him.

Atlas swiveled around. A tall man in a tan police uniform stood in the doorway. His sharp blue eyes pointed directly at Atlas.

"I'm a guest," Atlas explained.

"Where's Mommy?" A little voice drew his gaze down. A few pieces of her jet-black hair had fallen over her angular eyes. She looked just like a miniature version of the woman upstairs. But that grey color in her gaze—that was like looking in a mirror. He sucked in a breath. What a coincidence.

"Hey, guys." Jasmine's sweet voice smoothed over his skin like silk.

She came around the corner as the little girl ran towards her. Jasmine picked her up and kissed her before hugging her tight. The man still loomed in the doorway, eyes flicking between Atlas and Jasmine.

Jasmine was a *mother*. How had he not known that? Was this the baby's father? Jasmine's boyfriend? That burning sensation boiled in his stomach once again. Why should he care if Jasmine wasn't single?

The little girl slid down from her mother's arms as Jasmine asked, "How was your day at school?"

"So fun, Mommy! Then we got ice cream with sprinkles!" she shouted excitedly.

Jasmine smiled, looking up to the guy, appreciation and, fuck, was that love reflected in those green eyes? He clenched his jaw hard.

"Thank you for picking her up, Bently," Jasmine said.

Bently pulled her into a hug, narrowing his eyes at Atlas as he replied, "You know I'm more than happy to help."

Every muscle in Atlas's body tensed. He didn't like the look of her in another man's arms.

Jasmine pulled away, nodding.

"Who's this?" Bently asked Jasmine, as if Atlas hadn't already told him.

Jasmine's gaze flicked to him before she blinked and looked down. Her chin lifted as she spoke. "He's a guest. Bently, this is Atlas. He's staying with us for a couple weeks."

Bently gave him another hard look before he nodded.

Atlas had barely returned the gesture when Bently said, "Link called me. Said this car isn't worth fixin' again. Why don't you let me—"

"Let's step outside." Jasmine pulled her daughter's hand and walked out the back screen door.

Atlas kept his gaze fixed on Jasmine as she led Bently down the stairs. He wiped his hands on a dish towel and opened the cupboards closest to the back door, deciding now was a good time to search for a pasta roller or rolling pin as close to the trio as possible.

"I think it's time you get a new car. That junker isn't safe anymore. You and Zoey need something more reliable," Bently said as Zoey walked past them with a bucket and shovel she'd procured from a toy bin in one corner, then got to work digging in the sand.

"I can't afford a car payment right now. I can make do for a while longer." Jasmine's voice wavered on the last part.

He should feel happy to know she was desperate for money; it meant she'd be more likely to take his deal. But for some reason, seeing her like this made his stomach turn to stone and his chest tighten.

"And what about *him*? You don't think I'm blind, do you?" Bently said.

Seemed like Bently was jealous and possessive. Maybe he wasn't with her but wanted to be?

Jasmine turned towards the door and he quickly averted his gaze, closing the cupboard and opening another. He didn't want to make it obvious he'd been eavesdropping.

He took one more peek. Jasmine had walked farther down the sand path, her arms crossed defiantly in front of her as Bently shook his head.

"Are you making dinner?" Zoey asked, her little face pressing against the other side of the screen door.

Atlas smiled. "I sure am."

"When will it be ready? I'm soooo hungry." She rubbed her belly.

"You just had a big ice cream. How can you be hungry?" Jasmine said, scooping up the little girl from behind before raining kisses over her face.

Zoey giggled, dropping her spade as Jasmine opened the screen door and walked in. Her eyes flicked to his as a blush crept over her cheeks. Then she diverted her attention to Bently with a wave as he disappeared around the side of the house.

"Zoey, this is Mr. Atlas. He's gonna stay in one of our rooms for a couple weeks," Jasmine explained as she set her daughter in a seat at the large dining table, a small space away from where he'd been working.

"Hi." Atlas waved, unsure how he was supposed to respond.

Jasmine's eyes were glued to him as she pulled a juice box and bag of crackers off the counter and handed them to the little girl.

"Do you need help?" she asked.

He shook his head. "No. I got this. But you could make my day and tell me you have a pasta roller?"

Jasmine smiled. "Is that the silver thingy with the turny lever?"

"Well, I've never heard a more technical description of the tool, but yes, that sounds about right." He chuckled.

"My sister-in-law bought me one in the hopes of teaching me to cook. I think I still have it down here." She opened a low cupboard and reached way back before coming out with an unopened, dusty box. She handed it to him.

"Perfetto."

She blinked. "Is that Spanish?"

"Italian. My grandfather only spoke to us in his native tongue until we were fluent." Atlas closed his mouth. Why was he telling her so much about himself?

"So, you're Italian, then?" she asked, grabbing herself a glass and filling it from the tap.

"Both my parents are Sicilian. What about you?"

She walked over to the table and sat next to her daughter before she answered. He followed her, opening the pasta roller.

"My biological father was Korean, I'm told. My mother was Scottish and European." Jasmine pushed the juice closer to Zoey, whose mouth was full of orange crackers.

She was *told*? Was she adopted? "That's pretty cool."

She shrugged.

He cut the dough in quarters and began rolling out a sheet of pasta. "So, Bently is the sheriff here in town?" Was he too obvious?

Jasmine nodded.

"Uncle Bently catches the bad guys!" Zoey said.

"He's your uncle?"

Zoey nodded.

"Bently is my oldest brother."

Oh. The relief that hit his body was more noticeable than

it should have been. His muscles relaxed, and breathing seemed to come just a little bit easier.

"Are you a chef?" Zoey asked.

He smiled. "Only in my dreams."

Jasmine looked at him, her eyes flashing with something akin to recognition.

"If you work hard, your dreams can come true. Right, Mommy?" Zoey turned towards her mother.

Jasmine met her daughter's gaze, her face softening as she tucked a stray lock of hair behind the little girl's ear. "Absolutely, sweetheart."

The moment seemed so intimate between mother and daughter. It was obviously a conversation they'd had before. This precious exchange tugged at his heart. A piece of him wanted to be part of it.

"What are you making?" Zoey swiveled back towards him.

"Ravioli. I hope you like crab. If not, I can make some plain cheese ones." He hadn't exactly planned this dinner with a kid in mind.

"Do I like crab, Mommy?"

"We'll find out." Jasmine winked.

He got to work with his small captive audience watching him roll sheets of dough and slice them into squares. He used a Ziplock bag with the corner cut off to pipe the filling onto the squares of pasta. He made some with plain ricotta and cheese, just in case Zoey didn't care for the seafood ones.

"This is so fancy," Jasmine said.

Fancy was not a word he'd use to describe the mess on the table before him. But the more he learned about Jasmine, the more he wanted to know. What kind of life had she led? Where was Zoey's father? Did she ever have anyone who took the time to notice the way her eyes crinkled at the corners when she smiled?

"Can I help?" Zoey asked.

"Uh, yeah. I'm going to brush the edges with this egg wash. If you clean your hands first, you can help with that part."

Zoey clapped and scooted off her chair before running to the kitchen sink. Jasmine wasn't far behind, pulling out a stool that was folded up between the refrigerator and the counter. They joined him once again and he showed Zoey how to line the edges with just enough egg wash. Jasmine's gaze burned hot on him as he patiently showed the little girl how to press the second pasta layer on and get all the air bubbles out.

He'd never actually spent time with kids before. He was lost as to how to talk to her or what she was capable of, but Jasmine's smile never left her face, so he must have been doing something right.

Once he finished the Alfredo sauce and boiled the pasta, it was time for plating. He gave Zoey one crab ravioli and the rest cheese. Jasmine had moved the sunflowers to the center of the table and gathered drinks for them all. Water for her and Zoey, and a beer for him.

Atlas set the steaming plates of pasta in front of them before going back for his. He joined them, watching and waiting as they both took their first bite.

Zoey scrunched up her nose before spitting out half a ravioli on the napkin next to her. "This is yucky."

Jasmine's face flushed red. Her tone was firm, but kind. "Zoey Evans, that's really rude. Mr. Atlas spent a lot of time making us this dinner. Remember what you should say when you don't like something?"

Zoey looked down. "No, fank you."

"That's right."

"It's quite okay. Maybe you'll like the plain cheese ones?" Atlas offered.

Zoey looked at her mother. Jasmine nodded towards the plate. The little girl picked up a piece of cheese ravioli with her spoon and tentatively licked the edge. It must have been to her liking because she stuffed the whole thing in her mouth and chewed. She smiled and her eyes widened. "Mmmm."

Atlas chuckled. "Seems I've won over a critic. What do you think?"

Jasmine focused back on her plate and took a bite. Watching the fork disappear between those pink, glossy lips shouldn't have been erotic, especially with a child at the table. But goddamn, it was. She licked her lips and his cock stirred to life. A spark of lust lit inside, flamed with each tantalizing flick of her tongue. Forget dinner. He wanted to taste *her*.

"I have to say. You've proven my assumptions about your cooking skills wrong. That's the best thing I've ever eaten." Jasmine sipped her water.

I bet you'd be good to eat. Fuck! What was he thinking? She was the owner of the inn he was trying to buy. Not to mention a mother. He might not have much experience with kids, but he knew enough to know that you didn't get involved with a woman if she had a kid and you didn't plan on sticking around.

"Glad you like it." He picked up the glass bottle and drained half the beer. He needed to get a hold of himself, focus on the business, the opportunity of a lifetime for his career. He needed to prove he was good enough to his family . . . and himself.

They ate the rest of dinner with pleasant conversation including Zoey. Jasmine cleaned up, despite his protests, while Zoey wrangled him into coloring at the table.

"What color is your favorite?" Zoey asked.

Jasmine flit around the kitchen with ease—she made being a single mother and an innkeeper look easy.

"Mr. Atlas?"

He turned his attention back to the little girl. "I'm sorry. What?"

Zoey sighed with what seemed like a great deal of patience. "What is your favorite color?"

"Uh, blue."

She dug through the little box of colors and handed him a crayon and pointed to a blank corner of her page. "You can draw right there. Can you draw a mermaid?"

A mermaid? Was she serious? "I'm not very good at drawing, Zoey."

She grinned. "That's otay. Mommy says to get better we just have to pwactice a lot." Zoey nodded self-righteously, and was that a smile on Jasmine's lips?

"I'll help you. First, dwaw the tail." Zoey pointed again to the empty space before him.

"Okay. Here goes. One mermaid." He pressed the crayon to the paper.

He hadn't any real experience. But the little girl was happily babbling about little ponies as she scribbled across the paper, so he couldn't be doing too bad.

"Now draw the body. Here—" Zoey handed him a red crayon. "Make her have red hair like Ariel."

"Alright." He cringed at the final product—a stick figure with a fish tail and flaming red hair. He certainly wouldn't have a future in art.

"Yay! She is so pwetty." Zoey clapped.

At least the kid liked it.

"Mommy, can we go for a walk on the beach? I want to look for mermaids!" Zoey asked, peeking up from her drawing.

Jasmine dried her hands on the dish towel before rubbing the dark circles under her eyes. She seemed like she was going to fall asleep just standing there. She worked hard, that was for sure. She wiped a few strands of hair out of her face and nodded. "Sure, baby. Grab your jacket because it's a little chilly out."

"Are you going to come too, Mr. Atlas?"

He glanced up to Jasmine. Her eyes widened, and her brows creased. *Point taken.*

"Not this time. I'm pretty tired," Atlas answered Zoey.

"Otay. Come on, Mommy. Let's find some she-shells."

Jasmine's shoulders relaxed. She grabbed a coat from a hook by the door and helped Zoey get it on. She zipped it up and pulled on a grey hoodie with a couple of holes in it. They waved goodbye.

"Thank you again for dinner," Jasmine said as Zoey tugged her by the hand and out the screen door.

"It was my pleasure."

She bit her lip and nodded.

He watched them go, trailing down the beach, getting smaller. Zoey stopped every few feet to pick up something, collecting treasures and depositing them in the bucket Jasmine carried. She looked back after a while, and he waved. The farther away they got, the stronger the pull tugged on his heart. He wanted to go with them, but he was here to do a job and get back to New York. He had a billion-dollar company to run alongside his brother. As tempting as the thought was, Jasmine and Zoey didn't fit in his life. And he most certainly didn't fit in theirs.

7

JASMINE

Jasmine checked the quiche on the stove top, making sure it was set. A couple of the guests sat at the table with Zoey while she kept them entertained with her questions.

"Do you mind if I make the coffee this morning?" Atlas's deep voice sent a shudder through her.

Her heart skipped, and her belly leaped. Why did he have to affect her this way? She turned around and smiled. "Go for it. The grounds are in the cupboard right above the machine."

Jasmine focused her attention back on the quiche, slicing it into servings. She plated some for Zoey before she brought the casserole dish over to the center of the table.

"It's still hot, so be careful." She smiled at the guests and then returned to grab her daughter's breakfast. "Here you go, sweetheart. Eat up. It's almost time to leave."

"Do I like this, Mommy?" Zoey asked, staring at the bane of her existence—mixed food.

"You love eggs and sausage." Jasmine handed her daughter a fork. It seemed she was getting pickier by the day.

"Otay," Zoey said, sounding unconvinced as she started to dig in.

Annie and Steve joined them, and Atlas took a seat at the other end of the table with a fresh cup of coffee. Jasmine kept an eye on her daughter as she got started on the dishes. Her stomach grumbled. She'd see what was left and grab a couple of bites when everyone was done.

"This kind of food will make you grow big and strong," Steve said.

"It will?" Zoey asked.

"Oh yes," Annie agreed, and lowered her voice to a stage whisper. "Except for mushrooms. Never eat mushrooms . . . unless they're medicinal."

"Annie," Steve said, but there was no malice in his voice.

"Looks like a full house in here." Mikel's voice interrupted the chatter at the table.

Jasmine spun around. Her brother held Phoenix in his arms as her niece, Lyra, ran over to Zoey and gave her a hug.

"You're early."

Mikel's gaze flicked to Atlas before he turned to face her. "Yeah, we got a head start for once. Figured we'd hang out here for a few minutes."

Right. She could see straight through him. "Bently called, I imagine."

Phoenix squirmed in his daddy's arms, and Mikel gently set him on his feet. "Said Link had to come by."

Jasmine rolled her eyes. Was nothing in her life private? Did her big brothers think she was incapable of figuring out her own problems? She'd cost them enough in her lifetime. It was her responsibility to take care of Zoey and herself.

"Ready, baby?" Jasmine asked, focusing her attention on Zoey's backpack, making sure her snack and lunch were inside before zipping it up.

"Yes!" Zoey ran over and held out her arms. Jasmine gave her face a quick wipe and slipped the backpack straps over her shoulders. Then she kissed Zoey's forehead and ushered her out towards the front door before Mikel could say anything else in Atlas's presence.

Her brother followed her as the kids rushed outside.

"Wait on the grass," Jasmine reminded them. She walked out onto the porch, holding the screen door open for Mikel. The kids found the chalk in the basket and began coloring on the sidewalk.

"Is he Zoey's father? He's got her eyes," Mikel whisper-yelled.

"I'll tell you what I told Bently—I will handle this. This is my life. My choice." *My consequences.*

"I know it is. Just remember we've got your back no matter what. I'm here for you, Jaz," Mikel said, slipping his arm over her shoulders.

She nodded. "I know. But you guys have handled enough of my problems."

His brows furrowed. "What do you mean?"

She stared at him, searching his eyes for confirmation of the question she'd always been too afraid to ask.

"You're my little sister. I know I made a lot of mistakes and wasn't always here when you needed me most. But I'm back for good. Whether that's to loan you money for a car, pick Z up for school, or beat some sense into your baby daddy." He chuckled.

Jasmine laughed. "I don't think that will be necessary."

He shrugged and then released her. "Clean up, guys. Time to go."

The kids piled the bits of chalk back inside the bucket. Mikel walked over to Zoey and wiped the corner of her mouth where some bits of egg had been.

How did I miss that? Pinpricks of guilt settled in her chest.

She bent and opened her arms. "Can I have a hug goodbye?"

Phoenix ran into her arms first. She laughed and caught him. "Oof! You're getting so big, Phe."

"I'm strong wike Daddy!" He raised his little arms showing off non-existent muscles.

"You sure are."

Mikel picked him up, swinging him upside down as he giggled. "Come here, you little monster."

Lyra raised her hand. "I don't feel like giving hugs today. Just a high five."

"That works for me. Thanks for letting me know." Jasmine smiled and slapped her hand against Lyra's. The little girl had grown so much. Hard to believe she was already eight years old.

"Mommy, I want a high five too," Zoey said, raising her hand. Of course. She was always chasing her cousin's shadow.

A pang of loss tightened in her chest. "Sure, baby. It's your body." Jasmine lifted her hand and returned the gesture. "Can I have a hug and kiss too?"

Zoey tugged on her long hair. "Otay!" She wrapped her tiny arms around Jasmine's neck and squeezed hard.

"Wow! That's quite a hug. I think that will hold me until you get home." She kissed her daughter's forehead.

"Bye, Mommy."

"Have fun at preschool." Jasmine waved as Mikel corralled the kids into his SUV.

"Thanks, Mik."

"Anytime." He winked before shutting the kids' door. "Oh—Remy said to call her."

She waited until they'd driven out of sight before she

pulled her phone from her pocket. Remy's name flashed in her message inbox.

Remy: *Something you want to tell me?*

Damn. She'd probably hurt her best friend by not confiding in her, but why did they all feel the need to be up in her business? They acted as if she couldn't deal with anything on her own. *Maybe because they know I'm a failure.*

She walked back into the kitchen, pocketing her phone. Atlas stood by the screen door overlooking the back deck. His gaze turned intently to her as she cleared the table. Almost all the quiche had been eaten. She offered him a polite smile.

"Do you have a special container you want to put this in or do you just wrap it with plastic?" Atlas asked, motioning to the casserole dish.

"Atlas, you don't need to tidy this. Go enjoy your day."

"It's not a problem."

"I'm capable of cleaning up my own mess! You're a guest. Go do whatever it is you came here to do," she snapped, her anger boiling over. Her brothers' hovering, her friends' intrusiveness, and now him. It was too much.

Atlas lifted his hands away from the dish and backed up.

God, she'd acted like a bitch. What was she doing taking this out on him?

"I'm sorry. I shouldn't have spoken to you like that." She wiped her forehead, trying to fight the first signs of the migraine that was coming on.

"It's alright . . . Was that another brother?" Atlas asked.

She sighed. "Yeah."

Was it her, or did Atlas seem to relax after she answered?

"How many do you have?" he asked.

"Just the two. Well, their best friend, Andre, counts himself as an honorary big brother too. So, I guess that makes three."

Atlas nodded.

"What about you?" she asked.

"One brother."

"Does he think you're incapable of making decisions like my brothers seem to think of me?" She laughed.

He gave a curt nod as his gaze clouded over. Had she said something wrong?

"I'll see you later." He turned and left the room.

Great. I had to go and open my mouth and ruin this progress. Now he probably thinks I'm a raging bitch.

Later that afternoon, Jasmine went through the stack of paperwork that had been calling her name while Zoey twirled to the music blaring from Jasmine's phone in the common room. It was easy enough to lean over and peek around the corner to check on Zoey every few minutes.

While the few night classes she'd taken in accounting had helped give her a handle on things, they hadn't made balancing the books any more fun.

"Mr. Atlas, do you want to see my performance?" Zoey's little hopeful voice asked.

Jasmine held her breath, leaning forward to catch a glimpse of their exchange.

"I can't right now. I have some errands to run. But I'll catch up with you later, okay?"

Zoey's bottom lip stuck out as she looked down and nodded. "Otay."

Atlas walked past Jasmine, towards the front door, not bothering to glance her way. Jasmine took a sip of her water and checked the clock on the computer. She could finish this up after Zoey went to bed. She'd just add it to her never-ending to-do list. "Hey, Z?"

Zoey walked towards her, disappointment evident on her face. "What?"

"Wanna build a sandman?"

Zoey's mouth split into a smile. "Silly Mommy. It's a snowman."

Jasmine widened her eyes. "What do you mean? There's no snow outside, so we have to improvise. Let's go build a sandcastle before I make us dinner."

"Yay!" Zoey agreed, running towards the kitchen.

If she did one thing right, it would be to bring a smile to her daughter's face every time something in this world brought her down. But there would come a day when she wouldn't be there. When sandcastles wouldn't be the solution. When the real pain of Jasmine's past would stain her daughter's world. Would Zoey hate her for what she'd done to survive? How could she expect Zoey to forgive her for something she wasn't ready to forgive herself?

* * *

After building a sandman, with shells for eyes and driftwood arms, they walked down the beach collecting sand dollars and empty snail shells for Zoey's crafts. The waves crashed against the rocks as they searched the tide pools for new discoveries. A light, warm breeze tickled her face. Her loose T-shirt flapped against her skin. These moments were her favorite. If she could bottle them up and save them for the harder days, this was one she would keep forever.

Jasmine carried Zoey for the last part of the walk back to the inn. She set her at the table with her crayons and paper while she heated up some leftover pasta for them to share. Zoey stuffed her mouth full of cheese ravioli.

"You look like a chipmunk. Slow down." Jasmine laughed.

Zoey giggled. "Is so good."

"Hey, is it too late for that performance?" Atlas asked, leaning against the doorframe. His eyes flicked from Zoey to Jasmine.

Wow. It hadn't just been a brush-off earlier. He'd actually intended on following through. She bit her lip.

"Yes! I'm full, Mommy. Can I go show Mr. Atlas my dance now?" Zoey asked excitedly.

Jasmine nodded. "Sure thing."

"Can you put my song on?" Zoey asked Atlas.

He looked at Jasmine, helplessly.

"I got it, Z. You go set up." Jasmine pulled out her phone and stood.

Zoey ran from the room.

Atlas's attention was solely on her as Jasmine approached him. The air thickened with tension the closer she got. "I'm sorry if I upset you earlier."

His brows drew together. "You have nothing to apologize for."

If only that were true. "Thank you for entertaining her like this."

"She's quite the kid." The corner of his mouth turned up.

Her heart squeezed. He had no idea he was talking about his own daughter.

"Ready!" Zoey yelled.

"I guess we've been summoned," he said, chuckling. "After you."

She dipped her head and walked past him, his scent clinging to the air around him like the earth before a rainstorm. Jasmine entered the common room and took a seat on the grey couch.

Zoey pointed to the spot next to her. "Right here, Mr. Atlas."

He sat, the couch sinking with his weight. His proximity sparked to light the desire she'd thought she'd had under control. Jasmine's heart raced as she stiffened, doing all within her power not to lean towards him.

"Ready for the music," Zoey said, pulling a red, feathery boa around her neck and striking a pose that made her look like a starfish.

Jasmine scrolled through her music and picked the song "Into the Unknown" from the *Frozen 2* soundtrack. She smiled as the little girl spun and twirled, belting out most of the lyrics at the top of her lungs. Thankfully, her other two guests were out to dinner. She snuck a few peeks at Atlas. His eyes glimmered with amusement as he watched their daughter show off. Atlas was a good guy. *He deserves to know.*

"Thank you!" Zoey said, taking a bow as the song ended. It switched to something slower: "Beautiful Stranger" by Halsey.

"Your turn, Mommy." Zoey tugged Jasmine's hand.

Reluctantly, she got to her feet. "I think we've taken up enough of Mr. Atlas's time tonight."

"But, Mommy, you guys have to dance now. It's my turn to be the audience," Zoey pleaded.

Heat crept over her skin. Her eyes darted to Atlas's.

He shrugged. "I guess it's only fair." He stood and held out his hand to her. He seemed so much bigger this close. Her knees went weak. She looked down at her daughter. Zoey had climbed onto the couch, eagerly waiting for their dance, her big eyes ever watchful.

Jasmine inhaled a shaky breath and tipped her head to

meet Atlas's gaze. Their eyes locked as his hands gently wrapped around her waist. She slipped her hands over his broad shoulders. The zing of electricity vibrated up her arms, sending the rest of her body into a humming frenzy of lust whipped in desire. She let loose a tiny gasp. Molten heat spread from her womb to her limbs. He moved, sure and powerful, spinning her into a trance slowly around the small room. His grey eyes dilated and focused solely on her. His fresh scent was intoxicating, making her heady with need. Large palms burned her skin with his touch, drowning her senses with the burning need she'd ignored for too long.

His eyes widened as if he was as surprised as her by the overpowering combustion of their bodies together.

Something about the way he held her was different. This moment felt more intimate than anything she'd ever experienced. Like those grey spheres could see right through to her soul. How many times had she been in a man's arms, but never truly held?

Could she do this?

Can I trust him with Zoey and my heart?

Whoa. Where did that come from? Since when was her heart on the table?

His eyes flicked to her mouth.

Halsey's lyrics about it being finally safe to fall had never felt more true. It seemed like a sign.

Could she dare to hope? She licked her lips. His jaw tightened, and his hands gripped her hips closer. Atlas's head tipped down. He was near enough for her to taste his exhale.

As much as she wanted his kiss, this wasn't the place. Not in front of Zoey. She wouldn't be like her own mother. Her daughter would come first. Besides, what was she expecting? A two-week fling with her daughter's father?

If he was who she thought he was, he'd understand. It took all her self-control, but she backed out of his arms.

The loss smacked into her. She sucked in a staggered breath.

She had to be more careful. If her feelings for Atlas were this intense already, there was no telling the damage he could do if she truly let him in.

8

―――――――

ATLAS

Atlas blinked as the room came back into focus. Jasmine's face flushed and she avoided his gaze.

Zoey clapped. "Bavo, Mommy. You dance so pretty."

Damn. He'd forgotten they weren't alone. Hell, he'd forgotten anything else existed the moment Jasmine's tiny body pressed against his. What had he been thinking?

He hadn't been. That was the problem. At least not with his upstairs brain.

"Say goodnight to Mr. Atlas. It's time for bed," Jasmine said, her voice shaky and breathy.

"But, Mommy, I want to play."

Jasmine bent and picked up the few feathers that had fallen loose from the little girl's dress-up ensemble. "You can play tomorrow. It's time for your bath and then bed."

Zoey crossed her arms across her chest, her bottom lip sticking out. It was adorable. He bit back a smile. "Thank you, Mr. Atlas, and goodnight."

"Goodnight," he said.

"Don't let the bedbuggies bite." Zoey smiled.

Jasmine laughed. "That's probably not something we should say to a guest at our inn." Her eyes flicked to his, the remnants of the heated moment shared between them still burning like an ember in her gaze. "I promise this establishment is free of bedbugs."

He chuckled. "I'll take your word for it."

She picked Zoey up. The little girl looked so big in her arms. His instinct was to reach out and offer to help carry her, but he fisted his hands at his sides. This wasn't his family. This was temporary. *He* was temporary. He wanted to escape from their presence and clear his head.

He turned, rushing out the front door to his car. He needed a drink.

* * *

Atlas found himself at a club named The Shipwreck. He took an empty seat at the bar and waved the bartender over.

"What can I get you tonight?" she asked.

"I'll take over here," a man said, wrapping his brown sun-kissed arm around her belly, drawing Atlas's attention to the slight bump there. "You go up to rest while you still can. I can handle tonight."

"Finn, I'm perfectly capable—"

He kissed her, silencing her protest.

Atlas couldn't hold back the smile. These two were just as in love as his brother and Christina.

"Charli, baby, that was never in question. Let me do this for you while I have the chance before I leave on my trip."

She nodded and smiled. "Alright. Give this guy a drink on the house for having to witness your over-the-top PDA though." Charli winked at Atlas.

"Yes, ma'am." Finn saluted her. "Let me get his poison and I'll walk you to the car."

"Okay." Charli smiled.

"What can I get ya, bud?" Finn focused his attention on Atlas finally.

"Vodka on the rocks."

"Damn. Been a day, then, huh?" Finn grabbed a glass and filled it halfway with ice.

"You could say that."

A moment later, his drink was in front of him, and the couple had left together through the back door.

"You don't look like you're from around here." A saccharine sweet voice came from his left as a blond woman took a seat beside him.

"I'm not."

Her gaze raked over him. "Someone like you shouldn't be lonely." She put her hand on his thigh, making her intentions clear.

He should take her to her place and fuck her, get Jasmine out of his head. This was how he usually found women. His reaction to the innkeeper had to be because he hadn't scratched that itch in too long. *So why does this woman do nothing for me, then?*

"Are you offering to keep me company?" he asked, trying to get himself in the mood.

She smiled, her blue eyes flashing. "I can be very entertaining." Her hand moved up his leg.

He clamped his palm over hers, stopping the ascension. "I don't doubt that."

She looked down at the firm contact before her gaze flicked back to his. "You like to be in control? I can do that."

He shoved her claws away and picked up his glass before

draining the alcohol. He shook his head. "I appreciate the offer, but I'm good."

She pouted her bottom lip, sealing his resolve.

"Have a nice night," he said, getting to his feet and throwing a tip on the counter. What was wrong with him?

Back at the inn, he walked inside the dimly lit hall. A small light peeked out from beneath the adjacent door that was marked "Under Construction." Was Jasmine in there?

He backed up a step. No way was he going to ruin his career over a woman. *Even if she is the most beautiful creature I've ever seen.*

Atlas took the stairs as quietly as he could to his room. He needed to shut everything out for a while.

The window was still open, letting in a cool breeze from the ocean. The moon was half full, its light reflecting on the dark waves crashing against the shore. He rubbed a hand over his face and sighed. He pulled his shirt over his head and balled it in his hand. His heartbeat raced as the scent of Jasmine washed over him—like sweet rose and salt water. Even in his space, he couldn't escape her lingering smell. His cock jerked, aching for relief.

Atlas eyed the bed, this was better than the alternative. A fantasy wouldn't fuck up his career, but if he went downstairs, he'd ruin everything.

He lay on the bed, taking a deep inhale of the shirt. His scent mixed with Jasmine's heady feminine one. He slid his pants off and took his cock in his hand, pumping his fist up and down his aching shaft. He imagined Jasmine's green eyes, smoky with lust as he pulled her close. She'd taste like rain, soothing and lifesaving. He'd strip her until she was bare, laid out before him like a gift. He'd suck one of those pert nipples into his mouth. He groaned, squeezing harder, pumping faster. She'd get on her knees, and open her luscious mouth.

"I want to taste you," she'd say.

She'd run that pink tongue up his shaft before she swallowed him, root to tip, taking everything he had to give her. His stomach clenched. The base of his spine tingled. Every muscle in his body tensed.

"Fuck," he grunted. Ropes of cum shot onto his naked chest. He came hard.

He panted, catching his breath. He'd never orgasmed that powerfully on his own before. Looking at the sticky mess on his body, anger boiled to the surface of his short-lived euphoria. Jasmine Evans had too much power over him. She invaded his thoughts and desires. Since when did he turn down a willing blonde at a bar? Fuck that. He needed to do his job and get the hell out of here before he acted on something they would both regret.

9

JASMINE

Jasmine reached farther along the ceiling as she sanded the dried plaster back and forth. Her muscles ached, but she was almost done with this part. A bead of sweat trickled down her temple. She swiped her hand over her forehead, taking a moment to breathe. Upbeat music played softly in the background. The woman's voice sang about keeping on no matter how hard life was in the moment. The story of her life. She took another step up the ladder. It wobbled under her feet. She balanced herself before extending even farther out, carefully resuming her sanding work.

"Jesus!" Atlas's voice boomed.

She gasped. Tumbling forward, she squinted, bracing herself for the fall. The ladder crashed to the floor as two arms of iron caught her. She looked up into his grey concerned gaze. His heartbeat thumped wildly against her rib cage, matching her own. Adrenaline and lust mixed together in a cocktail, thrumming through her veins. His scent was heady, like a cool stream and man. He was so close. Her eyes flicked to his mouth.

"What the hell were you thinking?" he asked gruffly.

Anger burned in her chest, spreading out to her extremities. She pushed him away and stood. "Do you make a habit of sneaking up on people when they're on ladders?"

His jaw ticced. "Do you make a habit of doing this when you're all alone?"

Who else is going to do the work? It was all on her shoulders.

"I would have been fine if you hadn't come in and scared me," she snapped, putting her hands on her hips defiantly. Who did he think he was to show up here acting like he could tell her what to do? She had enough overprotective males in her life.

He shook his head, forearm and shoulder muscles flexing as if trying to restrain himself. But he took a step closer. He leaned in so his head was only inches from hers. "It was dangerous."

Not as dangerous as you.

A cloud of anticipation formed around and between them. Her body still drummed with hazy desire, intoxicated from the lingering effects of being in his arms. Her knees wobbled. She was rattled to her core. The way his eyes darkened as he focused so intently on her made her want to forget everything and jump into those grey pools and get lost in them.

She lifted her chin, but her voice was laced with breath. "Your concern is noted."

"Fuck." His hand gripped the back of her neck as his lips crashed over hers. The kiss took her by surprise like a rogue wave, all-encompassing and upending. She gasped as his tongue traced the seam of her mouth, tasting and taking. His lips were soft, but the kiss was hungry and rough. Like lightning and thunder all rolled into one.

She ran into the storm headfirst. Thinking could come later because right now, she was feeling.

Frantic hands moved of their own accord in a dance inspired by erotic hunger. She lifted his T-shirt, revealing his defined abs, and dragged it over his head before pulling him closer. His touch glowed across her skin like a beacon of light. His arms tightened around her, picking her up as she wrapped her legs behind his back.

He walked them over to the edge of the room, pressing her against the wall. She bit down on his lip. He growled, sending a shock wave of lust shooting through her core. Her body burned with white-hot desire. His tongue slicked along hers. His lips hungrily devoured her as if this kiss was more important than his next breath. How long had it been since she'd felt this wanted? *Never.*

Bruising fingers dug into her thighs as he ground against her. His arousal pressed to her sex. *More.* Scraping her fingernails into his shoulders, she pulled him closer. She needed this. Needed him. Atlas's groan was like an earthquake, shaking the atmosphere until it was unsteady and dangerous. He lowered her to her feet and spread his fingers through her hair, tugging it to the point between pleasure and pain. His possessive control was gasoline on the wildfire raging within her.

He lifted the bottom of her shirt, sliding his palms up her sensitive skin, searing her with his touch. She shuddered. Her flimsy bra did nothing to hide her stiff, aching nipples. As soon as his finger made contact with her breast, her inner muscles clenched. Wetness seeped into her panties. She whimpered.

The last time she'd had sex was in that bar bathroom four years ago with this very man. *But it didn't feel like this.*

Her eyes flew open as she froze. *No.* Back then she promised she'd never again punish herself with a cheap fuck that would only make her feel used in the end. But was this different?

Atlas pulled his face away from her. Chest heaving. Eyes glazed. Mouth glossy from their kiss. "Are you okay?" His voice was like gravel.

She shook her head. Why did she have to be so fucked up? Why did she have to overanalyze everything?

Because Zoey deserves better.

Atlas dropped his hands, taking a step back from her. A triangle formed between his brows as he bent to pick up his shirt.

Why was she so surprised he'd stepped away so quickly?

Because no one else ever took no for an answer before.

Atlas was a good man. He was also Zoey's father and he didn't even know. That was the number-one reason she shouldn't be doing this with him. Zoey would come first. Jasmine wouldn't repeat her mother's mistakes. And maybe Zoey could have both her parents in her life. But only if she ended whatever this was between her and Atlas until he knew the whole truth.

"Atlas." *How do I tell him she's his when he doesn't even remember me?*

He shook his head, fists clenched. "This shouldn't have happened." The anger in his voice made her wince.

A flicker of something flashed in his eyes before he turned and stormed out the door. Her stomach sank. The trigger of rejection and abandonment she knew all too well bled to the surface.

What have I done?

Dirty whore.

You're only good for one thing.

You tease me and expect me not to take what I want?

Jasmine cringed as memories assaulted her. The stink of

his sweat, and the groans. The ache in her jaw and the taste of her own vomit. She darted for the window, sucking in huge gasps of salty oxygen, forcing her eyes to the crashing waves. *Water, wind, sand, seagulls.* She pinched her arm, grounding herself with her senses. Her heart raced, and her eyes burned with panicked tears.

She was a mess. What had she been thinking kissing Atlas back? People like her didn't belong with people like him.

10

ATLAS

What the hell was I thinking? Atlas lay in his bed. His anger boiled over. How could he have been so stupid? Seeing her on that shaky ladder had made his heart lurch. Why would she do something so risky? Then that attitude, damn, had it ever got his engine revving. No one spoke back to him. Women bent to his will because they knew who he was. All in the hopes they'd become the next Mrs. Atlas Remington. But Jasmine was different. Fuck! He'd basically attacked her.

But she kissed me back. And what a kiss it had been. He'd never in his thirty-five years experienced anything like it. She'd removed his shirt. She'd wanted him too. *Until she hadn't.*

What the fuck was he doing? He was supposed to be buying her inn, not getting into her pants. What kind of asshole got involved with a single mother with no intentions of sticking around? And all for a deal. His family would never approve of Jasmine—why was he even thinking about that?

Bzzz. Bzzz.

Atlas pulled his phone out of his pocket and swiped the answer button. "Olli."

"Hey. How's your vacation going? Getting into any trouble out there?" his brother asked.

As a matter of fact . . . "Making progress," he lied. He'd probably just screwed up any chance he'd had.

"Bullshit. You and I both know it's a lost cause." Oliver chuckled.

Atlas gritted his teeth. "The more smack you talk, the more I know you're just worried I'll win the position."

"Whatever you say." Oliver sighed.

"Did you actually have a reason to call me, or did you just want to be a dick?"

"I'm checking on my little brother," Oliver answered.

"How's Christina?"

"At the spa for the day."

"Tell her I said hello," Atlas said.

"Will do. Oh—and, Atlas?"

"Yeah?"

"When I win the position, I'll still make you my CFO." Oliver laughed.

"Asshole." Atlas ended the phone call.

Soft footsteps padded past the floor outside his room before the door across from his creaked open and shut. His cock twitched and he looked down and shook his head at it. "You're my problem," he said to himself. He wanted her, more than he'd wanted anyone else in his life. That was the biggest issue.

He squeezed the bridge of his nose as the pressure built in his chest. He'd worked too long and hard for this to be the end. He was more determined now than ever. One way or another, this inn was going to be his.

Closing his eyes, he relaxed into the pillow. The steady

rhythm of the ocean forcing all other thoughts out of his mind as he slept.

Atlas opened his eyes to the hazy evening light, slowly bringing the room into focus. His stomach grumbled. He slipped his phone out of his pocket and checked the time. *6:30.* Sitting up, he rubbed the remaining sleep away. He needed a new plan. But first, he had to apologize to Jasmine if he had any hopes of getting this deal done. Women liked to be wined and dined. He'd invite her to dinner. A business dinner. Not a date. One where he could inquire about her goals and figure out the offer she wouldn't be able to refuse.

He washed his face and checked in the mirror that he looked presentable before heading downstairs. Women's voices filtered out from the dining room.

"I told you guys, I can't have this conversation tonight. I have my meeting, just like every other Wednesday night. That's why Zoey's at your house, Remy," Jasmine said.

He recognized the woman from the café as she spoke. "But you go every week. Surely you can miss one. Tell her, Belle."

"Her meeting *is* important." Belle, assumedly, sided with Jasmine.

He stepped forward, the wooden floor creaking under his foot. Four sets of eyes all focused on him.

"Hello," he said awkwardly.

Jasmine's gaze darted to the floor as her cheeks flushed.

"You came into the café earlier. Atlas, right?" Remy said, her eyes widening.

He nodded and smiled. "And how do you all know each other?"

"Belle and I are married to Jasmine's brothers." Remy

pointed between the woman with bright red lipstick and herself.

"And Mia is married to Remy's brother, so she's basically my honorary sister-in-law." Belle winked at her friend who held a squirmy baby.

"Where are you from, Atlas?" Mia asked with a heavy Spanish accent. She adjusted the little boy on her hip.

"New York City."

"That isn't far," Mia commented.

"*No tan lejos*," Atlas answered in Spanish.

Mia's eyes brightened. *"Tu hablas español?"*

He chuckled. *"Sí."*

"How many languages do you speak exactly?" Jasmine asked.

"Four, including English. It makes things easier in my line of work." *Anything to succeed.*

"What exactly do you do?" Belle asked.

"I'm in real estate." He shifted uncomfortably.

"Do you like Shattered Cove?" Remy asked.

"It's a beautiful town."

Jasmine's sisters-in-law all cast a conspiratorial glance between him and Jasmine.

"Are you staying long?" Belle asked.

"Okay, enough of this inquisition," Jasmine interrupted. The women all turned their heads to her.

Remy crossed her arms over her chest. "Oh, come on, Jaz. We came here for answers, and if you won't give them—"

"If you three don't stop, I swear to God I will tell your husbands what really goes down on book-club night."

Remy's eyes narrowed on Jasmine as the other two decided to look anywhere else but him.

Jasmine grabbed a purse from the table, slipping it over

her shoulder before walking over to him. "Was there something you needed?"

Three sets of eyes stared at them. He rubbed the back of his neck self-consciously. "I was hoping I could take you out to dinner."

Her eyes flicked to his chest. "That's not a good idea."

"I'd like it if we could talk." He needed to clear this up.

"I have plans tonight that I can't miss." She turned around to face the other women. "Come on. You're my ride."

Belle nodded towards the door. Remy gave Jasmine one more not-so-subtle look before she and Belle exited the room.

"Mia will be here if you need anything from the inn until I get back. Have a good night," Jasmine said, before walking out.

When had he ever been shut down by a woman? *Never.* Jasmine kept surprising him at every turn. She never did what he thought she would. Where was she going that was so important?

He pulled his keys out of his pocket and headed outside just as the taillights from the car trailed down the road. He'd go into town and stop for dinner. If he so happened to see where they went, it would be a bonus. It wasn't stalking if he was traveling the same way. At least that's what he'd keep telling himself.

He kept his distance, admiring the view as they wound around the road that bordered the ocean. The town was only a few miles from the inn. He pulled up behind them at a stoplight, just past the High Tide Diner. They turned right down a side street, stopping in an old church's parking lot. There were a few other cars parked about the place. He slowed down as Belle and Jasmine got out of the car and headed inside.

Where were they going? Was she religious? Was this some type of AA meeting? As always, he seemed to have more questions than answers when it came to this woman. *Why do I care so much?* It was not like he trusted many people. Everyone in his life had used him in some form for his family connections, or his bank account. It was natural to be suspicious of others' intentions. So why did seeking answers to Jasmine's secrets seem more like betrayal?

11

JASMINE

The next evening, Jasmine cleared the half-eaten dakgangjeong, or sweet crispy chicken, according to the Korean recipe book she'd borrowed from the library. She'd forgotten to swap out the gochujang with ketchup, and unfortunately her daughter didn't have the same affinity for spicy foods as she did. Was it hereditary? Her biological father surely would enjoy the spices from his nation. So it made sense that she did.

"Can I have more hobos now?" Zoey asked, taking a drink of her water.

"You mean hotteoks?" She laughed, picking up one of the sweet pancakes from the paper towel on the counter.

Zoey held her hands open, greedily. "Mmmm."

"Don't eat it too fast."

Zoey took a bite of the fried pastry, the dark filling spilling out over the edge.

"Try not to squeeze it while you eat it or it will drip." Jasmine traced her finger over the edge, sampling some of the sweet and nutty filling.

"I like this one, Mommy," Zoey said with her mouth full, a few bits of her dessert spilling out onto the plate underneath her.

"Stop talking with your mouth full, silly."

"Want some?" Zoey offered her half-eaten dessert.

"Just one bite." Jasmine leaned in as her daughter offered her the pastry. "Mmmm. You're right. So yummy."

"Hey, guys." Atlas interrupted and walked into the warmly lit kitchen.

She cringed. She'd been able to avoid him all day. It was probably better they pretend nothing had happened. Not that she'd ever forget that feeling of being alive for those few short minutes. *Maybe if I was somebody else.*

"What can I do for you?" she asked, switching into innkeeper mode.

He leaned against the doorframe, eyes flicking between Zoey and her as he crossed his arms over his chest. "I wondered if you had any recommendations on ice-cream shops?"

"Ice cream! I want ice cream too, Mommy." Zoey jumped up excitedly, dropping the Korean treat Jasmine had spent all afternoon learning how to make.

"You just had your dessert." This was going to be a losing battle.

Atlas shrugged, the corner of his mouth turning up. "I'd be happy to have company."

"Yay! Mommy, can we go to the diner? I want cotton candy—two scoops." Zoey tugged on her arm.

Jasmine looked to Atlas. He was full-on smirking now. She narrowed her gaze. *What is his game?*

She couldn't say no. It would offer them the chance to spend time together. Zoey was his daughter after all, even if he didn't know it.

"I don't have a car right now." Jasmine conceded.

"We can take mine." Atlas lifted the keys from his pocket.

She gave a resigned sigh. "I'll get her car seat." Jasmine grabbed her purse off the counter and Zoey's hand. Her stomach flipped with nervous butterflies. She had to tell him soon. But for right now, she'd let Zoey have this time with him. Just because someone was a father didn't mean they'd stick around.

* * *

"One cotton candy cone with rainbow sprinkles, and a double scoop of chocolate mint for me. What about you, Jasmine?" Atlas turned from the waitress and asked.

"I'm fine."

"My treat," he said.

Heat rose to her cheeks. She wasn't a charity case. And usually men wanted something in return. Nothing was free. "I'm good. Just ate dinner."

"What's your favorite flavor?" he persisted.

She crossed her arms over her chest. "I'm not hungry."

"Okay. Why don't you girls go get a table?" Atlas suggested.

Jasmine grabbed Zoey's hand and led her to an empty blue and white booth. Zoey slid in first, and Jasmine followed. Atlas joined them a few minutes later.

"Z, what do you say to Mr. Atlas for the ice cream?" Jasmine prodded.

"Fank you."

He smiled. "You're welcome."

Jasmine tried to look anywhere but at him. Zoey rubbed her eyes. It was close to her bedtime. She wasn't going to win any mother-of-the-year awards for pumping her kid full of sugar before bed, but this was a moment with her father Zoey could remember as she grew older. What Jasmine wouldn't have given to just meet her biological father—or even see a picture—to have some connection to Korea.

"How was your day at school?" Atlas asked Zoey.

"It was otay. I gots to paint with my fingers." She held up her little hands.

Atlas's eyes widened. "Wow. That sounds pretty fun."

"Here you go." The waitress came over with her hands full. "One cotton candy cone with rainbow sprinkles for the princess." She handed it to Zoey's outstretched hands. "I added some extra sprinkles." She winked.

Jasmine hadn't seen her around before. She flicked her eyes to the name tag. *Brynn.*

"Fank you."

"Sure, cutie." Brynn winked. "Here's your chocolate mint cone."

"Thanks."

"And your chai vanilla shake." She set the paper cup in front of Jasmine. Atlas's eyes were glued to her.

"Anything else?" Brynn asked.

"I think we're good." Atlas nodded.

"Enjoy." The waitress left them alone.

"I told you I didn't want anything," Jasmine said, eying the milkshake. *How did he know my favorite flavor?*

He shrugged. "No, you said you weren't hungry. I got you a shake so you can drink it later when you have room."

She inhaled a shaky breath. Was this pity? Was he attempting to make up for earlier? Was he just trying to get her to sleep with him?

"What else happened at school today, Zoey?" Atlas focused back on her daughter.

Zoey had licked all the sprinkles off and had a dab of pink

ice cream on her nose. Jasmine wiped her face with a napkin as Zoey answered.

"Denny kissed me."

Jasmine's hand froze. The blood in her veins turned to ice. Her chest squeezed tight as she held her breath. Panic skittered across her skin. "W-what did you say?"

"Denny kissed me." Zoey scrunched up her nose.

"Where?" Jasmine asked, her voice sounding more urgent than she'd intended.

Zoey looked up at her and pointed to her cheek. "Here."

Jasmine forced a deep breath in and out of her lungs as she softened her facial features. Smiling when it felt like you were free-falling was no easy task. She gentled her voice. "Did Denny ask if he could kiss you?"

Zoey shook her head. "No. He chased me and then did it."

Anger roiled inside her. Every muscle in her body tensed. "Did you tell your teacher?"

Zoey's shoulders drooped. "Miss Stevens said it meant he liked me."

Jasmine clenched her hands into fists, her nails breaking her skin. "That wasn't okay, sweetheart. No one can touch your body without asking and you saying yes, remember?"

Zoey lowered her head, her face downcast. "I'm sorry, Mommy."

Pink ice cream dripped down her chubby hands. Jasmine took it from her and set it on the pile of napkins on the table before cleaning her hands quickly and holding her baby girl in her arms. "Z, honey? You're not in trouble. You didn't do anything wrong. Denny didn't ask for your consent, and that was wrong."

"Co-sent?" Zoey asked.

Jasmine nodded. "Remember, it's the big word that means ask for your permission?"

Zoey nodded, her face buried in Jasmine's neck.

"Your teacher was also wrong. If a boy really likes you, he'll wait for your consent." She was suddenly aware of Atlas's intense stare on her. In her panic, she'd forgotten they weren't alone. It didn't matter. Some things were too important to wait.

Jasmine pulled Zoey away, cupping her sweet face in her hands. She considered her daughter's grey eyes. "You're not in trouble, Zoey. You did the right thing by telling me. You can always come to Mommy and tell me anything, and I will never get mad. Okay?"

Zoey nodded. "Otay, Mommy. I will."

Jasmine set her back down in the seat. "Now eat your ice cream before it melts."

Zoey picked up what was left of the cone and took a big lick.

Jasmine's eyes flicked to Atlas's. His own cone was dripping onto the table. She pointed. "You're making a mess."

He blinked twice before looking down as if just realizing it himself. He swept his pink tongue out, licking along the edge of the cone.

"Do you ask girls for co-sent before you kiss them, Mr. Atlas?" Zoey piped up.

He coughed. *Of all the questions to ask.*

Atlas's gaze shifted to hers, a flicker of guilt crossing them. *Is he going to lie?* Most adults did in this situation.

"Actually, no. I haven't."

He earned a little more of Jasmine's respect with his truthful answer.

Zoey's eyes grew wide. "You haven't?"

He shook his head. "But I promise I will from now on."

Zoey's eyes lit up and she smiled. "Good. That's good, right, Mommy?"

"That's very good." *Now if the rest of the male population could get on board . . .* She'd be having a talk with Miss Stevens on Monday.

Zoey focused on her ice cream, only managing a few more licks before she set it back onto the napkin. Jasmine excused them to go to the bathroom, and cleaned Zoey's hands and face with water. Her little legs were lagging on the walk back to the table.

"You guys ready to go?" Atlas asked, getting up from the table.

"Yes."

He handed her the milkshake. "Don't want to forget this."

She took it from him, a small smile curving the corners of her mouth.

Atlas held the door to the street open for them. The sun was low in the sky, a few clouds overhead making it a little cooler than when they'd entered the restaurant. She pulled Zoey's jacket from her purse, stopping to slip her arms inside.

"I'm tired. Mr. Atlas, can you carry me?" Zoey asked.

"Sure."

"I can—" Jasmine stopped. Does Zoey know? No. That would be crazy. She was just used to having her uncles around.

He shrugged. "I'd be happy to."

Zoey lifted her arms to Atlas. He glanced at Jasmine as if asking permission. She nodded.

Seeing the small three-year-old in her father's arms sent a shot of longing clamoring inside her chest. Zoey's fingers threaded around his neck as she hung on tight. His big, broad frame wrapped protectively around her. A piece of Jasmine's heart fused back together. She pulled out her phone and stepped behind them to snap a picture discreetly. Even if it all went to hell, Zoey could have at least one memory of her father holding her. Of being cherished by the man who was supposed to love and protect her.

But maybe Jasmine hadn't screwed everything up after all. Maybe this would be the best thing to happen to them.

A tiny spark of hope ignited deep inside her soul. A flicker of light amidst the darkest corners hidden in a wall of thorns. Hope was dangerous. But for Zoey, she'd put it all on the line.

12

JASMINE

Jasmine turned her face towards the bright sun, soaking in its warmth.

"Now bend forward and hug your legs." Mia guided the small group of ladies through the yoga poses.

Jasmine tried to empty her mind and focus on her breathing. The sound of the waves rushing on the beach helped. She needed this time to herself. To connect to her body rather than living in her head.

"That's it. Now move to your knees and get into Child's Pose. Tuck yourself together." Mia's soothing voice melded with the wind and waves and distant caw of seagulls.

Jasmine relaxed into the pose. *Inhale. Exhale. In with light. Out with stress.*

Mia directed them into a few more stretching positions before the final resting pose, Savasana. Jasmine's body relaxed onto the mat. Her eyes closed as she deepened her breaths. Sunlight kissed her exposed skin, color bursting behind her eyelids.

"How did that feel?" Mia asked.

"I'm ready for a nap now," Remy joked.

Jasmine opened her eyes and eased up to sitting.

"You're always ready for sleep," Belle teased.

Remy chuckled. "That's because I have two very active children at home."

The girls laughed together.

"So, Jaz, how goes it at the inn?" Remy asked, playing with one of her long braids.

Jasmine stood, picking up her mat and shaking the sand off. "Great. Everything is just fantastic." Everything at the inn *was* okay. It was her life that was falling apart at the seams while she barely held on.

Remy glanced at Mia, sharing some sort of unspoken message. Jasmine rolled up her mat as the other ladies joined her.

"I heard from Betty Lou, you and Z went to get ice cream last night," Belle pressed.

"Does no one in this small town have anything better to do than gossip about who I am seen with?" Jasmine snapped.

"Whoa. Down, girl," Remy said, holding up her hand.

"We love you, Jasmine. We care about you. But we know you like to keep things to yourself." Mia stepped forward, offering a kind smile.

"You and your brother have that in common," Belle joked.

"Both brothers. Must be a family trait." Remy smiled.

A pang of hurt sliced through her chest. *Because we had to.*

"We just want you to know that it's okay to talk to us. We're here for you. No matter what." Mia pulled her into a hug.

Jasmine relaxed into her friend's embrace. "I know you are."

But I'm done being a burden.

Mia smiled as she released her. "Alright, well. I'd better get to the studio for my next class. See you guys soon." She picked up her mat and waved.

"Me too. My mother has the baby so I can run some errands before I head into the bakery." Remy gave Jasmine a quick hug before she followed her sister-in-law.

Belle hung back until the other two had disappeared around the front of the inn. "Can we talk?"

Jasmine glanced at her phone clock. She still had two rooms to freshen up and prepare for the next guests. "I have a few minutes."

Belle took a deep breath before meeting her gaze. "You know I work as a sexual assault nurse examiner at the hospital."

Jasmine shifted uneasily, eyes darting out to the ocean. *Let's talk about literally anything else.* "Of course."

"But I've never shared with you why I chose that line of work," Belle said.

Jasmine wiped some sand off her mat.

"It's one way I can take my power back." Belle's gaze burned the side of Jasmine's face, but she didn't look up.

Her body flushed with heat as her heart thundered. The instinct to run grated on her nerves, her feet shifting, preparing to flee. "Okay."

Belle sighed. "I've been where you are. You must know that's why I'm at the meetings with you. If you ever want to talk to someone who really gets it, I'm here. Night or day."

Did Bently tell her the details? Would he betray my deepest, darkest secret? She trusted Belle, but still. She cringed. If they knew all the horrors she'd kept from them . . . they'd see how ruined she was.

She forced a smile, though her insides quaked. Pretending was a skill she'd honed since she was a child. Her survival depended on it. "I appreciate the offer. Truly, I am doing great. The inn is filling up. Zoey is healthy and happy. And I'm figuring out this thing with Atlas on my own." *I'm capable.*

Belle nodded, the corners of her mouth curving upwards for a moment. She probably didn't believe Jasmine, but at least she should drop it now.

"I'd better get going. I promised a certain sheriff I'd bring him his salad for lunch." Belle's eyes lit up when she spoke about Bently. If anyone deserved a happy ending, it was those two after the hell they'd been through. But happy endings were not realistic for everyone.

"Tell him I said he should get some of Betty Lou's mozzarella sticks once in a while." Jasmine laughed before heading over to the back porch.

Belle chuckled and waved, disappearing around the side of the inn. Jasmine's smile faded as she set her mat against the edge of the porch. She wiped her shaky hands over her face. Her heart still raced.

"Rooms. Go clean the rooms," she instructed herself, pulling up the to-do list in her mind of tasks she needed to accomplish for the day. She had to keep busy or her thoughts would go *there*. Back to the horrors she kept inside. Back to the memories. Back to her deepest shame.

* * *

Three hours later, both guest rooms were cleaned. She nodded along to upbeat pop music from the radio as she dipped the roller in fresh paint. The fumes of chemicals weren't as strong with the windows open, but she'd still need to keep Zoey out of here for the next couple of days. She turned, admiring the large room. Someday it would be a great personal living space for her and Zoey. She picked up the paint roller and slid it over the wall as she shook her hips to the beat, getting lost in the music.

Soon, the first coat was finished. She closed the cover on the bucket of paint and hammered it shut. Sweat trickled down her neck. Wiping her hands on her old shorts, she moved to the window, needing a gust of fresh air. A tall figure walking down the path to the beach caught her attention. *Atlas.* His hand dropped, holding a phone as he looked towards the sky. His head fell as his shoulders bunched and then drooped. What was bothering him? He ran a hand through his dark hair, turning his face towards the sea. His profile highlighted the sharp edges and square cut of his jaw —tragically beautiful.

Maybe I'm projecting. Atlas probably knew nothing of the pain she'd endured. All the more reason to keep her distance. Men like him deserved someone whole. Someone who could have a relationship. And that wasn't Jasmine.

"Jaz?"

Lincoln's voice made her jump.

"Sorry. Didn't mean to scare you." Link chuckled.

She waved her hand. "Not hard to do."

"I brought your car back."

She swallowed. *How much is it going to cost me this time?* "Great."

He gestured to the door. She exited first, and he followed as they made their way to the driveway.

"I got it running again, but I can't promise how long it will last. I think this might be the final time. I can't in good conscience have you and that little girl driving around in this hunk of junk." Link held out the silver key chain to her, his rich brown skin contrasting against the metal. "I got a call out to a buddy. Waiting to hear back about a vehicle. We can work on a payment plan and get you in something safer."

Jasmine's stomach dropped as she took the keys from him. She couldn't afford the cost of even the lowest of payment plans. There wasn't even twenty dollars to spare right now. "I don't know, but I'll keep it in mind. How much for the repairs?"

He sighed, hands in his pockets, looking between the car and her. "Bently already covered it."

She clenched her fists. Heat radiated in her chest as anger spiked. "Why? This isn't his car. I'll pay you. Give him back his money."

Link shrugged as if it was no big deal. "Already got paid. If you want to, pay him back."

"How much, Link?" She gritted her teeth.

"A hundred bucks." He looked off to the side.

Doubt it. "Towing costs seventy-five alone."

"Yeah, but you get the family-and-friends discount."

She should be thankful—and she was. But knowing she owed someone else something was too heavy. She didn't need special treatment or kid gloves. This was the life she had chosen and no one but her should deal with the burden.

"Send me the receipt and I'll pay him back," Jasmine said. "And thanks for helping me."

Link nodded. "Take care."

"Oh, I almost forgot. Emma said to tell you hello."

His eyes narrowed before he nodded. "Have a good afternoon."

"You too." Jasmine waved as he got in his tow truck and drove off.

* * *

Jasmine showered the grime and most of the paint from her body. A few flecks of light yellow clung to her hands and arms.

She pulled out one of the two dresses she owned and smoothed it over her body. She would do her best to look like a respectable mother. The emerald-green sundress flared a little as she spun around. It was a little wrinkled, but it would have to do. Hopefully no one would notice the small black stain on the hem.

She slipped on a pair of flip-flops and grabbed her purse before heading downstairs. In the kitchen, she grabbed a juice box and bag of crackers to tide Zoey over, stuffing them into her bag before heading out to her car.

The drive to the preschool was short. She dug in her purse and pulled out a ChapStick that was who knows how old. Rolling it on her lips, she took a deep breath. Speaking up and creating waves was not her strong suit. It drew too much attention. But for Zoey, she'd do whatever she had to.

Jasmine took a deep breath and climbed out of her car, shoving her weight against the door until it creaked shut. She righted her purse and headed inside. She was buzzed into the main lobby. Turning right, she entered the office.

"Good afternoon," she greeted the receptionist with a smile.

The woman seated at the desk gave her a scowl. Just her luck. Abby Tims—no, Abby *Peters* now. The woman who'd made her life a living hell all through high school. Teenager Jasmine's payback had been to fuck Abby's boyfriend, Jimmy, behind her back. The ultimate fuck you. Now Abby was married to him. A tinge of shame crept over Jasmine like a dark cloud. *That was the old me.*

"What do you want?" Abby snapped.

Jasmine swallowed hard and pressed on. "I need to talk with Miss Stevens if she's available for a few minutes."

"What about?" Abby turned her nose up.

"That's between Miss Stevens and me," Jasmine replied.

Abby huffed. "Fine. Wait over there." She nodded to the empty wooden bench.

Jasmine took a seat, looking around the small room. The walls were filled with shelves of craft supplies and artworks in progress.

"Mrs. Evans?" Zoey's teacher called a few minutes later.

"It's still miss, isn't it, Jizzy?" Abby said, throwing the old moniker at her like a slap.

Anger roiled inside her. But she tamped it down. Zoey was the reason she was here. "Yes, it is."

"Oh, sorry. *Miss* Evans. What can I help you with?" Miss Stevens asked.

Jasmine looked between Abby and the teacher. "Is there somewhere private we can talk?"

"Of course. We can use the teachers' lounge. Right this way."

Jasmine followed her into a room with a couple of folding tables and metal chairs. A microwave and dated refrigerator sat in one corner next to a coffee pot.

"I only have a couple minutes before the kids line up to go home," Miss Stevens said, taking a seat.

Jasmine took the one across from her. "I'll get right to the point, then. Zoey came home yesterday and told me one of her classmates kissed her."

Miss Stevens smiled and nodded. "Oh yes. The kids were having a bit of fun."

"Zoey didn't want to be kissed."

The teacher waved her hand dismissively. "Oh, it was just on her cheek. I promise there was nothing nefarious going on. Boys will be boys." She laughed.

Jasmine's nails dug into her palms. *Boys will be boys.* Over her fucking dead body. "Zoey said she did not consent. He never asked."

The woman crossed her arms, sitting forward. "Zoey laughed, so she must have enjoyed it."

Something snapped inside Jasmine. She rose to her feet, her chest heaving, body trembling. "Maybe I need to find another school for my daughter. One that teaches consent. One that doesn't perpetuate rape culture like *boys will be boys*." Jasmine scoffed.

Miss Stevens rose to her feet, face flushed. "Now, Miss Evans. I don't see how you can say such a thing. These are kids we're talking about. There's no need to make an accusation like that."

"Today, it's a kiss on the cheek. But what about tomorrow? If no one tells this little boy he must ask before he touches someone else, that even when someone laughs nervously, it must mean they want it, what happens when he gets older? Consent starts long before sex." Jasmine kept her voice steady, despite her shaky body.

"Oh, come on. Ever since the Me Too movement, we have to put this pressure on little boys. They're just kids. They shouldn't have to worry about that yet." Miss Stevens glanced at her watch.

The words were a punch to Jasmine's chest, sucking the air from her lungs. The back of Jasmine's eyes burned. She would not lose it here. She forced a breath in. "I'm sure the other parents at this school would think differently. And I'm sure the director might take my concerns more seriously."

Miss Stevens's eyes snapped to hers, her mouth going flat. "I'll keep your comments in mind in the future. Keeping these kids safe and teaching them is my number-one priority." Her tone was devoid of emotion and insincere, like a robot spitting out a prerecording.

Jasmine straightened. "I'd like to collect my daughter now."

* * *

Zoey was all smiles as she climbed into her car seat. Jasmine buckled her in and handed her the snack she'd brought. Her hands hadn't stopped trembling. Remnants of the adrenaline pumped in her veins. *What am I going to do?* The other preschool in Shattered Cove was private and cost an arm and a leg. Homeschooling wasn't an option. She had an inn to run by herself, renovations to finish.

She rubbed her temples; a migraine was coming on.

"Can we listen to music, Mommy?" Zoey's sweet voice broke through the panic, easing her soul.

"Sure, baby." Jasmine flicked on the radio, searching their favorite stations until she found something upbeat.

"Yay! I love this one," Zoey said excitedly, waving her hands and bobbing her head to Beyoncé's "Run the World (Girls)."

Zoey and Jasmine shout-sang along to the chorus.

"Girls run the world, Mommy!" Zoey yelled after the song ended. They both laughed.

Jasmine shifted the car into gear and drove away from of the parking lot towards the inn. They sang at the top of their lungs. She danced it out, pushing her cares from her mind for a few miles as they headed back to the one place she felt safe —her lighthouse in the storm. Their home.

13

ATLAS

Atlas tossed and turned in the soft sheets. He picked up his phone from the bedside table and glanced at the time. *1:03 a.m.* Sleep was elusive. He stood, walking around the bed to the giant window overlooking the dark beach. The moon was hidden behind the clouds, casting the earth in shades of grey and black. He took a deep breath of the salty air. Maybe a walk down the coast would tire him enough to sleep.

He pulled a grey hoodie on over his naked chest, and a pair of black sweatpants. Atlas slipped his phone into his pocket before he headed down the stairs as quietly as he could. It was something new to get used to—being in a house with other people.

Light shone from beneath the door marked "Private." *Back to the scene of the crime.* He peeked through the crack. *Does this woman ever stop?*

She lifted the paintbrush and swiped it over the blue tape around the edge of the window. A white baby monitor hung from her hip. He didn't want to scare her again, so he backed up and made some more noise retracing his steps to the door before he knocked.

"Come in." She turned around as he entered, her green eyes red and puffy. *Has she been crying?*

"Atlas? What can I do for you?" She set the paintbrush down, balancing it on the paint can.

He walked forward, and she took one step back. Fear flashed in her gaze. He stopped, holding his palms open at his sides, trying to show her he was no threat. *Something isn't right.* There were shadows in that green-eyed gaze. *Who hurt you?* "I —" His gaze dropped to a stack of paperwork on a metal folding chair. *Loan application.* His attention flicked to Jasmine.

She stepped forward, chin rising before she picked up the paperwork and flipped it upside down. "Did you want something?"

You. Even though I shouldn't.

She was a lot younger than he was, and a single mother. He should turn right around and leave her alone. "I wanted to apologize about the other day . . . about the kiss."

She blinked. "It's okay . . . but it can't happen again."

He nodded. Why did that hurt so much? He was here to do a job—not the innkeeper. But she wasn't just an innkeeper. Not anymore. She was an enigma. No piece of the puzzle of Jasmine added up. The more he learned, the more he wanted to know.

"Was that what was keeping you awake?" she asked, tipping her head to the side?

"No. I mean. Maybe that was part of it."

She nodded, turning around and bending over to put the lid on the paint. Her round ass was covered in partial hand-prints from where she must have wiped them. He balled his hands into fists and tried to look away, but his efforts were futile.

Jasmine stood, holding a brush in her hand. "Let me clean this and I might have something to help you sleep."

Jasmine walked past him towards the kitchen. He followed her out. She washed the paintbrush and set it aside to dry in the dimly lit room.

She opened a cupboard. Standing on her tiptoes, she reached inside. The clink of glasses broke the silence before she pulled out two small cups and a bottle of something clear.

"Come on." She nodded as she opened the back door, leading him outside. A few LED-powered lanterns surrounded the porch and led down the path to the beach.

She sat in one of the chairs, setting the glasses on the wooden table. He took the space beside her as she poured some of the contents of the bottle into the cups.

"To the ever-elusive sleep." She raised her glass, the corner of her mouth turning up.

He lifted the other and tapped his cup against hers. "To sleep." *What monsters keep you awake at night?*

He took a sip and coughed. The alcohol burned its way down his throat to his belly.

Light, honest laughter spilled out from her. It was music to his ears.

"I promise it gets better the more you drink." Jasmine was smiling, her eyes glittering.

He winced, tearing his eyes from her to look at the glass. "What is it?"

"Moonshine. A couple shots of this and you'll sleep like the dead."

Or I might die from internal melting organs. "Did you make it yourself?"

She snorted, and God it was cute. Jasmine covered her mouth, and he'd bet her cheeks were flushed. "No. A friend of a friend."

"And this is fit for consumption?" He chuckled.

She shrugged, her smile dropping. "I'm sure you're used to smoother and more expensive liquor. But in Shattered Cove, this is a treat."

Shit. That isn't what I meant. He sipped again, wincing. "You were right. It was a little better that time."

She nodded, staring at him in the darkness. The moon moved from behind the clouds, illuminating her. Tendrils of her black hair danced at the sides of her round face in the slight breeze. Her pale skin was highlighted in the shadows, her green eyes glowing in the full moon. She looked like she belonged in the sea—a siren sent to tempt the sailors. He couldn't take his eyes off her. His chest tightened, his body throbbing with awareness and desire.

"Glad it's growing on you," she said, her voice breathy. She felt this too. This impossible attraction.

"What are you turning that room into?" He wanted to know everything about her. And that never happened to him.

"It's going to be a space for Zoey and me. I wanted to create a separate area for us to live in. Then I can use our room as another guest suite."

Their room. Singular. As in they shared a room? They had this big house to themselves, and they shared a solitary suite?

Because she needs the income from the other rooms.

"You never seem to stop working. Wouldn't it be easier to just sell this place and find another house for you and her to live in? Maybe do something else? The real estate alone on a place like this would have you set for life," he said.

She turned towards the inn and then to the shoreline. "This place has been my dream ever since I was young. I promised Mrs. Jenson, the previous owner, that I'd do what we always talked about with the building."

"How did you meet her?" he asked, telling himself it was for the sake of business.

"I kept house for her. She was too old to take care of this whole thing by herself. She told me if I saved my money and got the funds together for the down payment, she'd sell to me at a fair price."

It was just below market value, actually. A parting gift from the old lady?

"It's a lot of work for you all by yourself."

She stiffened, turning back to face him. "Sometimes the things that take the most work are the things that matter most in the end."

Like you? Is she trying to tell me something?

"What about you? Do you love your job?" Jasmine asked.

He took another sip, feeling more relaxed as he settled into his seat. "No one has ever asked me that before."

Her eyebrows formed a triangle. "Then you've been hanging around the wrong people."

He laughed, free and full. When was the last time he'd felt like this? Her honest response was a rarity in his world. *Why couldn't Veronica be more like Jasmine?*

He took the last drink in his glass and licked his lips. Her eyes darted to his mouth. A warm buzz filled his veins. Maybe it was the alcohol and the darkness, but he felt like there was no one else in the world but the two of them. He wanted to share this part of himself with Jasmine.

"I've always wanted to be a chef, actually."

"Why not do it, then? You're a great cook from what I've tasted. Unless you're a one-trick pony." She winked before taking another drink herself.

He poured himself another small glass, chuckling. "Maybe if you're lucky, you'll find out just how untrue that statement is."

Her lids drooped as she licked her lips. She picked up the glass and drained the rest of her drink. "So, why not be a chef? Go to culinary school?" Her voice trembled slightly.

He shrugged. "In my family, we all join the family business. There is no room for fantasies."

"Atlas—" She reached out her hand to his, their skin touching only a moment. Heat bolted up his arm like an electric charge. She whipped her hand back and gasped.

"What?"

She shook her head. "Never mind."

He leaned forward, taking her hand once again in his. Potent lust and need radiated from their connection. "Say what you were going to say."

Tucking a strand of hair behind her ear, she said, "If it's important to you, then that's all that should matter. Why care what anyone else thinks? You really want to be a chef, that's what you should do."

He stared at her in the moonlight. The air was thick and humid with tension. His need coiled tight, threatening to snap. The grey clouds overhead moved, painting them in darkness once again. The wind picked up, the energy in the air shifting. The old house creaked as a rush of icy wind blew over them. A warning. A storm was coming.

The push-pull of his emotions clashed inside him. Her touch was intoxicating. A raw hunger unlike anything he'd ever felt roared in his veins. If he were a stronger man, he'd go upstairs, pack his things, and leave before this got too mixed up—admit his defeat and go back to New York.

He leaned forward. Her hand trembled in his. Jasmine's soft gasp made him freeze. Every muscle in his body was taut with unhinged need for this woman before him. A woman he had no business wanting.

"I-I'd better go to bed." She shot up from her seat, pulling her hand from his and disappearing into the house. His chest heaved as he gulped in fresh oxygen. His body vibrated. *What the fuck was that?* He eyed the bottle of moonshine and shook his head. What was he doing? He scrubbed his hand over his face and sighed. He was here to do a job. Every time he was around that woman, everything else left his thoughts. She consumed him. And it was only getting worse.

She needed the money, *his money*. She could start over, and make an easier life for her and her daughter. She needed a loan and, from what he'd overheard, a new car. He could offer her a solution. Offering her money would help relieve most of her stress. But why did that feel so wrong? Could he really trade everything he'd worked so hard for, all that he'd sacrificed, for Jasmine? She'd find another inn. Something smaller and in her budget.

But that isn't what she wants. No, this land meant something to her.

So where did that leave him?

14

JASMINE

Jasmine dug her toes into the warm sand as she picked through the pile of seashells she and Zoey had collected that morning.

"Is dere a tiny one?" Zoey pinched her fingers together squinting.

Jasmine laughed, sunlight warming her from the inside out as her chest expanded. "I love you so much, Z."

"I love you too much, Mommy."

Jasmine's laughter grew and Zoey joined in with her. "Don't ever change, baby girl."

Zoey picked up a small white shell from the pile and put it atop her sandcastle. "We needs a mermaid now."

As Zoey went to work digging into the bin of beach toys, Jasmine took the time to admire the bounce in her black pigtails. And the way those eyes glittered with a thirst for life and determination to experience every moment to its fullest. *Was I ever as carefree as this?*

Moments like this made all her hard work worth it. To see her daughter laugh and play, happy and safe—there was no greater honor. *I did this for her.* But how long could this go on? Soon they wouldn't have a car to get her to school. She could ask her brothers for help with a loan. *But it's not their job to take care of me and Zoey. It's mine.* Not to mention the issue with her teacher. Was her baby safe at school? Perhaps most other mothers would have let it slide, ignored the seemingly insignificant actions. But Jasmine wasn't other moms. *I might be a fuckup in a hundred ways, but my daughter will be safe and know what's right and what's wrong.*

And now Zoey might be able to have her father in her life. Jasmine had wanted to make sure he was a good person—and it seemed he was. She'd tell him . . . but not with her family around. Tomorrow. She'd tell him tomorrow.

"Anybody home?" Remy's voice called out.

Zoey jumped up and down excitedly. "Yes!"

Jasmine stood and dusted the sand off her shorts. Taking a deep breath, she prepared herself to greet her family and the questions she'd have to fend off all afternoon.

"Hey, guys." She waved as Zoey's cousins came barreling around the corner.

"Little sister." Mikel stepped down the porch steps and pulled her into a hug. "How are you doing?"

"Just peachy," she snarked.

"I think you try to make up for all the teen years I missed with your sass now." He chuckled.

She winced. It was a bittersweet reminder of the time he'd left—abandoned her like her parents had. He'd needed to heal, and she'd forgiven him. But the reminder still hurt.

Bently walked through the back door with Belle trailing him. Andre and Mia followed with their son, Matteo.

"I see the gang's all here," Jasmine said, giving everyone hugs.

Bently looked her up and down, worry creasing his brow. "You look thinner."

Jasmine rolled her eyes. "I guess it's a good thing we're having a cookout, then."

"Leave her be," Belle said, putting her hand on her husband's shoulder.

"I already stuck the enchiladas in the oven to keep them warm," Mia said, handing over the chubby, drooling baby to Andre.

"Perfect. Who's manning the grill?" Jasmine asked.

"I'll do it." Bently waved his hand and pulled the cover off.

"I guess that means we got kid duty," Mikel said, nodding to Andre.

Everyone dispersed to do their respective jobs. The women filed into the kitchen before setting up the various salads and fruit. Mia poured wine for them all. Jasmine gladly took her plastic cupful. She didn't usually indulge, except for the occasional five-dollar bottle of the cheap stuff. So this was a treat. After the week she'd had, she deserved it.

"So . . . where is he?" Remy whispered.

Jasmine tensed. "I don't know. His car is gone. He's a guest on vacation—it's not my job to keep tabs on him. Pretty sure that would be called stalking."

Remy crossed her arms over her chest. "Have you decided when you're going to tell him?"

Jasmine sighed. "No. And I would appreciate it if you stopped asking and minded your own business."

"She's just worried for you. We all are," Mia said.

Because you think I can't handle my own problems. "This is why I didn't tell you. Emma gives me space; you hover. It's like all your shyness disappeared when you and my brother got together, and it's morphed into nosiness."

Remy shook her head. "You see it as being nosy. I see it as caring about my best friend. *My sister.*"

Jasmine considered Remy's eyes before glancing at the faces around her. All different shades of brown. All full of pity. She stepped back and opened the refrigerator before pulling out two beers and a soda. "Gonna go give the guys a drink."

Remy sighed. "Jaz—"

She pushed open the back door and headed towards the grill.

"Here." She handed Bently the beer.

"Why thank you." He smiled. "I could run a background check on him if you want?"

Jasmine shook her head. "Isn't that illegal?"

His gaze hardened. "I'll do whatever I have to so I can keep you and Zoey safe. It might help to know if he has any skeletons in his closet."

She pinched the bridge of her nose. "No, Bently. And I appreciate you being so worried about this, but I can handle this situation by myself." She moved on before he could ask her another question or comment on her predicament. She walked towards Mikel and Andre. "Here ya go, guys."

"Beer delivery." Andre smiled before returning his gaze towards his son sitting at his feet, holding fistfuls of sand.

"Thanks for the soda." Mikel accepted the cold can before popping the top.

The kids were all working together to dig a hole in the sand with their little shovels.

"What are they up to?" Jasmine asked.

"Dre told them if they dug a hole big enough, he'd let them bury him up to his ears." Mikel chuckled.

"Ahhhhhh!" Phoenix cried.

"Zoey hit him!" Lyra yelled.

Jasmine's eyes snapped to her daughter. Zoey's face

reddened as her bottom lip jutted out. Her arms crossed protectively in front of her.

Mikel had already picked up the crying toddler and was soothing him. Andre had scooped little Matteo into his arms who'd started to cry, no doubt due to the other kids' screams. Jasmine approached her daughter. Zoey's eyes looked up defiantly towards her.

"What happened?" Jasmine crouched on her knees.

"He put sand on me, Mommy!" Her chin trembled.

"Did it hurt you?"

She nodded.

"I'm sorry you got hurt. But do you think hitting him was okay?"

Zoey looked down and shook her head.

"Hitting hurts. What do you think we can do to make this better?"

"I don't want to say sorry!"

Jasmine took a deep breath. "Well, what would make you feel better if someone hit you?"

After a minute, Zoey mumbled, "A hug."

"Let's ask Phoenix if he wants a hug."

She got to her feet, guiding her reluctant daughter by the hand.

Phoenix's tears had been dried and he slid from his father's arms.

"Phe, Zoey has something to ask you," Jasmine prompted, giving her daughter a nudge.

"Do you want a hug?" Zoey asked.

Phoenix opened his arms and clung to his older cousin. Zoey hugged him back and whispered, "I sorry for hitting you."

"Buddy, what do you have to say about throwing sand?" Mikel asked.

Phoenix said, "I sorry." The kids walked back to their work in the sand holding hands.

Jasmine exhaled a long breath before turning around to return to the inn and froze.

Atlas was on the porch, beer in hand, talking to Bently.

No. No. No.

Her brother nodded towards Jasmine before Atlas walked down the path approaching her.

"So, I finally get to meet the guy," Andre said under his breath. She didn't need to turn towards him and Mikel to know where their attention had been diverted. It was like the moments before a train wreck, seeing her two worlds collide.

Atlas stopped a couple of feet from her, nodding to the guys. "Your uh—brother told me to let you guys know the food was ready."

Jasmine swallowed. *The food is ready.* Sweat broke out on her forehead. She turned to the kids. "Come on, guys. Time to go wash up and then eat."

Zoey dropped her shovel and ran ahead, always wanting to beat Lyra. Jasmine turned back to Atlas. "Thanks."

He nodded.

Mikel clapped a hand over Atlas's back. "Come on in. Guests get first pick."

"I don't want to intrude," Atlas argued.

"You're not. But you might offend the ladies if you don't join and get a plate." Andre nodded towards the house, adjusting his son on his hip.

What were they doing? The last thing she needed was her family talking with Atlas. What if they said something before she had the chance to explain? Panic squeezed her chest as she shot Mikel a look that would kill any other mere mortal. He gave her a wink as he headed inside, Andre following right behind him.

"Is this okay with you?" Atlas asked, studying her.

No. "Of course," she squeaked, walking towards the inn. Her heart was pounding, and she had the feeling that it would only get worse from here on in. Her world was about to implode.

Her sisters-in-law got Atlas a plate and her family welcomed him into their fold. Bently's critical glare was the only abnormal thing about this get-together. That and the fact that her unknowing baby daddy fit right in. He laughed and kept up with the conversation, even answering the never-ending questions about living in the city from Lyra and Zoey. *He fits in better than I do.* His smiles seemed genuine. His laughter was pure. And every time his eyes landed on her, her heart skipped a beat. She was in trouble.

"So, you helped renovate the inn?" Atlas asked Mikel and Andre.

"Yup," Andre answered.

"Someone had to make sure it got done right and Jasmine was taken care of," Mikel said, his smile dropping just a little.

"You should talk," she snapped.

Mikel's shoulders sunk. Atlas flicked his gaze to her questioningly.

"Dessert, anyone?" Belle asked.

"I brought the Mexican wedding cookies." Mia set out the tray filled with white-powdered sweets.

"My favorite." Andre reached for one.

"And to think you turned them down once upon a time," Remy teased.

"How do you get them to taste so good?" Bently asked over a mouthful of cookie.

"Not from a cookbook." Mia laughed. "My great-abuela's recipe passed on down to my mother and now me."

A pang of envy sliced through Jasmine's chest. Mia knew

everything there was about her heritage. Jasmine spun around, considering her brothers' and Andre's faces. Though her family looked like the United Nations to everyone else, she felt out of place. No one looked like her. No one but Zoey. Jasmine fit with her family, but she didn't at the same time. She had nothing from her culture but her Asian features—no idea how to speak the language. Only her own poor attempts at following Korean recipes from the internet. *Just another missing piece of me.*

Maybe if she could find a way to connect to her roots, she'd feel more . . . whole.

Jasmine busied herself with passing out cupcakes and ice cream to those who wanted it. She drained the last of the wine in her cup as Zoey came up to her. "I want another cupcake, Mommy."

Jasmine shook her head. "Sorry, sweet pea, just one for now."

"Ahhhh!" Zoey let loose an ear-piercing scream, drawing everyone's eyes.

"Zoey Jane Evans," Jasmine said, warning in her tone.

"I want a cupcake! Now!" Zoey yelled, throwing herself to the ground.

The back of Jasmine's eyes burned as she fought off tears. She was at her emotional limit for the day. She knelt and scooped her daughter up.

"Does she need a nap?" Remy asked, somewhere behind her.

Her skin burned with the realization that not only was her family watching Jasmine fail at this, but Atlas was too. *He's going to think I'm a bad mom.*

"Let's go lie down," Jasmine said, turning to head inside.

"No!" Zoey lashed out, her tiny but surprisingly strong fist hitting Jasmine square in the jaw.

"Zoey! Stop!" Jasmine yelled, chest heaving.

The little girl erupted into tears as giant sobs wracked her body. Jasmine's tears fell too as she rushed in the door that Mia held open for her. She ran through the inn and up the stairs to the small bedroom she shared with Zoey.

Jasmine collapsed on the bed, cradling Zoey in her arms as mother and daughter cried together. How could such a good day have gone to hell in just a couple of hours?

After a few minutes, Zoey's cries subsided. Jasmine looked down and wiped the sticky hair from her forehead. Zoey's eyes closed as she drifted into sleep. Her long black eyelashes kissed her pink-tinged cheeks.

Jasmine leaned in and pressed her lips to her sleeping daughter's nose and forehead. "I'm so sorry, baby. I'm sorry for yelling. For not being patient. For not being enough." Tears slid over her cheeks, dripping onto her daughter's summer dress.

Jasmine held on a little longer before transferring Zoey to her bed, making sure the fan was rotating through the room. After walking into the bathroom, she splashed cold water on her face and took her hair out. Jasmine braided it quickly over her shoulder and stared at her reflection. She needed a minute to breathe. A moment to get out this pent-up energy. She glanced from the window. The beach was full of her well-meaning but overbearing family. Jasmine craved a break from here. Her eyes traced the golden coastline.

She went back into the room and turned the baby monitor on, keeping the portable one with her as she quietly exited the room. Closing the bedroom door, she turned towards the stair-case and froze. Remy stood at the top step and opened her arms before pulling Jasmine into a hug.

"I know these kinds of days are the toughest."

It was easy to forget that Remy had lived life as a single

mother for almost five years. If anyone knew how hard this was, it was her friend.

Jasmine relaxed into her hold.

"You're doing all the right things. Zoey is so lucky to have you," Remy encouraged.

Jasmine's shoulders felt a little lighter. "Thank you."

Remy released her. "Anytime, babe. I'm here, ride or die. I mean it. You need anything, I'm your girl."

"I know." Jasmine gave her a watery smile. "I need to go for a walk. Can you keep an ear out for Z?" Jasmine handed her the baby monitor.

"Of course."

Jasmine wiped her eyes one more time. "It sucks that Atlas had to witness me at my worst with her. Do you think he sees me as an unfit mother? Would he try to get full custody of her?"

Remy shook her head. "No way. The looks he's been sending you all afternoon were more like he wanted you. And then worried *for* you when you ran inside."

Jasmine nodded and took a deep breath to steady herself.

"I will try to stop asking so many questions about the situation. I just want you to remember, I'm here and I've been in your shoes . . . sort of."

"I know. I just need some space to figure this out on my own."

"I'll try to do that. But your brothers might have other ideas." Remy smiled mischievously.

"What do you mean?" Nerves buzzed in her stomach. "Remy—what did they do?"

15

———

ATLAS

Atlas dove to the ground, extending his arms upwards as far as they would reach. He made contact. *Oof!* Gritty sand sliced over the bare skin of his chest.

"Good save!" Mikel said.

"Out of bounds," Bently grumbled.

Atlas got to his feet and shrugged it off. It had been too long since he'd played volleyball.

"It's nice to finally be able to have two on two," Andre said.

His eyes flicked to the window next to his at the inn. *Is she okay?* He didn't know the first thing about kids, but anyone could see she had kept her cool under fire as long as possible. The way her eyes had flashed with regret before she'd taken off inside made his chest squeeze.

"Game point," Bently said, as he served.

Atlas snapped his gaze back to the sky, the white and blue ball coming towards his side. He hit it, knocking it over the net. Andre volleyed it back. Mikel jumped up to set it. Atlas spiked it down. Bently dove, barely recovering it. Andre swung his arm, sending it over both Mikel's and his head, scoring the final point.

"Ahhhh. Too bad." Mikel lifted his fist. Atlas knocked his against Mikel's.

"Sucker! You owe me fifty bucks," Andre teased.

"Best of three?" Mikel challenged.

"Can I play, Daddy?" Lyra asked Mikel.

He picked her up and put her on his shoulders. "Sure thing, princess. You can be on the winning team."

"Ha! You know you have to actually win to be the winning team, right?" Andre teased.

"Uncle Dre is jealous I'm faster than him," Mikel said.

"You're a comedian now too? Keep your day job." Andre snickered.

"Lyra, who's the best uncle ever?" Andre smiled.

"Uncle Bently!" Lyra yelled.

Andre's smile dropped. Bently burst out laughing. It was the first time all afternoon his expression had broken from a scowl—other than when he looked at his wife.

"That's right, and don't you forget it." Bently chuckled.

"Traitor," Andre growled at Lyra, who giggled.

He liked these guys. No one was talking about which million-dollar deal they'd just closed or which new car they'd bought their mistress. These were wholesome, fun-loving, dedicated family men. They stared awestruck at their wives, like these women had hung the moon. Was there something in the water in Shattered Cove? In his thirty-five years, he'd never seen anyone gaze at their spouse that way except Oliver and Christina. And the kids were all welcomed and included in conversation and events—not pushed off to the side with nannies and ignored.

"What work do you do?" Bently asked.

Atlas shifted on his feet. "Real estate."

Bently's eyes narrowed. "That sounds like a non-answer to me. What exactly is it you do?"

"My company acquires land and buildings. We work as a brokerage between companies who wish to expand."

"Like chain restaurants?" Mikel asked.

Atlas nodded. "Yeah, and companies like the online retailers who need shipping plants or manufacturing companies." *And hotels or resorts.*

A flash of movement caught his attention. Jasmine walked out the back door with Remy. The other women approached her and gave her a hug before she waved and headed down the steps. Her gaze locked with his before she turned and continued the other way down the beach, her hands wrapping around herself. She looked like she was drowning, and he wanted to be the one to pull her to safety. But that was in no way a part of the plan. Impossible didn't begin to explain the situation.

Someone cleared their throat. He whipped around. All three men were staring at him. It was clear from the overprotective-big-brother vibes Bently had going on that he thought Atlas was after their sister. Which he wasn't. But he couldn't keep his eyes off her either. *Although I did kiss her.*

"Tuesday we're heading to the ropes course. You should come," Mikel invited him.

Hanging out with these guys was great, but that wasn't why he was here. "I don't know."

"He probably couldn't cut it." Bently smirked.

The challenge burned his veins with determination. If there was one thing he'd like more than to wipe that smirk off Bently's face, he couldn't think of it at that moment. Besides, how many deals were made over the golf course? Time with her family would give him more insight into her, and how he could figure out what she wanted. So he could have the inn and get what *he* wanted: CEO position at Remington Empire. Along with the respect he finally deserved. *Only one week left to make it happen.*

"I'm game."

Bently nodded.

"Another round?" Andre asked, tossing the volleyball in the air.

Atlas's eyes flicked back to the beach. "Actually, I'm gonna go for a walk." He turned around, not needing to see the men's reactions. Something tugged inside him, leading him to the small woman in the distance. *I just want to check on her and make sure she is okay.*

* * *

Atlas caught up to Jasmine within a few minutes. She was sitting on a piece of driftwood on top of a sand dune facing towards the ocean.

"Hey," he said.

She wiped her face and turned around, her eyes red and puffy. "What are you doing here?"

"I wanted to make sure you were okay."

"I'm fine." She smiled, but it seemed forced. It didn't reach her eyes.

He nodded and pointed towards the makeshift seat. "May I?"

"Sure."

He took a seat and stared out at the ocean in silence for a few beats. "Your family seems pretty cool."

She chuckled, and it warmed his chest. "Don't tell them that. It'll go to their heads."

He smiled. "No one is that perfect, right? Tell me they have this dark, secret double life."

Her eyes dimmed. *Shit. What did I say?*

"They've all been through hell and came out the other side. They know how to hang on to something good when they have it."

And what hell have you known?

"Zoey's a great little girl. You're a good mom." He bit his tongue. *Was that too much?*

Jasmine smiled, turning to face him. "She really is. I'm happy to hear you say that."

"It can't be easy doing it alone." *Where is Zoey's dad in all this?*

Her gaze wavered before she turned back to the ocean. "Zoey's dad doesn't know anything about her. He never knew I was pregnant."

The air rushed from his lungs. Like all things with Jasmine, one answer led to more questions. *How is that possible?*

"How about your family? What are they like?" Jasmine asked.

He shrugged. He could give her the canned response, or he could share something real with her like she had. "My parents are . . . I'm always compared to my brother and I always come up short in his shadow. I can never seem to win their approval."

"That sucks. But in the end, it's your life to live, and you should do it according to your own rules. Do what makes you happy as long as it doesn't hurt anyone else."

"What about your family? Did your mother support your dream to run an inn?"

Her body tensed before she wrapped her arms around herself again. "She died when I was seven."

"I'm sorry." His stomach knotted.

"It was a long time ago. How is your life in New York City?"

"It's . . . uh . . . fine. I mean, it's great. Nothing extra special or overly negative about it. New York is a lot faster paced than here."

Jasmine tucked a strand of hair behind her ear and nodded. Her brows furrowed as she dug the sand with her bare feet. "Do you have a girlfriend?"

He straightened. The insinuation burned. "You think I would have kissed you if I had someone waiting for me back home?"

She turned, pinning her eyes to him. "I don't know you at all, Atlas."

"That's for damn sure."

"What do you want from me?" Her voice wavered, vulnerability flashing in her green eyes.

I should tell her about the sale.

"Is it just sex? A fling while you're on vacation? Because I can't do that. I have to set a better example for my daughter. That's not . . . me." Her gaze clouded over, hesitation in her voice like she wanted to say more.

He wasn't used to women being so blunt. Just one more thing he liked about Jasmine. She didn't seem to hold much back. She made it so easy to trust her—too easy.

She seemed lost and fragile. Like a tiny kitten in a storm. But even cats had claws. He'd do better to walk away now. But every time he was with her, it felt like he could breathe finally. He could be himself for once. He could share parts of him those closest to him had no idea about.

His eyes flicked to her mouth. Her pink tongue darted out, licking her bottom lip. He knew what she tasted like. His cock stirred, body heating. Everything inside screamed at him to take her into his arms and hold on to her. That she was the answer to every question he'd never been brave enough to ask. But she didn't fit in his life. She belonged with family cookouts, and love, not cold galas with fake smiles and rules of etiquette.

He reached out his hand, tracing the edge of her wrist. She inhaled shakily, her eyes boring into his. This growing attraction between them was something more. Something big. He had everything riding on this deal, but all he could think about was the feel of her mouth on his, and the way her legs had felt wrapped around him. Fuck it. He leaned in as she jolted to her feet. She tripped, losing her balance. Arms flailing in the sky, she fell forwards. He opened his arms, catching her against his chest. Her face stopped inches from his. She panted, eyes dropping to his mouth. The struggle creased her brows.

"We can't." Her voice was a pained whisper. Like it hurt her just as much to say as it did for him to hear.

"Jasmine?" Bently's voice interrupted their moment.

She jerked out of Atlas's embrace, clumsily getting to her feet. He gasped at the sudden empty feeling.

"Coming!" Jasmine said, jogging towards her brother, not looking back.

She sped away, something pulling him towards her. Why did it feel like they were tethered together somehow? Why did it have to be her? Atlas was going to figure this out. Whatever this was between them deserved to be explored even though he had everything on the line. It was worth the risk. *She* was worth the extra work.

16

JASMINE

Jasmine lifted the paint roller above her head, pushing it up and down to get an even coat of paint on the wall. She peeked over her shoulder. Zoey was busy coloring by the window on the far end of the room. The warm May breeze blew softly, airing out the long soon-to-be living room.

"What are you coloring?"

Zoey's pink tongue darted out in concentration as she scribbled the purple crayon across the paper. "A mermaid."

"Cool."

"Knock, knock," Atlas said as he stepped into the room, sucking out what was left of the oxygen.

She closed her eyes and inhaled a shaky breath before turning around. "Hey."

His dark hair glistened, fresh from the shower. A fitted V-neck shirt clung to his broad chest, highlighting the veins in his muscular arms. Dark-wash jeans must have been tailored to his specifications—they fit him so well.

"It's Sunday, and I thought maybe you guys would save

me from eating alone. I wanted to go back to the High Tide Diner." His gaze shifted to Zoey and then to her. A flash of vulnerability shone in them.

"I really have to finish this coat."

He turned his head, eyes roaming the room before ensnaring on hers. "Do you ever take a day off?"

"We just had a cookout."

"And you were up until after midnight in here," he said, gently.

Is he keeping tabs on me? "It needs to be done. Who else is going to do it?" she asked.

"So that's your only excuse?"

Her gaze narrowed. "It's not an excuse."

Atlas held his hands up. "I didn't mean it like that."

"How did you mean it, then?"

He smiled, showing off those perfect white teeth. "Put me to work, so we can go eat."

She blinked. He wanted . . . to help?

"You're my guest. I'm not—you can't—"

"I get to use my time how I like, and right now, that's painting this room so we can go get lunch afterwards, and maybe some more ice cream if Zoey is up for it."

"Ice cream?" Zoey perked up. "I want ice cream, Mama!"

She looked between her daughter and Atlas. She should be glad he wanted to include Zoey and spend time with them. But he didn't know she was his, so what was his ulterior motive?

"Now you've stooped to bribing my child?" She raised one eyebrow.

He stepped closer. "Let me help."

Her chest tightened, making it harder to breathe. A warm, melting sensation swirled in her belly and fluttered. "Okay. But your clothes might get ruined. You should go change."

He waved a hand. "I'll be fine. I have others."

She nodded, handing him the trim brush. "Have you ever painted before?"

He shook his head. Something about the fact that he was willingly entering completely new territory to help her made this moment much more meaningful.

Jasmine walked him through the basics and left him to his work as she finished the coat of paint on her side of the room. They completed the task much faster with the two of them.

"Did I do okay?" he asked, setting the brush on the paint can.

Jasmine came over and inspected the trim around the windows and base board. "Pretty good for a city boy who's never gotten his hands dirty before."

He chuckled. "I said I hadn't painted, not that I hadn't gotten my hands dirty."

She turned to look up at him. "Do tell?"

His grey eyes glittered with amusement. "I'd rather show you."

The air was charged with enough energy to short-circuit the whole inn. It was too easy to get caught up in whatever this was between them. Flirting with him was second nature. But having anything more would be disastrous. She backed up a step, looking over to Zoey. But she wasn't there.

"Zo—Ahh!" She jumped away as a cool slick of wetness slid over her thigh.

Zoey giggled. "Paint you, Mama."

Jasmine grabbed the paintbrush from her daughter's tiny fingers. "Zoey, this isn't the kind of paint we put on bodies." *At least it was only me who got painted.*

"Mr. Atlas's pants looks pretty now."

Shit!

He twisted, studying the side of his pants. The light yellow contrasted against his dark jeans.

Damn it to hell. Those probably cost more than I want to know. "I am *so* sorry."

He lifted his hand and waved it dismissively. "Don't worry about it. You warned me."

"Zoey, you ruined his pants."

She looked down. "I sorry. I was just trying to make it pretty."

He crouched down to look her in the eyes and smiled. "It's okay. They were kind of plain anyways."

She tipped her little chin up, eyes brightening before she looked cautiously over to Jasmine. "So, you not mad?"

He shook his head. "Nope."

"And I still get ice cream?"

He laughed. "If your mommy says it's okay."

They both turned towards her.

"I suppose." But she would be paying for lunch, even if it meant she had to skip a few meals herself. She owed Atlas that much.

* * *

Zoey pushed her plate away. "I'm full, Mommy."

Jasmine picked up a napkin and wiped the ketchup from Zoey's face. "I guess you don't have room for ice cream, then."

Zoey's eyes widened. "I am full of lunch, but I have room for ice cream."

"Ohhh. Let me see." Jasmine poked her belly as Zoey giggled. "Yes, there's your chicken nuggets, and the macaroni and cheese. Oh, yes, there's an empty spot shaped like ice cream."

Atlas laughed along with them. She met his gaze—it was

glittering with amusement once again. Jasmine tucked a tendril of hair behind her ear as the same waitress from the other day arrived.

"How was your lunch?" Brynn asked, clearing the plates.

"Great. I think we're going to get some ice cream," Atlas answered her with a smile.

"Cotton candy with rainbow sprinkles for the little one?" Brynn asked.

Atlas nodded. "Yes, and I'll take a chocolate shake for me. And a vanilla chai one—unless you want something else?" he asked Jasmine.

She shook her head. "That's perfect."

"Coming right up," Brynn said before walking away.

"I'm gonna run to the restroom real quick." Atlas stood.

He disappeared around the corner. Zoey pulled out the menu from the edge of the basket holding the condiments. She'd worked on coloring it before they'd gotten their lunch.

"Did you find all five starfish?" Jasmine asked, pointing to the hide-and-seek game on the paper.

"Almost."

A dark shadow appeared over the blue table. Jasmine looked up, her stomach sinking. *Not here.*

"Well, look what the cat dragged in. Been a while, Jaz," Jimmy said, his eyes roaming over her body. She tensed.

"Yup, here with my daughter. Have a good day." She turned back to Zoey, who was thankfully oblivious to her mother's former fuck-boy.

Take the hint and leave.

"We should get together sometime. Just like the good ol' days," Jimmy said, sliding into Atlas's seat across from her.

She jerked her head around. They'd already attracted an audience of accusatory stares. She didn't want this part of her past to touch her daughter. Panicked, she narrowed her eyes.

"As I've told you the last few unfortunate times our paths have crossed, it's not gonna happen. Besides, I don't think your wife would like that very much."

He smiled darkly. "Didn't bother you in high school."

"Well, some of us have grown and matured since then," she snapped.

"What Abby doesn't know won't hurt her. And we both know you're good at keeping your mouth shut and your legs open."

Heat rose to Jasmine's face as shame and embarrassment flooded over her. The barb was a hot and sharp poker driving through her heart, hitting its intended mark. She needed to get out of here. She searched the room wildly for an escape as her hand tightened around Zoey's shoulders.

"That's my seat." Atlas's voice had an edge to it.

She turned to look up at him. His jaw was tight, his muscles rigid. *How much of that did he hear?* Jimmy looked between Atlas and Jasmine and smirked, taking his time to stand. "Call me when this one leaves. You know I never minded sharing."

Jasmine's head snapped down, anger and shame roiling for dominance in her body. She trembled, tears burning the backs of her eyes. This was why she'd never have a happily ever after. Her dirty past. She was too broken and used. No one would want her after they knew the truth.

Atlas took the seat across from her. Her heart raced.

"You okay?" His voice was gentle, soothing, like he actually cared.

She nodded. *It's fine. Everything is fine. Swallow it down.* She lifted her chin defiantly.

His gaze roamed over her, not seductively, but more like he was checking to make sure she truly was alright.

Atlas was a good man. And he deserved to know something. If she could explain a small part, maybe he'd understand when the time came to tell him about Zoey. After all, he was no puritan either. He'd slept with a stranger in a bar, just like she had.

"I made a lot of mistakes when I was younger. He was one of them."

He nodded. "I think everyone does."

Her stomach flipped. Was he really this understanding? Did he sleep around as much as she had? Did he have other kids out there somewhere? A piece of her wall crumbled. She was beginning to trust him. Every time she expected him to run, he surprised her with patience and compassion. A man like Atlas cared about her despite her flaws, against all better judgement. But could he forgive her for the worst parts, the ones even she couldn't stomach to remember?

No one can.

"Ice cream cone for you." Brynn interrupted their moment, handing Zoey her dessert.

"Fank you."

"And two shakes," Brynn said.

"Thank you," Jasmine and Atlas said in unison.

"Let's walk to the park." Atlas stood.

"Yay! Can I swing, Mommy?"

"I guess so. Let me pay the bill first." She grabbed her purse.

"Already took care of it," Atlas said, taking Zoey's hand so she could jump from the booth to the floor.

"I was going to pay. It's the least I can do. You helped me today and—"

"Because I volunteered. Listen, I was raised to never let the lady pay. Mothers have this sixth sense. She'd know if I let you get the check and then appear here to ream me out. And we both don't want that, trust me." Atlas chuckled, leading Zoey outside.

This man. How was he so kind and good? Jasmine picked up a few extra napkins and slid them into her purse before jogging to catch up with them.

* * *

Zoey laughed as Jasmine pushed her on the swings. "Higher, Mommy! Higher."

"Any higher and you'll touch the clouds." Jasmine laughed.

"Yay! Oh—get me down. I want to play with trucks." Zoey pointed towards the sandpit where a few other kids were playing.

She slowed the swing and picked her out. Zoey ran off to the sandpit. Jasmine joined Atlas on the bench, keeping an eye on her daughter.

"We can go whenever you want to," she reminded him.

"She's having fun, and it's a nice day to be outside. I'm in no rush to get back," he assured her.

After a moment of silence, she asked, "If you had no limitations or expectations placed on you, you'd be a chef. But what else would you want in your life?"

He took a deep breath, turning to face her. "I've never thought about it. I've been raised for my place in the family business. There's actually a bit of a competition right now between my brother and me to become CEO of the company."

"That's what you want? Rather than being a chef?"

He shook his head. "A chef is a pipe dream for someone like me. It's not an acceptable job for a Remington."

"You mean it's beneath you." She crossed her arms.

He sighed. "My family thinks so."

"Do they control everything in your life? Who you date? Who you marry?"

He leaned forward, staring at his hands.

Had she struck a chord?

"They try to."

If being a chef wasn't a good enough profession for his family, she doubted a granddaughter whose mother was a struggling inn owner and had enough skeletons to fill said property would be accepted.

She closed her eyes.

"Ahhh!" Zoey screamed. Jasmine bolted forward, but once again Atlas had faster reflexes. A flash of grey rushed towards the sandpit as kids scattered. Atlas picked Zoey up and swung her out of the dog's reach.

"Waffles, stop! Sit!" A young guy came bounding after the dog. He grabbed the dog's collar. "I'm so sorry. She's friendly and loves to play, but she thinks she's still a small puppy."

"Keep her on a leash next time when there are kids around, or get some proper training for her," Atlas snapped, protectively shifting Zoey farther away. Zoey clung to his neck. He patted her back, soothingly. Was he even conscious of it?

"I'm sorry." The dog owner pulled the excited pup towards the other end of the park as it barked and jerked, trying to get loose.

Jasmine reached out and rubbed circles on Zoey's shoulders. "Are you okay, baby?"

She nodded.

Atlas's eyes flicked to hers.

"Thank you," she said.

"You're welcome."

"Why don't we get going?" Jasmine suggested.

Atlas carried her sleepy and scared little girl back to the

car. Jasmine buckled her in and climbed into the passenger seat. The smell of new leather was muted by Atlas's clean scent as he reached over to put the radio on.

He drove through town, taking the long way. Soon the rhythmic deep breathing of a sleeping child reached her ears.

"This is a beautiful little place."

"It is." It had seen its fair share of storms, but still the sun rose.

"You ever want to go anywhere else?"

She licked her lips. "I would love to visit Korea one day, immerse myself in the culture, find the missing pieces of my past."

"Would you move there?"

"No. I want to stay close to my family. The inn is my forever home."

He paused a minute as if struggling with something before he asked, "Would you ever consider selling the inn if the price was right? You could make a mint off the land alone."

She took a deep breath of fresh air. "No. This place is my hopes and dreams and everything I want to give my daughter all wrapped up in one home."

He winced.

"What are we doing? Why are you helping me paint and taking my kid and me to lunch and the park?"

He looked out his window before staring back out the windshield. "I just like spending time with you . . . I feel like me when I'm with you."

She nodded and closed her eyes. The steady vibration of the car relaxed her. They'd spent the day together like a real little family. He'd taken care of Zoey as a father should. But he didn't know he was indeed her father, and once he did, this would be over.

Was it selfish of her to want to savor these last few days

with him before she told him? If he walked away, Zoey would have some memories of her father, something Jasmine wanted so badly for herself. One less piece would be missing from her daughter's life.

She peeked in the back where Zoey was fast asleep. This was not the time or the place, but in the next few days, she was going to have to tell him. She just hoped he wouldn't punish Zoey for her crimes.

17

JASMINE

Jasmine turned the key for the second time before the car sputtered to life. Meeting with the administrator had been as encouraging as her conversation with Miss Stevens. Jasmine was not confident in the school, but what other choice did she have?

She drove out of the parking lot, towards the inn, her mind on everything else she had to do that day before picking up Zoey. Anything to try not to think of the fact that the anniversary of her mother's suicide was tomorrow.

The car lurched forward and stalled. "Damn it!" she screamed, slapping her palm on the steering wheel. She tried to restart it, and it made a horrible grinding sound before it choked to life once more.

"Just get me home and I promise I'll be forever grateful," she pleaded with the pile of junk that had lasted her far longer than it should have.

She made it home and parked. Letting go of the breath she'd been holding the whole trip, Jasmine got out. After picking up her phone, she texted Link.

Jasmine: *Find me a car that is cheap but will last. I'm ready to retire this one.*

Forced more like it. It didn't matter; she'd do whatever she had to do in order to make the payments. She had no other option. *Maybe I can pick up a few shifts at the bar with Charli on the weekends.*

She dialed Bently as she headed towards the kitchen.

"What's up?" Bently asked.

"Well, I need your help." She choked the words out. *Anything for Zoey.*

"You want that background check?"

"No. Not with that."

"Oh." He sounded disappointed. "What, then?"

She explained the situation with Zoey's school.

"I can talk to them if you want. Women's and children's safety are no joke. And I'm sure with a little pressure from the police department the school board will make the necessary changes," he said.

She smiled. As much as he was a pain in her ass, he'd always had her back. The only one who'd never abandoned her. But now he was building a life with Belle. It wasn't fair of her to push her problems on him anymore.

"Thank you, Bently."

"Anything for you, brat."

"Asshole," she retorted.

"You wound me." He chuckled.

She laughed. "Glad to know there are some chinks in your infallible armor."

He grew somber. "No one is perfect. Especially me."

"Belle has really done a number on that ego of yours." She brushed it off.

His deep laugh reverberated through the phone. "She's something else." His voice had a far-off quality to it.

"Okay, lover boy, enjoy your day. And thanks again."

"Sure thing. You too."

She hung up and tucked the phone into her back pocket. After brushing the hair from her face, she opened the kitchen drawer and found a hair tie. She braided her dark hair out of the way. Making her way to the linen closet, she then collected the items she needed to clean the rooms, as well as a fresh set of linens before adding it all to her cart.

She passed the window and stopped. Atlas was on the phone down below, shaking his head, his shoulders tense. He fisted his hands and slipped the cell into his pocket before dropping defeatedly to the sand, forehead bowed, posture slumped. *What's wrong, Atlas?*

* * *

Hours later, she pulled on a fresh pair of jeans and a T-shirt with the least amount of stains from little fingers.

Knock. Knock.

She headed over to her door and opened it. Atlas stood towering over her, his eyes a troubled stormy grey. His hair was tousled like he'd been running his fingers through it. He smiled, though it didn't reach his eyes.

"I wondered if you'd be up for dinner together?" His attention darted past her to her bedroom. "You and Zoey of course."

"I'm sorry. Tonight is book club with the girls. Zoey's at my brother's."

"Oh. Okay." Disappointment flitted across his features, his smile fading at the edges.

Her heart squeezed. The pull inside her—an overpowering need to comfort him—overrode her better judgement. She placed her hand on his arm as she asked, "Are you okay?"

He stiffened. *What the hell am I doing?* She loosened her hold, but his arms wrapped around her, locking her there. She held on in silence, his chest rising and falling with her own. The tension in the air was thick between them, anticipation zinging through her every molecule. Her skin broke out in gooseflesh. She shivered.

"Are you cold?" He let her go, holding her arms and looking at her more closely. His eyes roamed over her face.

"A little," she lied.

Atlas's eyes darted to her mouth before his arms dropped to his sides.

"I'd better go. Belle will be here soon."

He nodded, but didn't move. "So, what exactly happens at this secret book club?"

"If I told you, it wouldn't be much of a secret. And that's the key to blackmail." She winked playfully.

His jaw ticced, his face hardening. "I guess if you like that sort of thing."

"What do you mean?" she asked, confused.

"Forget it." He stepped back and left the room, the mood between them broken. Seconds later, his door shut with a little more force than necessary. She blinked, stunned. *What just happened?*

Later that evening, she was curled into a ball on Belle's couch.

"Pass the wine," Mia said before plopping on the cushion next to her.

Belle handed her the bottle. "I got this from a little vineyard in Vermont when we went a couple weeks ago."

"Oh, is that where the hard cider was from that Dre has in the fridge?" Mia asked.

Belle nodded. "Yeah. We stayed at this really cute place in the mountains. The Orchard Inn, I believe."

Jasmine's ears perked up. "I've heard of that place. One of my recent guests said her daughter helps run it."

"The couple who owns it was really cool. They had the cutest little girl running around and the woman looked close to popping with her second." Belle took a sip of her drink.

"Speaking of kids, how are the classes for foster care going?" Remy asked Belle.

"Good. We have a few weeks left. We could have a child placed with us in the next six months."

"You guys are going to be the best parents." Mia placed her hand on Belle's.

Belle's smile faltered for a moment. "I hope so."

"How about you, Mia? When are you and my brother going to give me another niece or nephew?" Remy asked, pulling a worn romance novel onto her lap from the coffee table.

Mia smiled mischievously. "We have our hands full with little Matteo. But I'll be more than happy to keep practicing for now."

"Eww. Sorry I asked." Remy covered her cheeks with her hands.

They all laughed.

"Speaking of sex, what did everyone think of chapter ten?" Belle asked.

"Oh, damn. That was a fun one to reenact." Belle fanned herself with her copy.

"Thanks for that mental image. I don't know why I bother coming here. You're all married to my brothers." Jasmine pretended to gag.

"I forget sometimes," Belle said.

Because I look different.

"We need to get you a man and then you won't complain so much," Remy teased.

Jasmine's stomach dropped. She took a sip of wine.

"How is that whole baby-daddy thing going? Have you and him . . ." Mia raised her eyebrows up and down. "You know, reenacted your own scenes?"

"No." Jasmine sat straighter. "He's her father and he doesn't even know. I can't complicate things with sex."

"She's right," Belle agreed. "I think that's smart."

"He seemed like a good guy. Andre really liked him," Mia added.

"Mikel did too," Remy said.

"He is a good guy. He's caring and patient, considerate and thoughtful," Jasmine admitted.

The girls exchanged a knowing look.

"Well, this sounds like a positive development," Remy said.

"You really like him." Mia pointed out the obvious.

Yes, she liked him. She genuinely cared for the father of her child. But that was the problem. She needed to make sure it didn't get any more complicated, for Zoey's sake. If only her heart would get the memo.

18

ATLAS

tlas sipped the coffee that wasn't half bad—now that he woke up in time to make it every morning at the inn. A cool breeze blew in from the screen door as Jasmine busied herself with cleaning up breakfast in between packing her daughter's lunch. She was quieter than usual today, focusing intently on her tasks. She didn't even make small talk with Zoey like she usually did in the mornings unless the little girl spoke to her directly.

Was it because of how he'd left last night? She'd joked about blackmailing her sisters-in-law, and it had triggered something in him. Veronica was the queen of blackmail, as were several others in their social circle. Secrets were ammunition where he was from. But after he'd cooled down, he'd realized that wasn't what Jasmine had meant. She wasn't like the socialites back home.

A few other guests milled about, planning their days or finishing up the simple pancake, sausage, and egg breakfast. A man he didn't recognize walked into the room, dressed in a military uniform—Navy maybe? He approached Jasmine who stood at the stove with her back to him and put his hands over her eyes.

"Guess who?" he said.

Atlas tensed. Who was this guy?

Jasmine's stoic expression morphed into the biggest smile he'd had the pleasure of seeing yet. His stomach sank like a rock that this guy was the one who'd pulled it from her.

"I'd know that voice and those hands anywhere. Turner! You're back?" She spun around and looped her arms around his neck.

Atlas's teeth ground together.

Turner's hands traveled down her back before slapping her playfully on her ass. It took every bit of Atlas's self-control not to tackle the man. He clenched his fists, every muscle in his body rigid.

"When did you get home? It's been years!" Jasmine asked, giving him a tight squeeze as he picked her up and spun her around. She laughed, light and free.

Atlas's gaze traveled from the blond-haired, blue-eyed man to Zoey. This guy seemed to be about Jasmine's age—young. Was he the father? Zoey looked up, her gaze fixed on her mother, eyes full of questions.

You and me both, kid.

Turner set her down, holding her hands as his gaze raked over her body. "Damn, girl, you look good enough to eat."

Jasmine blushed and swatted his chest. "You haven't changed one bit. I thought the Navy was supposed to make you respectable."

He waggled his eyebrows up and down. "I'm respectable everywhere it counts, and—" He leaned in and whispered in her ear. Jasmine's cheeks reddened even more as she giggled. He had never seen this woman giggle—not that he'd known her *that* long.

"Mommy?" Zoey asked.

Jasmine's attention darted to her daughter, a flicker of apprehension crossing her face. "Turner, this is my daughter, Zoey."

Turner walked over to the dining table and extended his hand. "Nice to meet you, Zoey. You look just as beautiful as your mama. I bet you're a little troublemaker too."

The little girl reached out and shook his hand hesitantly. Turner pulled a lollipop from his pocket and offered it to her. "Do you like sweets? I always carry a few of these with me just in case I find a fellow sugar-lover."

Zoey grinned as she looked to her mother for permission. Jasmine rolled her eyes and nodded. "Just this once."

"Fank you." She grasped the lollipop.

Turner straightened. His eyes flicked to Atlas and the other guests before offering a nod and focusing his attention back on Jasmine.

"Sorry, I didn't mean to interrupt your morning. I just know today isn't an easy one for you," Turner said.

What does he mean?

Jasmine's face dropped, her smile gone. "Oh, yeah. I appreciate it."

Turner pulled her into another hug.

His chest burned. Atlas wanted to be the one to know Jasmine's secrets.

"Do you like lollipops, Mr. Atlas?" Zoey asked.

For the first time, that name grated on his nerves. Why was he introduced as mister and Turner got to be just Turner? Who was this man to Jasmine? And why did he have to care so fucking much?

"No," he answered a little more gruffly than he'd intended.

Zoey's eyes widened and her mouth opened into an O. "I thought everybody liked candy."

"I prefer chocolate." He winked. It wasn't her fault he was rabid with jealousy over the man who couldn't keep his filthy hands off her mother.

"I noticed the grass needed mowing. I'll be back tomorrow to take care of it," Turner said, letting Jasmine go.

Hot anger wrapped around him and squeezed. He wanted to be the one to help Jasmine if she needed it, not this pretty-boy sailor.

"Oh, no. I got it covered," Jasmine argued.

"Already got the mower loaded into the truck and on the agenda for tomorrow. I'll be working with Dad's landscaping company for the rest of my leave. It's not a problem. Besides, I still owe you one."

She waved her hand dismissively. "Turner, I can't—"

"I insist," he ordered.

She nodded, conceding. "Okay. But then we're even."

He grinned. "Whatever you say, Trouble."

She smiled, and shook her head. "Don't ever change, Turner."

"I won't." He pulled her in again and kissed her cheek.

Pain radiated through Atlas's jaw as he clamped his teeth harder. He forced his eyes to his white knuckles. *She isn't mine.* His chest tightened, his lungs cinching together and cutting off his oxygen supply.

I'm just a guest. Temporary. But it didn't do anything to calm the riot raging inside him at seeing Jasmine in another man's arms.

"See ya later," Turner said before giving Zoey a wave and a wink as he left.

Jasmine walked over to clear the table, her eyes landing on his. Her brows drew together. "Are you okay?"

"Fucking fantastic."

Jasmine's mouth dropped open as her face flushed. Her eyes flicked to Zoey who was seemingly too focused on her candy to have heard his slip.

Atlas shot to his feet and darted out the back screen door towards the ocean. He needed some air. And a long walk to get this monster inside him under control.

Hours later, he wandered back to the inn. He owed Jasmine an apology for losing his temper and saying what he'd said in front of her daughter. But he also wanted to be put out of his misery and know who the fuck Turner was to her.

Was he an old boyfriend? Zoey's father? Not that it should matter because he was leaving in four days. *But it did.* Technically he'd gotten his answer from her about the inn. She wouldn't sell. The only trick left up his sleeve was to come out and tell her why he was here and offer her an embarrassing amount of money. Not many people could turn down the offer when they saw their name on a check with so many zeros. But he didn't want to do that because it would mean his time here really would be up. Jasmine would look at him differently. And he wasn't ready to let go just yet. He liked the Atlas he got to be here in Shattered Cove. No one had expectations of him. No one thought less of a man who had humble dreams. And *she* was here.

That little girl was worming her way into his heart too. He'd actually miss Zoey when he went back to New York. Since when did he give a child a second thought?

He pushed open the screen door and walked through the empty kitchen. Voices came from the other room.

"We planned this weeks ago. Come on. You can handle one afternoon out with everyone," Remy said.

"I know what you all are doing. And I appreciate it, but I just want to be alone today," Jasmine replied.

"It's not only for you. They need this distraction. *They need you.*"

Jasmine huffed. "Fine."

What is today? Atlas walked the rest of the way into the inn. Both women turned to look up at him. Remy smiled, but Jasmine's gaze darted away.

"I'm gonna get Zoey's overnight bag," Jasmine said.

"Are you ready to go?" Remy turned to him.

Jasmine froze. Mikel and a herd of children came through the door with an older couple and a woman he recognized from the bar.

"Hey, man." Mikel raised his fist to bump Atlas's. "Ready to go?"

Oh, shit. I forgot.

Jasmine's eyes darted to her brother's. "What do you mean?"

"We invited him at the cookout. Come on. It will be fun." Mikel turned back to Atlas.

"So, he got a few days' notice, and you drop it on me today?" Jasmine snapped.

Mikel offered a sheepish smile. "I knew you'd run away if we told you."

"Running away is your MO not mine," Jasmine said, a flash of anger and then regret in her eyes.

Mikel's jaw tightened.

"Jaz," Remy warned.

What is going on?

Jasmine's gaze clouded over, her face stoic as if a mask had been slipped on. "I'll get Zoey's stuff." She turned and jogged up the stairs.

The couple exchanged glances before Remy gave Mikel a hug. "She'll come around."

The other woman stepped forward. "You must be Atlas. I

think I recognize you from the bar, right? I'm Charli."

He smiled. "Yes. That's right."

"Are you going to the ropes course too?" Atlas asked her.

She shook her head and ran a tattooed hand over her small baby bump. "Oh, no. I'll be manning the inn while y'all go have fun."

"Is Finn coming later?" Mikel asked.

"He'll be picking me up." Charli said with a smile.

"Isn't he leaving soon?" Remy asked.

Charli nodded. "Yeah, he and a buddy of his from the Army are going fishing in Washington in a month or so. Still working out the dates."

"Alright, kiddos, go to the bathroom and then we gotta get going. Papa Stone has got popsicles for you all in the freezer at home," a woman who looked a lot like an older version of Remy said, moving her way over to Atlas.

Her kind eyes met his and her mouth dropped open. A man whom he presumed to be Papa Stone came up next to her. His eyes widened.

Why are they so shocked?

"Mom, Dad, this is Atlas. He's a *guest* at the inn," Remy said, sliding in front of him. Her father's gaze darted to her and then he nodded.

Her mother smiled politely. "Nice to meet you, Atlas."

"You too."

After the awkward introductions, Atlas sat back as the kids ran around. Their parents ushered them out to one of the waiting SUVs.

"Come on. You can ride with us. We're gonna take one car and meet up with everyone else at the course." Mikel patted Atlas on the back.

"Maybe I shouldn't go. I don't think Jasmine—"

"Trust me on this. She needs it more than she knows," Mikel said, giving him a gentle push towards the car.

He climbed into the back and buckled up as Remy turned the radio on from the passenger seat.

Atlas peeked out the window as Mikel got in and reached across the console to hold his wife's hand as they waited. Jasmine left the inn, a pink bag over her shoulder. She entered the SUV with the kids, coming out a moment later without the luggage. Not looking up, she walked to their car and slid in. Jasmine sat as far away from him as she could after shutting the door.

Mikel pulled onto the road.

Atlas glanced over at her. Jasmine's attention stayed glued out the window, her eyes empty and glassy. Like she wasn't really there in the car with them. Who had been the one to cause her pain?

He was helpless. An awkward outsider. What could he do? It wasn't rational, but he wanted to be the one to pull her close and hold her while she released whatever it was she was holding inside. To wipe the stubborn tears when they eventually fell. The man to make it all better and earn one of those wild and free smiles that felt like sunshine in the dark. But had he already missed his chance? Would Turner be that man for her?

Over my dead body.

He had no idea what this was between them, but it was time he did something about it. Their relationship was a storm he wasn't prepared for, strong enough to drown him. It was time to jump into the deep end. She'd been the siren who'd drawn him to her. He'd just have to hold on tight and hope it wouldn't wreck him—that *she* wouldn't sink him.

19

ATLAS

"Always keep one of these attached to the line. Only remove one at a time and pull to make sure it's secure. Got it?" the instructor asked.

"Got it," they all said in unison.

"Okay, go for it. Have fun. And be safe."

Bently and Belle led the way up the stairs before attaching their gear to the ropes course line. Remy and Mikel followed them.

"I don't know about this," Mia said, grasping her husband's arm for dear life.

Andre attached his clip to the metal rope and then hers. "It's completely safe."

Jasmine hung back, staring up at the highest level of the ropes course. Atlas held out his arm. "After you."

Her green eyes flicked to him, flashing with apprehension. "It's a long way to fall."

"I'll catch you. I promise." His words had never felt truer.

She blinked away and headed up the stairs, attaching her gear. He followed as she passed the first floor and moved past the second, all the way to the third. He peeked out the window, his stomach flipping. *It's a lot higher from up here.* She continued on the stairs, up to the highest course, almost like a challenge. Whether it was to see if he could back up his words with action or to prove something to herself, he didn't know.

She moved her hooks to the first cable above them and climbed the rope ladder. Her round ass swayed as she moved farther on. He followed once she was at the top. She'd chosen a tire obstacle. Her little body reached out to the rope as her feet jumped from one tire to the next. He swallowed hard and took his turn. The other couples laughed and screamed occasionally from below. No one was up here except them. A light breeze blew over him. Sweat beaded on his forehead.

The next option was a wooden plank or a line of large hoops. He wiped his brow. Jasmine stood panting only inches from him. She turned towards the hoops. His stomach dropped. Of course she chose the scariest obstacle. Her hands trembled on the line.

"I'll go first." The words left his mouth before he'd thought it through. But something inside him told him she needed this. Needed to see him prove his words true.

He slipped his arm across her, putting one clip on the line in front of hers before repeating the process with the other. With little room on the platform for maneuvering, he brushed against her. He grabbed the swaying ring, trying his damnedest to not look down.

He turned back to Jasmine. Her vulnerable eyes were glued to him, her cheeks reddened from the exertion. "You don't have to do this one."

"Are you going to?"

She nodded. "I'm feeling a little reckless today."

More unflinching honesty from this lost beauty.

"I told you, I got you." He grabbed the other side with his

hand and leaped. The feeling of free-falling only lasted a second. Both hands grasped the edge of the wide hoop.

She gasped from behind him. He fought hard to find his balance, but it was impossible. The hoop wiggled under his feet. He had two choices: jump to the next one and cling for dear life or go back. Failure was not an option. He pushed himself forward and grasped the plastic.

"Oh, shit," Jasmine said. He couldn't turn around and look because his primary focus was not to fall to his death. He grabbed the metal cable attached to his gear and held on as if his life depended on it. After a few shaky moments, he was able to center his gravity. He only had three more of these to go. *Only.* This had to be safe. But his body screamed at him in self-preservation to go back.

"You got this," Jasmine encouraged.

A surge of determination washed over him. He reached for the next ring and leaped. He grasped the hoop and looked down. Big mistake. His stomach lurched and flipped. His head spun. He clung to his gear and tried to find his balance once again. Atlas was directly in the middle of this death trap. It was just as far back as it was forward. He closed his eyes and took a deep breath.

"Almost there. What's your worst fear?" Jasmine asked.

"Is that supposed to make me feel better right now?"

"Just answer!"

"Falling to my death," he answered deadpan.

"Other than that."

"Snakes."

"Like, little garter snakes? Or pythons?" She giggled.

He pushed out a puff of air, the corner of his mouth curving up momentarily. "All snakes. Big or small. No fucking thank you." He reached and jumped to the next one. His body swayed on the hoop as he readied himself for the last jump. But her distraction was working.

"What fear keeps you awake at night?" she asked.

He closed his eyes. "Failing."

"That's gonna make getting to the other side that much sweeter."

The last jump was almost harder than the first. They seemed to be farther apart. But once he reached the wooden platform, he wanted to kiss the ground with relief.

"Wooo!" he yelled instead, turning around.

Jasmine's hand dropped from her face revealing a huge grin. "You fucking did it!"

It was impossible not to smile seeing her amazed expression. He laughed. "Now it's your turn."

Her eyes darted down, all her visible joy going with them.

"Or you could take the plank and meet me on the other side over there," he offered.

Her chest rose and fell as she lifted her chin with determination. "No, I got this." Her voice wavered like she didn't believe herself.

She reached out towards the hoop.

"Grab the edges, slip your feet on, and then use your gear cord to get your balance," he directed.

She hesitated another moment before she leapt, doing as he said. The color drained from her face as she squeezed her eyes together. "Oh my God!"

"That's it. You got this. Focus on the next one."

She reached out, her gaze dropping towards the earth far below. Jasmine whipped her hand back to her gear, stark fear etched across her expression.

"Don't look down. Look at me," he ordered.

Her eyes darted to his as he looked on helplessly. He'd do

the course again just to rid her of the terrified look on her face.

"That's it, honey." The endearment slipped from his lips. "Look at me. It's just us up here and there is no rush. You got this."

She nodded and reached forward, moving stiffly to the next hoop.

"Yes. You got it!"

The hint of a smile turned the corners of her mouth up before she reached for the next one. Each ring she conquered, her confidence seemed to grow.

"This is it. Last one and then you're safe." He cheered her on. It was also the hardest one because the lead cord went up at an angle to the platform and she was at least a foot and a half shorter than him.

She lifted her arm and jumped, her foot barely making purchase before it slipped. She fell, arms flailing. But he caught her in an iron grip before she slid down the cord. He hauled her onto the platform, tucking her safely against his chest. Her rib cage heaved as she clung to him the same way Zoey had when the dog at the park had scared her. But this time his body reacted to the closeness. A mixture of arousal and adrenaline coursed through his veins. His ears rang, blood pumping like a jackhammer. He rubbed his hand in a circle on her back while holding onto her waist with his other arm.

"Thank you for catching me."

"I told you I would. I'm a man of my word."

"I'm beginning to see that."

An hour later, they joined the other couples back on the ground. His muscles ached in places he hadn't known existed, and the hint of rope burn stung his hands.

"It was so scary," Mia said, taking a sip from her water bottle.

Andre laughed. "You stayed on the first level."

She glared at him. "I did not. This is the first level." She pointed towards the area where a few young children took turns.

"That's not even a level. That's the kiddie area." Andre chuckled.

Mia crossed her arms over her chest and everyone in their group laughed.

"I'm gonna find a bathroom," Atlas said, turning to walk towards the porta-potties lined up along the gravel walkway towards the forest.

After he'd relieved himself and used the hand sanitizer, he walked back into the warm sunshine. He hadn't smiled this much, this often, since . . . when? When had he ever been this carefree?

He neared the edge of the group, walking behind Jasmine. The atmosphere had shifted. The others looked down as if they'd rather be anywhere else but there. The only two looking at her were Mikel and Bently, sorrow, anger, and confusion reflecting back.

"She knew! She knew what he did to me and left me there. Don't try to pretend a few good moments make up for that."

Her brothers' faces drained of color before turning red.

What the hell have I walked into? Should I go before she sees me? But more importantly, who was the fucker who'd laid a hand on her?

20

JASMINE

Jasmine swallowed. The burn of the alcohol was dulled by the numbness that consumed her. She turned her face towards the dim sky. Even the moon was hiding tonight. Seventeen years had gone by since the incident, and this day hadn't gotten any easier. *Happy birthday to me.*

"How could you leave us?" Jasmine swiped the tears that fell without permission. Grief and sadness threatened to swallow her whole. She'd kept them behind a locked door for so long—unable to afford to let them out, to feel them. They would drag her to the deepest darkest depths of the ocean and drown her. She couldn't fall apart. Jasmine had Zoey to think of. Zoey needed a mother who wouldn't check out. A mother who would protect her.

"How could a mother leave her child with a monster?" Her voice broke. *I would never do that to Zoey.*

She took another swig of the moonshine, her head spinning. Sticky, hot anger roiled from the depths of hell in her soul. The cool breeze wrapped around her like sickly, cold, dead fingers everywhere all at once. Goose bumps coasted over her flesh. She slapped the air, spilling the bottle. Shooting to her feet, she shivered. A million invisible bugs crawled over her skin as the scent of stale cigarette smoke and his acrid breath assaulted her.

"It's not real. It's not real," she cried, wrapping her arms around herself.

The memory crashed over her like a rogue wave, unforgiving and overpowering. *The tang of his salty release as she choked, bile rising in her throat. Her stepfather's grunts as he forced himself deeper, cutting off her oxygen. The gasp from the doorway as her mother's shocked and horrified face locked on to them.*

"Shut the fucking door, Marie," her stepfather growled.

Her mother hesitated only a moment. Jasmine pleaded with her eyes. Please help me.

Marie dropped her gaze and left. And that violation felt worse than any other she'd endured at the hands of her stepfather. That was the moment her body shut down, locking away anything tender and childlike. That was the day she realized she was truly alone and no one would save her.

"It's time you earned your keep. Dirty little whore. This is all you're good for," her stepfather said, over and over and over until she started believing him somewhere along the way.

Four hours later, Bently found their mother hanging in the basement. Her final abandonment.

It was my fault. I killed her.

Jasmine gasped for oxygen. She stumbled down the stairs, falling to the ground as her stomach emptied onto the sand.

She wiped her mouth with a shaky hand and looked up towards the inn. The only place that was truly safe and untainted by her past. A light flicked on. *Atlas.*

Her chest ached, pain lashing it. The physical torment was agonizing. The weight of shame crushed her chest. The anger at herself, the situation, her mother, and her stepfather made her skin burn hot. She needed relief—no matter how temporary. An escape. And to punish herself the only way she knew how.

Jasmine stumbled into the inn, making her way up to her bathroom where she brushed her teeth. She glanced at the reflection staring back at her with glazed eyes. She didn't even recognize herself. Jasmine tucked her wild black hair behind her ear.

You're only good for one thing anyways.

She washed her tear-stained face, removing the evidence. Only the cruelest men liked to fuck girls with tears, and Atlas wasn't one of them.

Jasmine inhaled a shaky breath to steady herself as she walked out of her room and across the hall. Her heart raced. Each beat reminded her that, despite herself, she was alive. She was trapped in a living hell that had chosen to break out from the door she kept it locked behind tonight. Needing to escape this fresh pain from old wounds, she took another deep breath and knocked. There was no turning back. Atlas could take her where she needed to go: a break from reality and the punishment that she craved more than anything else. She truly was depraved, just like her stepfather had said.

The door opened, light shining into the dark hallway, casting Atlas's face in shadows. He was a silhouette edged in hope. Everything she could never have. The ultimate torture.

"Jasmine?" The worry in his voice sent her over the edge.

She didn't need him to care for her; she needed him to use her.

Crashing her mouth onto his, she kissed him like the world was ending—and for her, it was. He hesitated, frozen in the doorway. She slicked her hands over his chest. He gripped the back of her head and pulled her into the room, slamming the door closed behind her. His kiss was all-consuming, lust branding her with each flick of his tongue. She slid her palm over his cock through his pajama bottoms.

He jerked away, wrenching out of her arms. His chest heaved, his eyes dark. "You taste like that shitty moonshine. What's going on?" he rasped.

"You don't want me again?"

His brows scrunched up. What had she said?

"Again? Honey, you're not making any sense."

She reached out, tracing his jawline. "Just tonight. Help me forget."

"Help you forget what?" His fingertips burned into her hip.

The urge to tell him everything bubbled up. She hadn't told anyone. *Ever.* She'd held it all inside. Not even her brothers knew it all. Only what Mikel had seen. But if she told Atlas, he'd never look at her the same. The desire in his eyes would turn to pity. The want that powered his grasp would release with disgust. He'd see how broken she really was.

His hands cupped her face as he searched her eyes, as if her secrets were hidden there. But it was all in vain because she kept them buried in the deepest darkest recesses of her soul. And even she didn't go down there.

"What do you need to forget, baby?" he repeated.

She closed her eyes, unable to look into the same grey orbs that her daughter shared. Zoey was tucked safely in bed at her grandparents'. Tonight Jasmine would allow herself this dirty pleasure mixed with pain. She'd pay for it tomorrow. *I always do.*

"Everything. Help me forget everything," she pleaded.

His forehead leaned against hers. His hot breath tickling against her mouth.

"You don't know how much I'm tempted, beautiful. But

even a blind man could see how you're hurting. And you're drunk. I won't take advantage of you like that."

She whimpered, the loss and rejection too much. Jasmine pulled away, but he held her firmly, wrapping her against his chest.

"*When* I make love to you, it's gonna be when you're sober. I want you to remember every single moment. And I want to know it's what you really want."

Fat droplets fell from her eyelashes, soaking his shirt. Tiny sobs wracked her body. But he only held on tighter.

No one had ever treated her like this. Cherished her. No man had ever turned down no-strings-attached sex before. They didn't care about her mental state, nor her alcohol consumption. But not Atlas.

"Ssshhh. I got you. You can let go. I'm here to catch you," he said, picking her up in his arms and carrying her over to the bed. The sheets smelled like him. The mattress dipped as he climbed in next to her, pulling her against his warm chest.

She had no idea how much time had passed, but eventually her tears dried. He gently stroked her hair. She relaxed into him, head pounding from the crying. But for once in her life, she felt safe. She'd hang on to that feeling however long it lasted. Safety had always been fleeting at best.

"Today's my birthday," she said.

His hand stilled. "I have a feeling you don't want me to say 'happy birthday.'"

She shook her head. "My mother killed herself seventeen years ago today."

His grip tightened as he exhaled into her hair. "I'm sorry."

"I don't know why I'm telling you this. Maybe because I don't want you to think I'm a total mess for no reason."

He kissed her forehead and her heart melted.

"I'd never think that."

If you only knew.

"Can I ask you a question?" His voice was like gravel.

She nodded.

"Who hurt you?"

Her breathing hitched. "That's a long list." And most were because she'd let them. Her own way of hurting herself—a sick attempt at redemption through pain.

Her eyes fluttered closed against his comforting chest, her breathing matching his. Drifting off, she said, "Please don't hate me."

"Why would I hate you?"

"Because of Zoey," she answered.

Somewhere in her alcohol-hazed mind was a warning that she had just slipped up. But she couldn't find it in her to care, because for the first time in her life, she felt completely safe in a man's arms. She would worry about tomorrow when it came. Every single one of her actions had a negative consequence. And this time would be no different.

21

ATLAS

The early morning rays of the sun peeked in through the curtains Atlas had left open. His eyes fluttered open. His arm ached from being in the same position all night, but waking up to the warm body beside him was worth it.

He studied Jasmine as she slept. Her dark tendrils of hair spilled over the pillow. Her long, dark eyelashes fanned over her lightly freckled cheeks. Her mouth was open at the edge, drool leaking on his arm. He grinned. Seeing her like this, so vulnerable, was adorable. She was breathtaking from afar, but up close she was like a dream. His chest squeezed. Since when did he have a woman in his bed who actually stayed the night? It had been years since . . . *Veronica.*

He dipped his head, breathing Jasmine in. He was drunk on her closeness, intoxicated by her scent. His cock was rock hard, begging for release. But that would have to wait. He'd endure torture if it meant he got to keep this woman in his arms a little longer.

What did she mean last night about him hating her

because of Zoey? Did she think he was that shallow of a man to think less of her because she'd had one bad night? As far as he knew, Zoey was safe at her family's. She hadn't been reckless. Why did it bother her so much what he thought of her anyway?

After the little he'd learned about her, every protective instinct inside him made him want to keep her close. He yearned to hold on to her and not let go, be the one to keep her safe. He wanted this woman, but he needed to take care of her. She'd obviously seen so much hurt in her life. He wouldn't be the asshole to add to that. Despite what she seemed to think of herself, Jasmine was a fucking warrior. She lived life according to her own rules, and he admired the shit out of her. But she seemed to have blinders on when it came to seeing what a kick-ass woman she was.

Jasmine stirred, covering her eyes with her arm and groaning. She probably had one hell of a hangover.

"Hey, Sleeping Beauty."

She jolted up. Wincing, she held her head. "Oh my God. Did we?" She motioned her finger back and forth between them.

"No. We did not. I promise it'd be more memorable," he teased.

She sighed with what looked like relief. "I'm so sorry. I'm a terrible innkeeper, sleeping with—or next to—my guest. I don't usually get sloppy drunk like that. Not since . . . well, before Zoey."

"What about with Turner?" Now was as good a time as any to find out exactly what was between them.

Jasmine frowned. "Turner?"

"You seemed mighty close when he stopped by yesterday."

"He's my best friend from high school," she said, her eyebrow quirking up.

"Did you and him ever . . ."

"Not that it's any of your business, but no. He was one of the few who never tried." She rubbed her temples.

"Could have fooled me," he grumbled.

"Are you jealous?" she asked, amusement sparking in her green eyes.

He pulled the back of her head forward as he kissed her. Jasmine's lips locked together, but she melted softly against him.

"I have morning breath and it feels like I swallowed sand." She blushed.

"That would be from the moonshine I'm guessing." He got out of bed and grabbed a bottle of water from the tiny fridge before handing it to her. She unscrewed the cap and took a sip while he dug out a few painkillers from his bag.

"Thank you." She stood, tucking her hair behind her ear. She glanced at the clock. "I should get going. I'm sorry to intrude."

He cupped her face, forcing her to meet his eyes. "I'm glad you came to me. I'm gonna take a shower and then I'll be down to make you a hangover cure for breakfast."

Her brows creased together like she was trying to figure him out. This woman wasn't used to being taken care of, and it made him want to be the one to take up the job all the more. He kissed her again before opening the door for her. She hurried over to her room, giving him a nod before closing herself inside.

Walking into the bathroom, he took a look at himself in the mirror. The stupid grin on his face was new. He turned the shower on and stripped naked before climbing in.

* * *

Two hours later, he'd fed Jasmine, making enough for the couple of other guests sharing the inn. She'd left to pick up Zoey, and he took the opportunity to go for a jog down the coast. It was a lot harder to run in sand than on his treadmill in his home gym. His muscles ached as he sped up into a sprint.

Beep. Beep. Beep.

He slowed down to a walk, gasping for breath as he picked up the call. "Hello?"

"Did I catch you at a bad time?" his mother asked.

"Just out for a run. What's up?"

"Seriously, Atlas, I raised you with better etiquette than that," his mother snapped.

He rolled his eyes. "Sorry, Mother. What can I help you with?"

"For starters, you can come back to the office. Quit your fool's errand at that inn and return to do some actual work."

Right. The whole reason he was here. How had he let his goal fall by the wayside? Those green eyes of course, and the little grey ones that were never far behind.

"I'm working on it. I have three days left."

"Just get it done or come home. We have plans to make. Veronica's parents are going to stop by next week for dinner, and it would be a good time for us all to talk about the next steps for you two."

He gritted his teeth. "Mother, that's not—"

"You are so stubborn. Look at Oliver. He's quite happy with our little arrangement. Christina is just who he needs on his arm. I sent something to the inn to make you remember why you need to get back here. Be on the lookout for it. Wouldn't want it to get lost."

"Moth—"

"I have to go now. See you soon, darling. Ciao." The call ended.

He pulled his phone from his ear and stared at it. What the hell was he doing? Maybe this town had gotten to his head. This place was temporary. But that CEO position was forever. It was what he'd wanted more than anything . . . Wasn't it? He shook his head, slipping the phone back into his pocket, and jogged back towards the inn.

I'll ask her once and for all and then if she says no, I'll stay my three more days and go back to reality. And then . . . what? Could he go back and forth? *Yeah, right.* That would never work with his schedule. It would be better if he left her alone. She deserved someone who could be there for her and her daughter. Maybe he should leave sooner.

Zoey's giggle erupted from behind the beach grass. Atlas slowed to a walk, hands on his hips. Jasmine tickled the little girl. The smile on Jasmine's face sucked the breath from his lungs. She was radiant.

"Stop, Mommy!" Zoey pleaded.

Jasmine immediately stopped. "Is that enough tickling?"

"Yes. I want to build a sandcastle now. Mr. Atlas!"

Jasmine's head whipped up, her gaze meeting his. A slight pink colored her cheeks.

"Hey, sweetheart."

"Will you build a sandcastle with me?" Zoey asked, holding her hands out in front of her like a prayer.

He couldn't say no to that little face. "Sure."

She giggled and grinned. "Yay! Okay, you can sit here on our banket."

For the next forty-five minutes, he took instructions from a very excited three-year-old, trudging buckets of water back and forth from the sea. They worked together to create whatever castle Zoey had constructed in her little mind.

"It's perfwect!" She clapped.

They took a break for water and a picnic lunch of simple sandwiches under an umbrella on the beach. The waves and blue sky were the beautiful backdrop for the most perfect afternoon.

The low hum of a mower was the only sound out of place. Jasmine waved to Turner as he packed up the machine. Atlas felt a little better knowing the guy's history with her. But a man could tell when another male wanted a woman. And Turner had his sights set on Jasmine.

"Do you want an extra sandwich?" Jasmine asked.

"No, thanks," he said.

Jasmine nodded, brushing her hand over Zoey's sweaty forehead. The little girl's eyes fluttered closed with her head on her mother's lap. Her tan arms wound around Jasmine's waist. An outsider looking at the three of them would assume they were a little family. A twinge of something foreign tugged at his heart.

That wasn't for him. Not this. Not with her. And it was time he did what he came here for.

"This inn is something special."

She smiled, glancing at the white building behind them. "I'm glad you agree."

"You don't think you'd ever be willing to sell it?"

Her forehead bunched as she studied him. "You keep asking that."

"I'm in real estate. I know a place like this could go for a cool one and a half million. I know you could use that cash."

She turned to face the beach, silently watching the waves for a few moments. "Tell me about the restaurant of your dreams. What would it look like?"

He shrugged. "I haven't thought about it."

She cut him a disbelieving look that called his bullshit.

"Something rustic but modern. Farm to table. Fresh ingredients. Family friendly, but also higher class. Somewhere anyone would fit in."

She closed her eyes as if imagining it. "What would you call it?"

"Atlantis."

Her lips curved up. "What would the menu be like?"

"Seasonal. Fresh seafood from the fishermen at the docks, proteins from local farmers, along with most of the vegetables."

"And after you found the building—the one that felt like the perfect fit. The one where you had to tear up the horrible shag carpeting and replace it with actual wood flooring—you'd move all the tables in and get your kitchen equipment. You'd set everything up just how you wanted it. It would be back-breaking hard work, but you'd know it was worth it. You'd have the menu designed and tested. You'd have your first customers, and they'd love the food. You'd have a fuller crowd every night as word spread of your awesome restaurant and the chef behind the magic."

He nodded. The picture of where she was going with this becoming clear.

"If someone walked into your restaurant and handed you a check for one and a half million dollars, would you sell it? Knowing it would be knocked down and made into something less yours?"

He swallowed, a punch to his gut at the thought of having all he'd dreamed of and then trading it for cash. "No."

"Why?"

"Because it's not about the money. It's about the dream," he answered, disappointment and understanding spiraling inside. That answered that. She wouldn't sell, and he'd have to find another way to prove his worth to his parents and grandfather.

"What's holding you back from doing that? From owning your own restaurant?" Jasmine asked.

The thought scared him as much as it excited him. "I'd have to risk it all, and in the process, disappoint my family. If I failed, I wouldn't get another shot. The Remingtons are expected to live a certain life, work at the family business, dress a specific way, and marry the right kind of people."

She winced. "That sounds exhausting."

"It is."

"Why do it if it doesn't make you happy?"

He turned to face her. "I never said that."

"Your face doesn't light up when you talk about real estate and your family like it does about Atlantis."

He reached out, tucking a stray lock of hair behind her ear. His hand lingered against her cheek. Her green eyes locked on his, vulnerability flashing in her gaze. How could this woman see through him? Unearth things even he was blind to?

"You see me."

Her eyes darted to his mouth.

"Can I kiss you?"

She licked her lips, gaze flicking to her sleeping daughter before returning to his. "Okay. But there's something I need to tell you."

"I'm all ears." He leaned over, brushing his mouth against her soft, pink lips. She tasted like sunshine and strawberries. Heat melted him from the inside out. His heart raced, his pulse jumped. He'd never felt anything like it: complete and utter rapture from just the slightest touch of this woman. She pulled away, resting her head on his shoulder. He wrapped his arm around her, Zoey sleeping between them. Never had he felt this complete, this *right* before.

What are you doing to me?

"Atlas?"

His spine stiffened. That whiny voice was unmistakable. He turned around and stood. Veronica sneered from the porch. Her designer handbag was clutched to her chest with her perfectly manicured nails.

What the fuck is she doing here?

Mother.

"There you are. I missed you." She clicked her heels down the wooden stairs. Her eyes narrowed on Jasmine. He needed to get Veronica away from her. The socialite was vicious when she wanted to be.

"What are you doing here?" he snapped, walking over to her.

"Your mother told me where you were staying. I thought I'd surprise you and we could talk about the engagement party." Her voice rose.

Atlas cut a look towards Jasmine. Her face fell before resignation transformed her expression into a stoic mask.

Shit.

"You wasted your time. Let's go. I'll show you the door." He grabbed Veronica's arm and pulled her towards the inn, away from Jasmine and Zoey. He needed to get them out of Veronica's sight before his two worlds could collide.

22

JASMINE

Jasmine buckled her half-asleep child in the car. The backs of her eyes stung, and her chest felt as if someone had punched a hole through it. But that cheating bastard didn't deserve her tears.

Of course he would be engaged to *her*. Whoever she was, she clearly came from the same circles as Atlas—if her designer shoes were any indication. Her bag probably cost more than Jasmine could ever dream of affording; it screamed money. She was tall, pretty, and model perfect like he'd picked her out of a catalog. *Everything I'm not.*

Atlas belonged with someone like that. And to entertain the thought of keeping him for herself was clearly a fairy tale. She'd thought he was different. *Guess that's what I get when I open my heart up.* Jasmine winced. The worst part was, she had begun to trust him.

So where does that leave Zoey? Had she truly fucked this up for her daughter? Had this all been an act from Atlas to get into her pants?

No. He'd turned her down. So, what did he want?

"Jasmine." Atlas's voice brought a fresh wave of pain slicing through her.

"Leave me alone." She shut Zoey's door and went over to hers before lifting the handle to open it.

Atlas's hand clamped over hers. "Please let me explain."

She shook her head, glancing at Zoey to make sure she was still sleeping. Jasmine lowered her voice, emotionally drained. "I can't for the love of me figure out what you want. What are you doing here if you have a fiancée like *that* waiting back home for you? Do you get off on manipulating people?"

"It's not what it looks like—"

"It never is. What do you want from me, Atlas? It isn't sex or you'd have not been so chivalrous last night." Jasmine searched his face.

The only other thing he'd talked about was her inn. He was in real estate.

"Is it the inn?" Her voice broke. Was this all to get her to sell?

He hesitated and closed his eyes, running a hand over his face. "No. It's not about the inn. I came here . . . and then everything changed. I wasn't expecting . . . you."

Why did that have to make her heart flutter? Why did he have to seem so perfect? But he wasn't. He was engaged!

"Well, I wish you the best for your engagement." She opened the car door and slipped inside.

He held it open, conflict written across the hard lines and edges of his face. His eyes flashed to Zoey before he lowered his voice. "Veronica isn't my fiancée."

She pulled the door, and he stepped into the opening, lowering himself to look her in the eye. "When I was young and stupid, I thought I loved her. I haven't been with her since I was twenty years old. Since I found out she had been cheating on me with my best friend."

"You don't need to tell me this." She inhaled a shaky breath.

"But I want to. My family is the one pushing for us to get married now, even though I have no intention of doing that—I *never* did."

His grey eyes seemed sincere, his words true, but how could she know for sure?

"I'm gonna be late," she lied.

He bowed his head defeatedly, shoulders slumped as he backed away. She turned the key, hoping it would start and that she'd filled her humiliation quota for the day.

The engine turned over with a squeal, and she winced. She glanced to his sparkling new Mercedes as she backed out of the driveway—yet another reminder of how different their worlds were. Only they did share one thing.

Zoey's dark hair caught her attention in the rearview mirror. It was time to tell him everything and face the fallout.

* * *

She parked the car outside Belle and Bently's large home. After opening the back door, she unbuckled her daughter. Zoey's eyes blinked open.

"You go ahead inside. I'm gonna make a call real quick and be right in." She kissed Zoey's cheek.

"Otay, Mommy." Zoey rubbed her eyes before she skipped down the walkway. Belle opened the door and waved. Jasmine pointed to her phone and held up her finger. She waited until the girls were both inside before she turned towards the street and typed out a text to Remy.

Jasmine: *Thank you for coming to the inn early to cover for me. I appreciate it. I know it was last minute.*

Remy: *No problem. Atlas was looking for you. I told him you'd be back later.*

Jasmine swallowed the ball of emotions she didn't even want to start sorting through. She closed her eyes and pinched the bridge of her nose. After a few deep breaths, she grabbed Zoey's sleepover bag and walked inside.

Bently got home from work with *non*-birthday cupcakes for them to share—her family at least respected her wish to not celebrate her birthday on the actual day. But in the days that followed, they usually stopped by with their own treats and surprises in increments. She said her goodbye to Zoey.

She climbed in the passenger seat of Belle's car as her sister-in-law drove them to the old church.

"Everything okay?" Belle asked.

"Just peachy." Jasmine turned the radio up and stared out the window.

Belle didn't say anything else as they weaved through the roads towards the meeting. Jasmine was grateful for the silence. Her stomach was in knots, churning with a mixture of doubt and pain.

Once they arrived, they walked into the building together.

"Jasmine?" Belle asked as they climbed the old cement stairs.

"Yeah?"

"Would you prefer if I don't join you tonight?" Belle asked.

Jasmine opened the door and held it open for her. "Why would you think that?"

"Because in all the months we've come here, you've never shared your story. If you'd prefer I find another meeting, I can have a different SANE nurse to take my place."

Jasmine shook her head. "It's not you. I've never . . . told anyone."

Belle nodded. "Speaking my truth was huge in my healing journey. It was one of the hardest things I had to do, fighting that shame. But I felt lighter after. Like the more I told, the less power it had over me."

Jasmine looked down. She'd heard Belle's story. The trauma she'd endured at the hands of her mother's boyfriends or drug dealers. If anyone would understand her, it would be Belle, and the other women at this Sexual Assault Survivors meeting. But every time she got the urge to open up, the words stuck in her throat like a ball of shame. A sinking feeling that maybe, unlike these women, she had deserved what happened to her. Maybe she truly was a bad person. *That's why Mom left me.*

"Don't listen to them." Belle's strong voice interrupted her thoughts.

"Who?"

"Those voices that tell you what you don't deserve. The ones that tell you you aren't good enough. Don't let him hold any more power over you," Belle said, walking inside.

Jasmine stood stunned, conflict rioting inside her every cell. The urge to flee rose with each pained breath. She turned back to the car, hands raking through her hair. She could do what she usually did, and go in and sit quietly to listen to everyone else share. Or she could turn around and face this for the first time in her life. If anyone could help her, it was these women.

She took a deep breath, gathering all her courage. If she was going to be a better mother for Zoey, she needed to work through her issues.

One shaky step in front of the other, she walked into the church.

Jasmine was the last to arrive. She took an empty seat next to Belle. Charli waved from across the circle of chairs, next to

Brynn, the woman from the diner. *Oh no. Her too?* She recognized a few other women from previous meetings.

"Did everyone get refreshments?" Cassidy Clark, the group therapist, asked.

The ladies nodded.

"Okay, well, I thought we'd start the meeting with some meditation and then affirmations."

Cassidy led them through fifteen minutes of grounding themselves and speaking strength and resilience aloud.

"Is there anyone who wants to share today?" Cassidy asked.

Jasmine's chest tightened. Her leg bounced up and down, nerves and anxiety rushing through her. She wanted to, but could she?

Belle placed a hand over hers and squeezed. Her silent support meant everything.

"I-I think . . . I'd like to say something." Jasmine struggled for breath.

All eyes turned to her.

"Go ahead. We're listening. This is a safe space," Cassidy encouraged.

Jasmine stared down at her hands. "I was triggered recently. I had a really bad night. I was so weak."

Belle's thumb rubbed over the soft flesh of her hand, soothingly.

"I used to use sex as a form of self-harm. I felt I needed to be punished, so I'd seek out men who would only use me. I felt so powerful in that moment, letting them do exactly that to me, because I was the one who was really pulling the wool over their eyes. I was letting myself be used, so I had the power. Then . . . after . . . the shame would be my ultimate punishment. I'd prove him true."

"Prove your abuser true?" Cassidy asked.

Jasmine nodded.

"Abusers commonly use shame and threats to keep their victims under control."

"Well, during that weak moment, I gave in. I just wanted that temporary escape—no matter what I had to pay the next day. I almost erased four years of progress."

"What stopped you?" Cassidy asked.

Her eyes met Belle's; nothing but sympathy reflected back. "He did. The man, I mean. He said he wouldn't take advantage of me because I was drunk and hurting."

"He sounds like a good guy," Cassidy observed.

She closed her eyes, tears escaping. "I don't know. How would I know? How does anyone ever truly know? My brothers are good men and they both hurt the women they loved."

"Being a good person does *not* equal perfection. Let me ask you something: do you think you could be self-sabotaging a possible relationship with this man?" Cassidy asked.

Jasmine blinked. "There's so many other factors. It's so complicated."

"There usually is. Just be aware of what is keeping you closed off. Is it that you truly feel he is an unsafe person, or is it because you believe you are unworthy and afraid of the vulnerability that comes with loving someone romantically?"

Jasmine wiped her face. "I'm not sure."

"You're not alone, Jasmine. Every woman here has experienced sexual trauma in some way. I myself have. Don't be discouraged because you had a bad day. Healing is not linear. It's messy and unpredictable. You can go years without any major hiccups and then the next day it can feel like you're back at square one. But you're not. You've made it this far, and you can keep on going. Talking about it is the beginning of your healing journey. You will begin to see the light at the end of the tunnel."

"Talking about it makes it feel more real. I don't know if I'm ready for that," Jasmine confessed.

"Baby steps. No one is asking you to go into the details of your trauma, especially if it triggers you too much. But piece by piece, you can unpack this. The more you share, the more you're letting go. You're taking away your abuser's power. By doing your inner work and letting go of the responsibility for the perpetrator's actions, you stop holding yourself accountable for things you had no control over." Cassidy took a sip from her coffee cup before continuing. "And it's important to be aware of these feelings and not push them aside when they come up."

Jasmine swallowed hard, willing the ball of nerves in her belly to calm down.

Cassidy crossed her legs. "A piece of your childhood was stolen. To heal, it must be recognized as a loss and then grieved. You can reclaim your power. Remember, you're not a victim; you're a *victory*. And you're not alone. Every seventy-three seconds, someone in America is sexually abused. Every nine minutes, that victim is a child. You. Are. Not. Alone."

I'm not alone. I'm not alone.

Belle turned to her. "Sometimes, when we make progress or something new happens that triggers our self-protective responses, it can feel like we go backwards. Old wounds open, memories and flashbacks seem to come from nowhere, pulling us into that darkness."

Jasmine met her gaze. "But what if that darkness feels like it's coming from inside me?"

Cassidy offered her a warm smile. "Shame is a powerful weapon. It keeps the victim oppressed. You are not your trauma.

You are Jasmine. It happened to you, but it isn't the core of who you are. Reshape those thoughts when they come. When those voices tell you you're unworthy. When they say you're nothing but a whore for sleeping around, change it. Say to yourself, 'I made some decisions that were not best for me before, but it doesn't mean I'm a bad person. Everyone makes mistakes. I'm not a failure. I made a mistake and I'll try better next time.' Change your mindset. Flip your thoughts around until they stop focusing on you being the problem and instead change the behavior itself."

"Okay. I can try that."

"Is there anything else you want to share?"

Jasmine shook her head and leaned back in her chair.

Brynn spoke up next, sharing about her abusive ex. But all Jasmine could do was run through what Cassidy and Belle had said to her. Was she sabotaging this thing with Atlas?

His explanation made sense. He'd never kept how much his family expectations had been a thorn in his side a secret. How they didn't see eye to eye. His actions said he was a man worthy of her trust. He'd even sent Veronica away, telling her she'd wasted her time. Should Jasmine give him the benefit of the doubt? Could she trust him with her heart?

Fear sluiced through her at the thought. Maybe this was what Cassidy meant. Maybe this was where she pushed the urge to run in the opposite direction and walked towards something good, towards Atlas. Her tiny beacon of light in the darkness of her relationships. A lighthouse in the storm.

But first, she had to tell him about Zoey.

Tonight she'd tell him everything.

23

ATLAS

Atlas swiped the screen of his phone open with one hand and brought the bottle of amber liquid to his mouth with the other. He'd need some liquid courage for this call. The purchase of the inn was not going to happen, and that probably meant the CEO position wasn't either.

He tapped his contacts. Should he call his grandfather with the news? Go straight to the decision-maker? Or his mother and father?

He checked the time. His grandfather was surely asleep by now. The old man's schedule was like clockwork. In bed by ten, up at five.

"Mother dearest it is," he grumbled and clicked her name.

It rang twice before she answered. "Hello? Hold on. Let me put you on speaker phone."

"Mother."

"Atlas, Veronica called and said—"

"Why did you send her here? Veronica and I will never

happen despite what you and Dad wish. She's a snake. I'll never be with someone I can't trust."

His mother huffed. "Oh, come on now. What happened years ago has no bearing on who she is now."

He gritted his teeth. *She knew about the affair.* The floor creaked outside his door before the one across the hall opened and closed. *Jasmine.*

"Look, Mother, I called to tell you the deal won't go through here. We'd be better off finding another spot for the resort farther down the coast."

"I told you that place was a waste of time. Oliver already tried." His father's voice came through.

He bunched his fist at his side. *Of course. If their favorite son couldn't do something, that deemed it impossible.*

His mother huffed. "It's just as well. Oliver already secured an old hotel near the Hamptons that would be perfect. And it only took him two days."

He cringed.

"Really, Atlas. I don't know why you'd waste so much of your time over there. It was clear from the beginning it was a dead end," his mother added.

"I wanted to show you that I deserve the CEO position. I thought it was worth one last effort." He tried.

"Son, we've made a decision," his father said, sounding hesitant.

No.

"Oliver will run the company as acting CEO, and you will work directly under him." His father delivered the final blow. The air was sucked from his lungs as he dropped to his knees. Blood rushed to his ears, making them ring.

"Come back home and we'll talk about the next steps for you at the company. Oliver said he wanted you by his side, and we agree that it's for the best—oh, I have another call coming through. Talk to you soon," his mother said before she hung up.

The phone slipped from his hand onto the floor. Defeat weighed his shoulders down. He trembled with anger. "They fucking chose him again." *Why did I ever assume I had a chance?*

He'd failed. Just like they'd all said he would. The whole reason he came here was to buy the inn and earn the position. He should pack up and leave. It was all over anyways.

He grabbed the bottle of whiskey and took another gulp of the burning liquid. He wasn't used to this cheap stuff.

Why couldn't he be good enough? Why did he always have to be second fiddle when it came to his family? His phone buzzed from the floor, Oliver's name glowing on the screen.

His brother didn't deserve his anger. He was a good man, a good friend, and a good brother. *But I need some space.*

He hit ignore.

Warmth flooded his body; it buzzed from alcohol. He wasn't drunk yet, but relaxed. He stared at the door. If there was one person who he couldn't bear to think less of him right now, it was Jasmine. He'd thought they had something. Those steel walls of hers had begun to fall. But then Veronica had come and ruined everything. Maybe he had one more shot at happiness before he had to go back to reality.

Shaking his head, he got to his feet. He left his room and held his hand out to her door. Atlas drew in a deep breath and knocked lightly.

Her footsteps padded closer, halting on the other side. Their tension wound thick despite the door separating them.

"Please," he whispered his prayer into the dark hallway. Begging was something he'd never done before. He could blame it on the whiskey, but the truth was Jasmine made him willing to do things he'd never once considered—like stay.

The door handle creaked as she opened it. Light spilled out from behind her, casting her in a glow. His eyes roamed across the threadbare T-shirt with the Seacoast Construction logo across the chest and down her sexy, naked legs.

"Atlas?" Her voice was a whisper.

His gaze snapped back to hers. Primal urges, carnal lust, and something more powerful than both of them wove together and imbedded itself deep inside his soul.

"Where's Zoey?"

"She's having a sleepover at my brother's."

He took a step forward, into her space. She stayed her ground. Her chin tipped up, need and conflict highlighting in those green orbs.

"Do you know how goddamned irresistible you are?"

She shook her head.

"I look at you and I want . . . I want things I shouldn't."

She swallowed, her throat bobbing delicately with the motion.

He reached out his hand and traced his finger over her collarbone. She shivered.

"You are so beautiful. And strong. And everything I never knew I wanted. Never knew I needed."

His cock pressed against his zipper. Desire splintered through him. His body quaked with warning. He was about to make a choice at this fork in the road that would change his life forever. He knew it, like a premonition. This woman would suck him into this dangerous cyclone brewing between them. And he must be insane, because he'd gladly drown in her.

"I want to dive into you and just forget." His heart hammered. Blood rushed in his ears like a furious wind whipping. The air was so thick with anticipation he could reach out and touch it.

Jasmine's eyes fluttered, darkening. She licked her lips and gazed up at him. "Forget what?"

He threw her own word back at her. "Everything."

She sucked in a tiny gasp. Every one of his senses was in rapt attention of her tiniest movements. He was depraved, lost in this powerful lust. The room was silent, but inside each cell screamed like a hurricane roiling.

"I want you too," she whispered.

"I can't commit to more than this. But I'd like to make good on my promise to make love to you." He'd be honest even though it killed him. Because she needed to know as much as he wanted this—wanted her—this could only ever be temporary. His family would never let him go, and the last thing she needed was them interfering in her and her daughter's life.

Her gaze locked on him, hesitating as if warring inside. She closed her eyes, and when she opened them again, there was no trace of the conflict.

"Okay." Her voice trembled.

"Yes?" he clarified, clenching his fists at his sides. There was no way he could touch her and remain in control.

"But there's something I need to tell you first."

"Will it change things between us?"

She nodded.

"Then I don't want to know. Don't tell me yet." He crashed his mouth over hers, swallowing whatever she was going to say. Her hands gripped his shoulders as he picked her up, shutting the door behind him with his foot. He carried her over to her bed and laid her down gently.

He began to lift her shirt, but she held his hand in place. "Atlas, the last time—"

"Shhh. Let's just focus on right here and right now. You're perfect as you are. I don't care about your past." He rubbed his thumb over her cheek. Her eyes grew glassy with emotion as her expression softened. The lines on her forehead disappeared as she nodded.

"Let me unwrap you like the gift you are." He kissed her once more and pulled back.

Her face flushed pink, and he couldn't wait to see where else she turned that color. He drew her shirt up over her head and sucked in a breath. She had no bra on—just a scrap of pink silk underwear.

"You're breathtaking." His eyes roamed over every exposed inch of her nakedness, from her green eyes to her swollen, plump lips. The curve of her slender neck down her smooth flesh. Her two perfect handfuls of breasts with light brown nipples. Her soft stomach, decorated with silvery lines, marks from carrying that sweet little girl. He gripped the edges of her panties and slipped them off her toned legs, her pussy glistening with her desire.

"Now it's my turn." She stood and lifted his shirt off, torturously slow. Her hands skimmed his hot flesh. He shuddered. He'd never been this turned on in his life. *What are you doing to me, little siren?*

She unclasped the button on his pants, unzipping them and pushing them down. Her eyes widened, and a bolt of pride shot through him.

"You don't wear underwear?"

"Sometimes." He smirked. "You don't wear a bra?"

"Not when my only plan was going to bed." Her lids were hooded.

"Any regrets?"

She swallowed and shook her head. "None."

She reached out, but he clasped his hand over hers. "Don't touch me or this will be finished before it starts."

She nodded, her eyes dark with lust. He leaned down. Hot

lips weaved between his. He dipped his tongue into her mouth, and she tasted like Pandora's box: forbidden and enticing. Elusive and devastating. Urgency roared within him. He pulled her towards him. Her naked flesh slapped against his. Her soft against his hard. They were made to fit. She held on to him like she was just as afraid that this would disappear as he was, like a dream. He stepped forward. The back of her knees hit the bed. He crawled over her, settling in the middle of the mattress. He rubbed his rough stubble against her neck as she gasped. He sucked and nipped, kissing his way along her throat and between her breasts.

"Oh, God."

He cupped one breast and lapped the other into his mouth before releasing it with a pop.

She whimpered. "I need you inside me."

"Not yet, beautiful. There are many more parts of you I want to taste." He licked her nipple as she squirmed beneath him. Her hand shot out, reaching for his cock. He caught her arm, locking it above her head as he chuckled. "I promise I'm gonna give it to you until you can't form words anymore. But first, I'm gonna suck on these delicious tits."

She bit her lip.

"Then I'm gonna work my way down, making you come in as many ways as I can think of, until your sexy body flushes as red as your cheeks."

"Fuck," she whined.

"I take my promises very seriously. Now, can I get back to work?"

"Yes!" She nodded emphatically.

He nipped, and flicked, and scissored his teeth over her nipples as she writhed beneath him in the most ancient rhythm known to man. He'd give her this—worship her body until he lost control.

He ran his hand over her soft belly to the patch of dark curls. She tensed as he touched all around the place she wanted him most, drawing out the anticipation.

She whimpered. "Please, Atlas?"

"Please what?"

"Fuck me with your fingers."

He ran his finger over her clit. Jasmine's core pulsed and she arched her back like she was reaching for her orgasm. She gasped, her eyes slamming closed. He swirled his finger around her aching nub as he pinched her nipple and kissed her mouth.

"Atlas!" she cried.

He flew off her before spreading her thighs and diving into her juicy center, licking up her juices.

"Mmm." He hummed his appreciation.

Her thighs squeezed around him. He forced her knees apart, leaving her wide open for his feasting. "You taste so fucking good."

He added two fingers inside her. She shot off like a rocket, quaking around him.

"Atlas! Fuck. Yes!" Her hands pressed his head down as she rocked her hips, riding out her orgasm.

He loved a woman confident enough in bed to take what she wanted. His body burned, his cock rock hard and aching.

"That's it, baby. Come on me." He rubbed the rough stubble on his chin over her slit. Kissing her thighs, he continued to pump his hands in and out, curving his fingers to reach that spot that would make her—

"Oh, God! Fuck!" she screamed before slapping a hand over her mouth. He'd been all over the world, but seeing that pretty pink spread over her chest as she came undone was probably the sexiest thing he'd ever witnessed. He hurried off the bed and grabbed the wallet from his pants. After pulling out the condom, he made quick work of opening it and sheathing himself. He climbed back over her.

Her hazy gaze focused on him.

"It's my turn." She sat and pushed him onto his back. She wrapped her hands around his cock, making it jerk.

"Fuck. Jasmine. Baby. I'm not going to last, and I really want to feel that pussy around me," he warned.

One side of her mouth quirked up at the side, challenge flashing in her eyes. She lowered herself onto him. He hissed. Her warm, tight channel squeezed him. *Bliss.* This was pure bliss.

"Don't move yet." His fingers dug into her hips.

She leaned down and sucked his nipple into her mouth, giving him the same torture he'd put her through.

"Okay." He gave her permission.

She rocked against him, agonizingly slowly. Her long hair flowed wildly over her shoulders. Her tits bounced each time she came down on him. He reached out, cupping her breasts. She gripped his wrists, pinning them over his head with a sly smile. "How does it feel to be able to look but not touch?"

He chuckled. "As long as you keep riding my cock like that, I'll do whatever you want."

A flicker of something passed through her expression before she lowered her mouth to his. They stayed lip-locked as she rode him in slow motion. It was the most sensual experience he'd ever had. Her touch seared his skin, branding his soul. Her pace increased while she chased her next orgasm. Her whimpers grew louder each time she slammed over him.

"That's it, baby. Give it all to me," he commanded. "Take what you need."

She sat up, releasing his wrists. She rocked her hips faster. Her inner muscles clenched over him like a vise. He reached out and pinched her nipples. She came undone. She threw her head back in ecstasy as her breasts bounced. His spine tingled with his own impending release. She closed her eyes, tensing, her body locked up.

"Open those eyes, baby. Let me watch you come."

Her eyes flew open, glazed and wild. She peaked. She moaned, vibrating with her own euphoria. There was no turning back. Pleasure gathered. His balls tightened.

"I'm gonna come. Are you ready for that?" he groaned out.

She nodded. "Yes!"

He pulsed inside her. Every nerve ending caught fire.

"Jasmine!" he roared. His stomach muscles contracted as he emptied himself inside her. He came with an unbridled force he'd never known existed. He pulled her against him as they both came down, their chests heaving against one another.

She lay limp in his arms, sated. He'd just had his entire world rocked. Jasmine had destroyed any sense of normalcy.

In another life, he'd be able to make her his. But she didn't need him complicating her and Zoey's life.

But how was he supposed to let her go now? She kissed his chest. He ran his hand over her naked back. Reality would come soon enough. Until then, he'd hold her while they waited.

24

JASMINE

Jasmine's eyes fluttered open. White curtains billowed in the early-morning ocean air. The fiery horizon cast her room in an orange hue. It almost seemed like any other morning. Except for the warm body curled around her and the delicious soreness between her thighs. She slammed her eyes shut and waited for regret to wash over her. But it didn't come. Its absence was unsettling. Even though the wave of shame after her sexual encounters was the worst part, at least it was predictable. *So, what does this mean?*

Atlas stirred, snuggling closer, his hard cock pressing between her thighs. She bit her lip. Her core throbbed, wanting more. *But what if he wakes up and regrets everything? Or worse—what if he thanks me for the good time and leaves early?* But more importantly, would she be okay when he walked away in a few days?

She still had to tell him about Zoey. She'd tried. But he'd made a strong case, and then after that kiss she just hadn't been able to focus on anything except his body on hers. She shook her head. *Because I'm weak.*

Cassidy's face flashed in her mind, reminding her to reframe the self-talk.

I had a moment of weakness, but it doesn't mean I'm weak.

Self-correction felt awkward. Maybe, with time, it would get easier.

"What are you thinking about so hard over there?" Atlas's voice was still thick with sleep.

"I'm wondering what your plans are for the day?"

He pulled her so that her head landed on his chest, and he kissed her forehead. She melted with the sweet gesture. For the first time in her life, she felt cherished.

"I guess that depends on what you have planned. Unless you're sick of me." He chuckled, but there was a hint of vulnerability in his voice.

How could one man affect her so much? "I have a group of teenagers from our friend Aaron's Hope Facility coming over for a cookout and a day at the beach."

He quirked an eyebrow.

"It's a center for homeless LGBT+ teens and kids from rough backgrounds. Aaron gives them a safe space to live in, hang out, get resources, or whatever they need. I have to set up and help cook when the volunteers get here."

"So . . . I could help too?"

Again with the heart melting. "You don't have to. You're still my guest."

"I want to spend the day with you. And if that means I help feed a bunch of hungry teens, that's what we're going to do."

She smiled. "Okay."

And she would tell him about Zoey before then—the truth about his daughter. Or maybe she should just tell him now and get it over with.

"But first, I want breakfast." Atlas pulled his arm out from under her and crawled down her naked body.

"Oh—oh!" Jasmine said as he spread her legs. His idea of a morning meal was just fine with her.

His tongue delved between her folds, the fluttering sensation lighting her up with yearning. He coaxed his finger inside her as he lapped at her clit. She wriggled her legs closed. The sensations were too much, her sex oversensitive.

His fingers gripped her thighs and pressed them apart. The scruff of his beard raked across her tender flesh, tantalizing and teasing. His tongue was torturously gentle. Conflicting sensations spun her up. Pressure built. He added another finger, sliding in and out of her slick pussy, fueling the ache. She writhed. Her hands grasped the sheets. Her eyes closed. Tension cinched tight. Heat bloomed, starting in her womb and blanketing her in an all-out blaze. Icy sparks coasted over the fine hairs of her body. Pleasure gathered before spilling out as a warm gush of liquid gushed from her.

"Fuck yes," he growled, sucking her clit. He curled his fingers, hitting that sensitive spot, sending her flying towards the heavens.

Her eyes burst open. Vivid color blinded her. Every muscle clenched as her orgasm rocked through her. Shattering. Splintering. Obliterating everything she'd ever known.

"The most beautiful thing I've ever seen is watching you come," Atlas said, sliding his slick fingers out of her. His eyes darkened, his chest muscles taut. His large cock head was rock hard with a drop of arousal glistening at the tip. He was beautiful. A god chiseled from alabaster stone. Much like the myth he was named after, the man seemed to have the strength to carry the world on his shoulders.

Could he be strong enough for me? Hope sparked. And she was too blissed out to smother it before it could grow. *What if this could be my new normal?* Her chest tightened. Waking up in bed every day next to this man? Sharing her body, sharing his, and merging their lives?

He climbed in next to her once more, pulling her close and holding her. She closed her eyes, fighting the happy tears that wanted to fall. Every part of her was warm, fuzzy, and relaxed. For once, she actually wanted to return the pleasure for him. Maybe if she didn't think about it, she could do it. If anyone deserved her attempt, it would be Atlas—the man who'd given her so much without even knowing. Who'd made her feel cherished and worthy. The man who'd given her Zoey.

She kissed his chest and down his toned abs, licking through the dips of his muscles and along his hip. She gripped his cock. He hissed before gritting his teeth.

"Fuck, I might come from just the image of your mouth on me." He ground out.

She smiled seductively, a rush of confidence shooting through her. If she kept her eyes open, maybe she could stay present. His arousal dripped from the tip. She spread it over the head with her thumb. His dick throbbed in her hand, hardening even more than she'd thought possible. She leaned down and licked the top, tasting his salty essence.

"Jasmine," he groaned.

I can do this.

She slipped her mouth over the first few inches before bringing her mouth back up.

"Fuck, yes!"

Pride surged through her. Her confidence grew. She hadn't tried to give anyone a blow job since she was thirteen and that had ended in a panic attack.

She sucked him farther in, keeping her eyes on Atlas. His hands fisted the sheets. Grey eyes gazed upon her like she was the most beautiful thing he'd ever seen. His mouth glistened with her release, like she'd marked him. Like he was hers. His stomach muscles tightened. His cock twitched against her tongue. Empowered, she sucked a little harder, took him a little deeper.

He wove his fingers in her hair, driving her deeper.

"That's it, baby. Take it all."

She froze. Panic shocked her out of her body.

Grunting noises echoed, getting louder. The tang of her stepfather's rancid sweat soured in her mouth. She gagged, trying to beg him to stop, but her mouth was too full to make a sound. Survival skills took over as she focused on stealing breaths against the prison of his hands pushing her head down. She floated above, watching as if it were happening to someone else.

But it wasn't.

It was happening to her.

"Jasmine!" Atlas's voice sent her rocketing back to reality. He shook her. He came back into blurry focus. Wetness spilled over her cheeks.

"Baby, what happened? Are you okay?" he asked, frantically searching her face.

She clenched her eyes closed, embarrassed and ashamed. This was why she couldn't have a normal relationship with anyone. What man wanted a woman who couldn't give blow jobs because they triggered her? Especially when they found out why.

"I'm sorry," he said, pulling her against his chest. "I'm so sorry."

Why was he of all people apologizing? She was the one who was broken. It only made her silent tears turn into sobs. He held her as she fell apart, stroking her hair and whispering, "I've got you. You're safe. No one will hurt you again. I've got you."

If anything had held her back from this man, it was gone —obliterated by his tender care. He knew. And still, he stayed. She sobbed harder as he held her even tighter. His presence grounded her as she expelled some of the shame and pain she'd held in for so long.

Her shaking turned to slight trembling. Her sobs subsided.

He picked her up and carried her into the bathroom. After turning the shower on, he kissed her forehead, tucking her closer while they waited for it to heat up. He stepped into the hot spray and set her to her feet. Water sluiced over her, washing the tears and the memories away. He grabbed the shampoo and squirted some in his hands before lathering it in her hair.

He took up so much space, barely fitting in this small shower with her. But his touch was gentle. He held her like she was precious. He rinsed out the shampoo, tilting her head against his chest before repeating the actions with her conditioner, massaging her skull. He picked up her body soap and squirted some on the loofa before carefully scrubbing every inch of her body. Starting at her feet, he worked his way up her legs. His hands swirled over the pinkening of her skin as if he could wipe the memories clean. The gentle sensation of her sponge dipped over her sex and across her hips. His eyes flashed to hers every so often as if to make sure she was still okay with him touching her. He used his other hand to massage her back as he washed her stomach up to her breasts. Taking care, he brushed the soapy material over her arms and towards her back. The tension left her body as the soap dripped down the drain.

Her chest squeezed. Her heart melted into a gooey puddle. Warm affection radiated from every pore. What if Atlas was the man for her? The one who knew all her secrets . . . and stayed? "Atlas?"

"Yeah, baby?"

I'm falling in love with you. "Thank you."

His brow creased. "Anything for you, honey."

She closed her eyes, fighting off another bout of tears. He stood, wrapping his arms around her. He held her like that until the water turned cold. She still had to tell him about Zoey. Would he hate her for keeping her from him? Monday was only two days away, and he'd have to leave. But for now, she'd savor this. Maybe it was selfish of her.

But when you'd been starved of love your whole life, you hung on to it with a viselike grip when you finally got it. Because death was better than having to live life without the richness of genuine love.

Atlas left her to get dressed and went to his own room to do the same. He told her not to worry about the guests' breakfast, that he had it handled. She was on strict orders to relax until she had to come down for the event with the teens. So, for the first time, she let someone else take over her duties with the inn without protest and rested.

* * *

Jasmine blinked her eyes open. The warm sun shone on her. She'd fallen back to sleep. Picking up her phone, she checked the time. *Shit.* She was late. Clicking the waiting message, she shot out of bed.

Atlas: *Aaron and his crew are here. I've got everything covered until you're ready to make an appearance. Take your time.*

Could this man get any more perfect? She smiled, tucked the phone in her pocket, and headed into the bathroom to brush her teeth and relieve herself before getting changed.

She made her way downstairs, following the voices bleeding out from the kitchen. Atlas stood in front of the stove, laughing and joking with Marge. The older woman was the main cook at Hope Facility, and she was a riot.

A few of the younger male volunteers stood nearby, ogling Atlas from afar. She didn't blame them; he was a sight to behold. Especially in the laid-back look of board shorts and a tight-fitting T-shirt.

"So what's the secret to the sauce?" Atlas asked Marge.

She put her hands on her hips. "You know a lady never reveals her secrets." She winked, reaching out to grab his bicep. "Even if the one who's asking is as fine as you."

He chuckled again, his gaze meeting Jasmine's. "Hey, sweetheart. Marge here was just showing me how to make a proper chili dog sauce."

"She makes the best in town." Jasmine smiled.

Marge cut her an unimpressed look. "In town? Honey, you know my shit's the best in the state."

Jasmine laughed. "You're so modest."

Marge brushed her long, grey dreads back. "Modesty is for boring people."

Atlas stirred the large pot.

"Why don't you make yourself useful and bring these out to Aaron. I got this handled." Marge gave the platter with the packages of hot dogs to Atlas.

"Yes, ma'am." He took it as Jasmine opened the back door, holding it ajar for him.

"Jaz!" Aaron said, holding out his arms for a hug.

She walked over to him, reached up on tiptoes, and squeezed him back tightly.

"You're too short to hug. I feel like I need to pick you up like a kid." Aaron laughed.

She pulled away and slapped his chest playfully. "Maybe you're the one who's too tall. Remember, great things come in small packages."

He chuckled.

"Have you met Atlas?" she asked.

Aaron nodded. "Yeah, we met earlier. Thanks for the help, man."

"My pleasure. Is it okay if I throw these on the grill?"

"Yup. It's hot and ready," Aaron said, opening the top.

After lunch, the group of teens spread out on the beach. Some played volleyball while others tossed the Frisbee back and forth. A few of them were brave enough to swim in the cold Atlantic waters. Zoey would love this when she got home from Bently's.

"These kids are pretty cool. This seems like a great program."

"Thanks," Aaron said.

Atlas pulled out a black card from his pocket and handed it to Aaron. "Give me a call next week. I'd like to donate something to your cause."

She eyed the matte card with the words *Remington Empire* written in glossy writing.

"I'll hold you to it." Aaron smiled and reached out his hand to shake Atlas's.

Two of the volunteers walked over.

"He can grill my meat anytime," Ted joked.

Atlas flashed them those pearly white teeth.

"Yeah. You can slip your wiener into my bun." Dan winked.

"I'm flattered. Truly. But I'm afraid I'm taken." Atlas winked at Jasmine.

Her heart soared. He'd just publicly acknowledged her as his, even after the mess upstairs. Could this be real? Did he want this to last longer than Monday?

"Lucky bitch." Dan hip-checked her.

She laughed. Jasmine was the lucky one for once, and she

was going to bask in the light as long as it lasted. But what would happen when she told him about Zoey tonight?

Over the rest of the afternoon, her smile never seemed to leave her face for long. She played with the kids. A few of them asked about part-time jobs and helping around the inn. And she promised to keep them in mind. She needed the help for sure, but her funds were too low to hire an employee just yet. She passed out the food when it was done.

Atlas's eyes never strayed far from her. Where she'd expected pity, there was instead some unnamed emotion shining back in his grey gaze. He eventually joined a game of touch football with the kids, and they had no problem piling on him in a tackle. He didn't seem to mind, laughing and joking along with them, clearly comfortable despite being surrounded by almost all gay men. It only made her respect for him grow. Maybe for once in her life she'd made a good decision. Maybe this was her second chance.

Atlas came over, wrapped his arm around her, and kissed her temple. "How are you doing?"

"Amazing."

And it was the truth. Nothing could bring her down from this elation. It was like she'd swallowed sunshine.

25

———

ATLAS

tlas opened the door to the restaurant, holding it for Jasmine and Zoey. They picked a small booth by the window and slid in.

"Smells good in here," Atlas said.

"Pirate's Pizzeria have the best pizza. Gloria and Vincenzo immigrated from Italy," Jasmine said, handing him a menu.

"I want extra cheese!" Zoey clapped.

"Please," reminded Jasmine.

"Peas!" Zoey smiled, showing off all her baby teeth.

"What toppings do you like?" he asked Jasmine.

"I'm not picky. But pepperoni and mushrooms are my favorite."

"Sounds good to me," he agreed.

The waitress came over to their table. "What can I get you?"

"One large pepperoni and mushroom pizza, and another large cheese and anchovy for the little girl."

"Ewww!" Zoey scrunched her face and plugged her nose.

He chuckled. "What? No anchovies?"

Zoey shook her head adamantly. "No, fank you."

He shrugged, turning back to the waitress. "I guess just cheese on that one."

She smiled and wrote it down. "Anything to drink?"

He turned to Jasmine, who said, "I'll take a hot black tea and a chocolate milk for Zoey."

"And I'll take a beer—IPA if you have it."

The waitress nodded and scribbled on her pad of paper. "I'll bring the drinks right out."

"Today was fun," Atlas said, turning his attention to her as the waitress left.

Jasmine tucked a piece of her hair behind her ear. "Aaron's kids are great."

His phone vibrated in his pocket. "Excuse me." Atlas pulled out the phone, Oliver's name flashing on the screen.

His stomach sunk. He wasn't ready to face reality just yet. His brother's call was like a storm cloud hovering over this beautiful day.

Zoey giggled. Her laughter was like the sunshine parting the clouds, warming his chest. He clicked "ignore" and put his cell away.

Jasmine and Zoey were coloring a page together. The way she focused so intently on her daughter, anyone could see that little girl was her whole world. She was so selfless and giving. But who took care of her? *No one.* And after what had happened that morning, this woman had an immeasurable amount of strength. It didn't take a genius to piece together the fact that she'd been sexually assaulted. Was that why she stayed so guarded and closed off? *But she let me in.* Her green eyes met his, and she smiled. Something a lot like love clattered around his rib cage, forcing its way into his heart.

"What is it?" she asked.

"Just admiring the view."

Her smile faltered. *Yes, baby. I don't know how to handle this either.*

The waitress returned with their drinks.

"Do you ever drink coffee?" he asked, motioning to her tea.

She shook her head. "Not really."

"That explains it."

Her forehead wrinkled.

"Your coffee was pretty terrible at the inn." He chuckled.

Her eyes grew wide. She looked so much like Zoey in that moment. All except the eyes. Those grey orbs of Zoey's matched his. A pang of longing he'd never experienced before grew inside him.

"Maybe it's not up to your snobby tastes. But I'll have you know guests love my coffee." She crossed her arms in front of her.

"Taste it tomorrow morning, then taste some that I made and tell me what you think." He shrugged.

"Oh, it's on." She smirked.

"Mr. Atlas?" Zoey's sweet voice interrupted their challenge.

"Yeah, sweetie?"

"Wouldn't it be cool if it rained pizza whenever we wanted?"

"So cool," he agreed.

"And then snowed ice cream for dessert." She smiled, her face lighting up.

"I'm guessing that means you want ice cream for dessert?" He laughed.

She nodded vigorously. "Yes, peas!"

"You're going to turn into an ice-cream cone one of these days because you eat so much," Jasmine teased.

"Can I have sprinkles as hair?" Zoey asked.

Jasmine giggled. "Oh, the mind of a child."

Atlas wiped a hand over his face. He was tired in all the best ways. A long night of making love, the early-morning events, then an afternoon in the sun and sand. Now dinner with two people who were by far his favorites. To say he was attached was an understatement. A stranger walking by might assume they were a family. And something about the idea just fit. Monday wasn't the end. This was real.

After their meal, Atlas threw enough cash on the table to pay the bill and tip. He stood, stretching his tired muscles. A small group of women cut their eyes towards Jasmine, speaking loud enough for them to hear.

"I can't believe she'd use her child to take advantage of a man like that. Look at him. Someone should tell him what a whore she really is."

He clenched his fists, turning towards them. Jasmine's hand shot out and grabbed his.

"Don't," she pleaded.

The woman continued, "My son said she came on to him. She was the reason he and Abby almost broke up in high school. Now she wants to break up their marriage?"

"Disgusting," another woman agreed.

Jasmine's hand tightened. "Let's just go."

"You can't let people talk about you like that and spread lies."

She looked down and then grabbed Zoey's hand. She stood, turning to face him. "Everyone is going to have an opinion about me. And in this town, there's more who agree with them than there are on my side. But the only opinion about me that matters is my own. Only I know what I've been through, and why I did the things I've done. They aren't worth the energy." She led Zoey out the front door.

He stood there, staggered by her statement. This woman

was a power to behold. A force unknown to man. A true warrior. If only he could adopt her self-confidence when it came to his parents' view of him. But it wasn't like a switch. He couldn't just shut it off.

He cut the old women a look that could kill. "You should be ashamed of yourselves. That goddess"—he pointed at the door—"is a hundred times the person you'll ever be."

Their shocked faces turned to anger as he stormed out, ignoring their snide responses.

The car ride back to the inn was quiet after they got ice cream. Jasmine stared out the window as Zoey played with the doll she'd brought. He didn't want to end the day like this. But he wanted to give her space if she needed it.

He parked at the inn and opened Jasmine's door and then Zoey's.

"Why do you always open Mommy's door? She's a big girl. She can do it," Zoey said.

He chuckled. "Well, sweetheart. When you go out with a man, he's supposed to open the door for the lady. And he's the one who should pay."

"Unless she wants to pay," Jasmine argued.

He held his hands up. "He should make sure the woman he is with is taken care of, whatever that looks like for them."

Jasmine's expression softened. "I'd better get her in for her bath. It's almost bedtime."

"Bath!" Zoey yelled, running towards the inn.

Jasmine and Atlas followed.

When they reached her bedroom door, she opened it while he hung back leaning on his. Zoey disappeared into the room.

"Get your clothes off and in the hamper, and I'll be in to run you a bath in a minute," Jasmine directed. She spun around to the sound of little footsteps retreating and tucked her hands in her shorts pockets. "Thank you for dinner. And this afternoon. And . . . before. I really appreciate everything you did. And I understand it if you need some space from me now."

He frowned. *What?* "I don't—"

"Mommy!" Zoey called.

"Just a second," she answered, backing into her bedroom.

"I don't want—"

"Mommy! I'm cold," Zoey persisted.

She sighed. "I have to go take care of her."

He nodded.

"Goodnight," she said before she closed the door.

He took a deep breath and ran his hand through his hair. Frustration and unease slithered around him. He unlocked his bedroom door and walked inside. He needed a shower himself.

An hour later, he was clean and had changed into a pair of sweatpants. He was too hot to bother with a shirt. There was no way he was going to sleep until he and Jasmine cleared this up. He slipped out of his room and went downstairs before opening the door to the room that was always under construction.

She'd cleaned up everything except a few cans and brushes with a drop cloth. Jasmine had painted the second coat of trim around the windows. He busied himself, opening the can and stirring the paint like he'd seen her do. He dipped one of the smaller brushes he'd used last time into the bucket and wiped the excess on the side. He stroked the brush across the wood panel, getting lost in the hypnotic work.

He'd finished all three windows in the room before the door creaked open and Jasmine walked in. Lines appeared between her brows as she studied him. She'd changed into another faded T-shirt and sleep shorts.

"What are you doing in here?" Her lips curved into a small smile.

"Finishing up for you," he said, setting the paintbrush down. He closed the lid to the paint bucket.

"Thank you. You do so much for me. And I owe you . . . everything."

Hardly. Does she really not see how special she is?

She rubbed her hand up her arm. She was so vulnerable. He stepped closer and tipped her chin up to look at him. "I'm sorry for trying to get into your business earlier. It pissed me off—what those bitches said about you. I don't understand how people can be so vile and spread vicious lies."

She winced. "Thank you for caring enough to want to do something. No one's . . ." She hesitated, holding in whatever she was going to say, like he assumed she did with so much else.

He traced his thumb over her bottom lip. She shivered.

"I care a lot more than I probably should after just a few days with you."

She closed her eyes, leaning into his touch. "Me too."

A spark of hope lit, burning bright. "Maybe this doesn't have to end Monday when I return to the city. I can come back. We can see where this goes?"

Her green eyes darted to his. Disbelief, indecision, and hope flashed across her expression like a work of moving art. "Atlas, I'd love that. But—"

His mouth crashed over hers, elation spinning in his chest. Hope and warmth. Nothing had felt as right as this in his life. There was no room for "buts." He wanted her. He yearned for her like no other before. And she'd just said he could have her. *Jasmine is mine.*

She was the one good thing in his life, untainted by his family or the expectations imposed on him. Jasmine saw *him*. She didn't think he was second best. For once in his life he didn't have to be compared to his brother. She was separate and beautiful. Goodness and comfort. Light and love. And he'd do whatever it took to hang on as long as she'd let him.

26

JASMINE

Jasmine held on to Atlas as he carried her up the stairs to his room. His lips fused to hers, and she trusted him to get her safely to his bed in the dark. A tremble rocked through her. She *trusted* Atlas. She *loved* him. He made her feel safe. And beautiful. And worthy. For once, she wasn't worried about tomorrow because he'd be there when the sun rose. Even once she told him the women weren't lying, once she told him the truth about Zoey, she was certain he would stay. Their love was bigger than the past.

He set her to her feet and opened the door before pulling her inside. It shut with a click as she removed the baby monitor from her waist and set it on the dresser. The only light from the room came from the bright moon. Nature's spotlight on his bed. His gaze was dark and consuming, his face cast in shadows. Each rise and fall of his naked, muscular chest sent a pulse of need throbbing in her sex.

Atlas was so perfect it was hard to believe he was real. And nothing like her. Could he love all the versions of her? Even the ones she kept hidden?

Their tension swirled, the air between them carrying a powerful energy like the wind before a storm. Anticipation sparked like a live wire.

"Take it all off," he commanded, his voice gravelly.

Her limbs trembled and knees knocked. She grabbed the hem of her shirt and lifted it over her head. Her flesh burned with the heated grip of his gaze. Next, she slipped the sleep shorts down her legs and kicked them off. She stood exposed and vulnerable, waiting.

He clenched his fists at his side. "You're so beautiful."

She looked down.

His finger lifted her chin, his grey orbs serious. "You're so stunning, you take my breath away. I always thought that was some cheesy line, but you make it hard to breathe. You're the most beautiful person in here." He pointed to her heart. "And here." He tucked her hair behind her ear and tapped her forehead. "Your body is fucking paradise."

She swallowed the emotion that rose, her every molecule burning with a wildfire of swirling want, need, and pure unadulterated love for this man. She blinked back the tears that threatened to fall.

He cupped her face, searching the windows to her soul. "If you need me to stop at any time, tell me."

She closed her eyes, taking a shaky breath. Would this man ever cease blowing her away with his tender kindness? There was no pity in his eyes or disgust. Only concern. He still wanted her. And he cared enough about her to go at her pace.

She nodded. "Okay."

His thumb traced her bottom lip before his mouth descended upon hers. His kiss was soft, melting her insides and setting her body ablaze. His hands pulled her close, strong and reliable. She slipped her tongue inside his mouth and he groaned, deepening the kiss.

He spun her around, backing her to the bed. The soft mattress was cool to the back of her knees. She climbed on top, kneeling. He tugged his sweatpants off, leaving him bare. Wrapping her arms around his neck, she pulled him over her. His weight settled on her. Burning skin against hot flesh. Soft planes against steel ridges. Wide dips against smooth curves. The past and the present woven together.

He kissed her neck, making gooseflesh flood over her. She curled her spine.

Jasmine gasped. "Atlas."

He trailed kisses over her throat, and shoulders, and down farther still.

"Let me do the work. Let me show you how you deserve to be worshipped." His deep voice reverberated through her.

She'd never done this. She'd fucked many men. But he was the first she'd made love with. *And hopefully, he will be the last.*

His mouth swiped over her breast, sucking, nipping, while his hand kneaded the other. She ran her hands over his shoulders, needing to feel all of him, but settling for what she could get.

He took his time, stoking the fire within her, arousing her with patient devotion. His hands slipped over her hips. His finger dipped inside.

"Oh, God!" She sucked in a breath, using her arms to sit up halfway.

He inhaled her sex. "You smell so delicious. Let me taste you. Can I do that?" Atlas's gaze snapped to hers for her consent, and just the knowledge that he was waiting on her permission sent her a rush of excitement.

She was empowered and safe.

Jasmine nodded. "I want you to taste me. Make me feel good, Atlas."

He grinned wolfishly before his large hands pressed her legs farther apart. She stayed sitting up, as his head lowered to her pussy. He kissed her thighs, then her lower lips. She gripped the sheets in her hand, her body tensing in anticipation. His tongue lashed out over her clit and she gasped, panting for breath as he licked and stroked, savoring her like she was his last meal. His head bobbed up and down between her thighs. The sight was erotic and powerful. She reached over and gripped his dark hair. His fingers dug into her hip on one side as he slipped another digit inside her with his other hand. The pressure built, throbbing and burning. She writhed, rocking her hips, seeking her release.

He sucked her clit into his mouth. Throwing her head back in reckless abandon, she bit down until she tasted blood to keep from crying out. Desire puddled and pooled within her. Her legs itched with the impending icy-hot sensations of her release. "I'm . . . I'm going to . . ."

"That's it, baby. Come! Come for me." He sucked harder —fucked her deeper.

His fingers hit the most miraculous spot inside her as she came apart. Flashing, blinding light flooded her vision.

"Atlas!" Every muscle tensed as her orgasm ripped through her.

He crawled over her body before tucking her against him, holding her in a viselike grip. His heart thudded against hers, matching it beat for beat.

"You're fucking perfection," he growled, nipping her ear.

"I need you inside me. Right now."

He climbed off her and grabbed his sweatpants. Her arm shot out and grabbed his. "I wanna feel *you*. I promise I'm clean and I have an IUD."

He hesitated.

Shit. "It's—you don't have to—"

He dropped the pants and crawled back onto the bed. "Okay. I'm clean. And I've never gone bare before." He trusted her too.

"Me either."

He nodded, leaning down to kiss her again. She wrapped her legs around him, running her hand down his hard shaft. His whole body tensed, the muscles on his back bunching under her other hand.

"You want my cock inside you?"

"Yes. I want you. Every inch."

He lined up at her entrance and gently, inch by delicious inch, slid to her womb. Slowly, he was stretching her. She kept her gaze on him. She didn't want to miss a moment of this. He buried himself to the hilt, filling her up in more ways than one, before he began to rock her back and forth. She pulled him closer, kissed him harder, and held on to him as tightly as she could. His lips locked with hers as they spun and writhed, slammed and gasped. Nails raked, pressure built. This connection was unstable and intense. Possession stirred. Passion blurred. Every sense was sharpened. Time slowed. The world fell away until all that was left was his soul merging with hers —a beautiful rhapsody known only to them.

His arm tightened around her, his forehead dipping to hers, their eyes locked.

"Come with me," she commanded.

"Jasmine!" he roared, pulsing and filling her a moment later.

She soared off the edge of the cliff, flying, weightless, basking in the light. There were sparks and shimmers and then a warm wave of euphoria crashed over her. And she floated back to earth, light as a feather, descending in a cloud of bliss.

He pulled out and rolled next to her on the bed, tucking

her against him. For the longest time, there was only the sound of their breaths. She turned around, memorizing his face. His closed eyes, relaxed body. Watching him sleep, joy and hope burst inside her. For once she hadn't screwed up. Atlas was the best man in the world she could have asked to be her daughter's father and share her bed. He was someone Zoey could be proud to call daddy. She let the tears fall.

"I love you."

Her only answer was his light snores. She slipped out of bed and covered him with the comforter before going back to her room. Tomorrow, she'd have Remy pick up Zoey for a few hours. She'd sit him down and tell him everything. He'd understand why she hadn't told him right away. Her stomach flipped. If anyone would understand, it would be Atlas. The man had won her love and her trust, both of which she'd thought impossible.

27

JASMINE

Jasmine packed Zoey's lunch bag as Atlas told the little girl a joke that had her giggling. She smiled, her heart so full at seeing father and daughter enjoying this moment. It felt right—meant to be. She'd gone and had a baby with a stranger, then met him again years later and fallen in love. She'd done it so backwards. But when had her life ever gone according to plan? Normalcy was a perception after all, not a set rule.

"Better eat that breakfast so you can grow big and strong." Atlas grinned at Zoey.

She picked up the breakfast burrito and shoved a big bite in her mouth. He chuckled and shook his head as he brought his empty cup over to the counter.

He flicked his gaze to Zoey who was happily oblivious to them as she chatted with another guest, a woman with long, red hair who Zoey had already said reminded her of Anna.

Atlas pressed his hand to the small of her back, discreetly bringing his nose to her neck and inhaling. "I missed waking up to you this morning. Sorry I fell asleep."

She smiled. "I missed that too."

She peeked another glance at her daughter as he kissed her temple.

"Aunty Remy is here!" Zoey exclaimed, pointing out the window.

Jasmine zipped up the bag and walked over to Zoey. She wiped Zoey's mouth before guiding her outside and into Remy's waiting SUV. She kissed Zoey's cheek and shut the car door.

"Thanks again for this," Jasmine said to Remy.

"Anytime. Good luck." Remy gave her a squeeze before she climbed into the SUV. Jasmine waved as Remy drove off.

Jasmine's stomach tumbled and twisted. Knots of anticipation and nerves mangled inside her. She put one shaky leg in front of the other, heading back into the inn.

Atlas was waiting where she'd left him, leaning against the counter. The other guests had cleared out. It was just the two of them.

"Come here," he said.

She walked over, each step harder than the last. Her body grew hot with nervous excitement. This would be a shock and then he'd have to process it. But hopefully in the end, he'd see this as a good thing.

His brow wrinkled as she drew closer, like he could read her apprehension. "Are you okay?"

She nodded, her words stuck in her throat.

He leaned down, capturing her mouth in a kiss. She melted against him, savoring this moment before she shattered his perfectly manicured world.

His hands drifted over the back of her shirt before coasting down to her ass. He picked her up and set her on the counter, stepping between her thighs. "I can't keep my hands off you."

"I need you to try. There's something I have to talk to you about," she tried.

"I know."

"W-what?" she asked, holding her breath.

"I know this is a lot more than we both bargained for. But I want you to know that what I feel for you, I've never felt for anyone. I'm in this, regardless of what that means. I've got you. And . . . I love you."

She blinked, her chest tight. The well burst in her heart. "I love you too." Jasmine kissed him. He squeezed her harder, grinding himself against her.

She broke away, panting, smiling. They could overcome anything together. Finally, Jasmine was ready to jump overboard because he would be there to catch her. "Atlas?"

"Yeah, baby?"

She took a deep breath. *Here goes everything.* "Four years ago, I was in a really bad place. I'd use sex as a way to make myself feel better for a moment and . . . punish myself at the same time. I met a man in a bar and we hooked up in the bathroom—"

"I don't need to know this." He cupped her face.

She searched his eyes—the same grey orbs that had met hers that night so long ago, promising escape. They hadn't exchanged pleasantries. She'd caught him staring and nodded towards the restroom. He'd met her there.

"I do. You need to know. That man is Zoey's father. I never knew his name. I couldn't look for him."

"Why are you telling me this now?"

She trembled. "You really don't remember me?"

His brow furrowed. "Remember what?"

"We met at the Pink Drink bar, four years ago, in April. You're Zoey's father."

He shook his head, face paling. His arms dropped to his side as he backed away from her.

She slid off the counter, reaching out to him. "Atlas—"

He jerked from her touch, running a hand through his hair and tugging.

"I didn't tell you right away because I wanted to make sure you were a safe person for Zoey."

He blinked before settling his gaze on her. His eyes narrowed, turning to ice. "I was never in New Hampshire four years ago."

Her phone chimed in her pocket, signaling that someone had come into the inn. She blinked. She was *sure*. There had to be a mistake. He had to be confused. Maybe he'd been too drunk?

Footsteps thudded closer. The new arrival entered the room. She looked up at the figure standing in the doorway and gasped. Her eyes flicked back and forth between carbon copies of the same man.

Atlas was an identical twin. And if Atlas wasn't Zoey's father, then that meant . . .

The wall behind Atlas's grey eyes slammed shut. His expression was unreadable.

28

ATLAS

Atlas didn't need to turn around. Her reaction confirmed everything. Her eyes flicked back and forth between Atlas and the man who had finally stolen everything from him. Oliver had been chosen over him, *again*. Zoey's true father. Jasmine had thought he was Oliver all along. She'd wanted the parent of her child. And Atlas had played right into her hands. None of it was real between them. Anger rose—his only protection.

"I think you've already met my brother, Oliver." His voice was like steel.

Jasmine stepped backwards as if the truth had been a physical blow. Fear flashed in her eyes. She reached out to Atlas, but he jerked away, grasping her wrists.

"Atlas?" she pleaded.

Oliver chuckled, oblivious to the earthquake shaking Atlas's world off its axis. "I see why you didn't hurry back home. She's hot. But sleeping with the new inn owner won't get her to sell this place to you. Give it up already."

Jasmine backed up as if she'd been slapped. He got a tiny

bit of satisfaction from that. *Now you know what it's like to feel used.*

"What? That's why you were here?" She ran a hand over her forehead. "That's why you kept asking about the inn and money." She whipped her attention back to him, eyes blurring with tears. "I *trusted* you. You betrayed me."

"Guess you know how it feels," he snapped.

"You look familiar. Have we met before?" Oliver asked, stepping closer to Jasmine.

Her green eyes searched Atlas's face, the unspoken plea flashing. *Please don't tell him about Zoey.* He gave nothing away in his expression. She'd used him, and what was the most vile, she'd made him fall for her. Then she'd ripped his heart out, committing the worst possible sin. It had been Oliver she was hoping for all along. Her gaze dropped, shoulders slumped as she wrapped her arms around herself. She looked so fragile and broken. A part of him wanted to comfort her—hold her and tell her it was all going to be okay. And that made him even more angry. She still held power over him.

Atlas turned his anger towards Oliver. "You cheated on Christina."

Recognition flashed in Oliver's eyes as he flicked his eyes back over to Jasmine. "That's right." His eyes raked over Jasmine's body.

Atlas clenched his fist, grinding his teeth until his jaw screamed in pain.

"That's why you look so familiar. Wait—that old lady wouldn't sell to me because of *you*? You're the one she turned my offer down for?"

Jasmine winced. Hurt was written across the curves of her face. Pain shone in her green eyes. Atlas stepped into Oliver's space, shoving his chest against his brother's.

"Hey!"

"Does Christina know?" Atlas demanded.

"I mean, a man has needs, Atlas. Surely you know that. You fuck anything that moves and never more than once."

"I'm not the one who's married." He slammed his hand against Oliver's shoulder.

Oliver held up his hands. "I was drunk. She came on to me."

Atlas turned to Jasmine. "Is that true?"

She turned her face to the floor. "I didn't know he was married." Her voice was so small. Another spear through his shredded heart.

"Good to know you have *some* standards," Atlas deadpanned.

She squeezed her arms tighter; tears dripped down her cheeks.

Every part of him ached, screaming at him, pulling him in different directions. His heart told him to wrap her in his arms and hear her out. But his mind kept flashing back to what her ex and those women had said in the restaurant. Had the whole town been laughing at him? Had those women actually tried to warn him?

He pushed Oliver aside and rushed upstairs to his room. After tearing out his suitcase, he started packing.

"Atlas?" Jasmine's voice cracked.

He wouldn't turn around and look at her. "Get out."

"Let me explain? Please?" she begged, and something cracked inside him.

He spun around, grabbing her shoulders. Her eyes widened, fear flashing as she winced.

"Why? So you can tell me more of your goddamned lies? So you can manipulate me some more?"

She shook her head, fat tears glistening over her face. Her expression hardened. "You can't handle my truths! No one can. You wanna know why I didn't tell you when you first got here? You were a stranger. I had to make sure my daughter would be safe. I understand better than anyone that someone who is supposed to be a father can hurt you in ways no human would want to imagine. So no, I didn't think just because I thought you were her father, you had a right to know."

The only reason she started any of this was because she thought I was Zoey's dad. So once again, I'm chosen second. She'd wanted something from him, just like everyone else in his life had. He shook with rage, his skin burning. His hands gripped her harder, pinning her against the wall. He didn't want to hear this. He couldn't believe a word out of her mouth. He'd seen women use their own children to manipulate men before.

"You have no idea what it's like to find out you're pregnant from a stranger with no way to contact him. To raise a child, a human solely dependent on you to meet all her needs. To put a roof over her head, and food in her belly, and love her when all you want to do is lie down and never get back up again." Jasmine's gaze didn't waver, though her body shook.

"Enough."

"You have no idea what it's like to see the man you thought was her father walk into your inn and not remember you. To wonder if you should tell him, if he's safe? If he's trying to take the one person I love most in this world. My job is to protect Zoey first and foremost. That's why I didn't tell you right away. I tried . . . that night."

The night he'd come to her room. He should have listened, rather than let his dick do the thinking.

"I shouldn't have waited so long to confess. Before things got so . . . tangled."

"I would never have slept with you if I'd known you fucked my brother first," he snapped.

Her face paled, pain lashing across her expression. Her

head dipped, gaze pointed at the floor. "Did you mean any of it? Was this all just to buy the inn?"

It was too fucking real. But the truth would leave him vulnerable. And he'd had enough heartache to last him a lifetime. "How does it feel to have secrets kept from you?"

She shook her head. "That's not . . . I trusted you." She tipped her chin up. Her eyes were red from crying. Through the pain and the betrayal, she was still so tragically beautiful—stealing his breath, making his own body war against itself. The siren, dragging him down to the deepest darkest depths of the ocean, sending him to his death. He swallowed the feelings that threatened to overflow, locking them away tight as he'd been trained to do all his life, until he felt nothing but icy aloofness and hot rage. "It's obviously not the first terrible mistake you've made."

She blinked, a blank mask falling into place. "Let me go."

He stepped back, hands dropping to his sides. His heart lurched, stomach knotting. Bile rose. *What have I become?*

She ran out of the room, tugging at whatever invisible force tethered them together. It cinched tighter with every footfall, until it snapped.

He sucked in a staggered breath, running his hands over his face. Heavy footsteps climbed higher on the stairs.

Oliver walked in, crossing his arms. "You look like shit."

Atlas closed his eyes, trying to block his brother out. "Shut the fuck up."

"Come on, At. She's a slut. Don't waste—"

Oliver didn't get to finish his sentence. Atlas's fist met his brother's cheek with all his pent-up rage behind the punch. Oliver crashed to the floor, holding his hands out.

"What the fuck! Asshole. This is what I get for coming to check on you?" Oliver held his face.

"Why are you even here?" Atlas demanded.

"You ignored my calls. I wanted to make sure you were okay. I know you wanted that position so badly. I figured you'd need my support."

Atlas shook his head. "You have a fucking kid with her."

"This happened before Christina got pregnant."

"With Jasmine, you fucking idiot," Atlas snapped.

Oliver's face paled. "No—I can't." He shook his head vehemently. "I'll lose the shares in the company. And my position. Grandfather said—"

"Well, I guess you should have kept it in your pants," Atlas interrupted. Blood boiled at the thought of his brother's hands on Jasmine.

Four years ago, I was in a really bad place. I'd use sex as a way to make myself feel better for a moment and . . . punish myself at the same time. I met a man in a bar and we hooked up in the bathroom.

Was that all he was to her too? What did she think she was doing? Making him fall in love with her so he'd marry her and then she'd live like a queen? Although the back child support from Oliver would have her set up for life. *No. Jasmine isn't like that.* At least that was what he'd thought. But then again, she'd kept a huge secret from him the whole fucking time—thinking he was Zoey's father. He wasn't Oliver. He never would be. And now she knew the truth, chances were she wouldn't want him but the real deal.

He threw everything else in his bag and zipped it up. He needed to get out of here, away from everyone. He walked out the door, leaving behind all he'd come to fall in love with in less than two weeks. This place was everything he hated now. Jasmine was the one person untainted by his life in New York City and his family. And it turned out, even that was just as much a fantasy as mermaids were.

29

JASMINE

Jasmine sipped the tea Belle had brought her, tasting nothing. She wanted something stronger. Alcohol that would burn hotter than the searing pain in the place where her heart should be.

She peeked out the window. Zoey was happily playing with her cousins. Her sisters-in-law and Mia all sat around her on Belle's bed in silent support. Andre had gone to the inn, in case her other guests needed anything. Bently went with him, but apparently Atlas's room was empty when he arrived, both brothers nowhere to be found. Mikel and Bently were in the backyard playing with the kids. Bently's eyes wandered up to the window every few minutes, worried.

Jasmine closed her eyes, fighting off the tears. Embarrassment heated her skin. She'd let her guard down for the last time. She was just getting used to being loved by someone and then the rug had been ripped out from under her. A rogue wave of reality came crashing over her, pulling her so deep into the depths of the dark sea that it seemed easier to give in than swim up. Oliver was actually Zoey's father. *Atlas's twin.*

She'd fucked one brother and fallen in love with another. How much more of a slut could she be?

Shame weighed heavily on her shoulders, wrapped around her neck like a millstone. Zoey deserved a better mother. Maybe she'd be better off without her.

"Jaz? Do you want to talk about it?" Remy asked.

No. She absolutely did not want to tell them what a whore she was.

You're nothing but a whore.

Sucking me off—it's all you're good for.

You're nothing but a tease.

Useless slut.

A warm hand rested on her thigh. She blinked her eyes open. Belle offered her a sympathetic smile. "We're here for you."

If anyone was going to understand this, it would be Belle. "Atlas isn't Zoey's father."

The women exchanged confused looks. "What do you mean?"

Jasmine sighed. She'd made choices and now she had to face the consequences. "His twin brother is."

Remy clapped a hand over her mouth.

"*Dios mio,*" Mia said.

"Why don't you start from the beginning," Belle suggested.

Jasmine explained what had happened as the women grew more outraged.

"*El cabron!*" Mia swore.

"I'm so sorry, Jasmine." Remy pulled her into a hug.

"I'm the one at fault here."

"How do you figure that?" Belle asked.

"I fucked his brother and was such a slut I didn't even know who Zoey's father was."

"This is just one huge misunderstanding. You and Atlas can work it out. I'm sure—"

"He doesn't want anything to do with me. He said if he'd known . . . he would never have started something with me. He was just here to buy my inn."

Mia clicked her tongue and crossed her arms.

"There's no way how that man looked at you was fake. He cared about you," Remy said.

Cared. Past tense. "If there was anything, it's gone now. I poured my heart out to him. I risked everything. I told him more than I've told anyone, and he threw it all back in my face."

"Bastard!" Mia snapped.

Jasmine looked around the room, taking in the three concerned faces. Her sisters' support never wavered. "I feel like the dirtiest person. I'm a failure as a woman, as a mother. I'm a slut just like *he* said. My mother knew it, and that's why she killed herself." The words tumbled out of her mouth. She gasped in an attempt to suck in oxygen. A weight settled over her chest, making inhaling impossible. Panic strangled her.

Three sets of arms surrounded her, holding her close.

"Deep breaths, Jasmine."

"We got you, sweetie."

"We're here."

"You're safe."

"You're so much stronger than you know."

"You're not a mistake. You're a survivor."

"Deep breaths—one, two, three, four. Now let it out. Four, three, two, one," Mia guided her.

Her sisters' voices offered her comfort. It conflicted with the voices inside screaming that she wasn't good enough. That it was all her fault. The shame that had seeped into her bones had consumed her since her earliest memories. Her sisters quieted the voices as the women held her tight. Their tears mixed with her own. She closed her eyes, clung to their combined power. She'd be safe to let it all fall apart while they kept guard.

* * *

Five days had passed since Atlas had left without a word. It was a struggle to get out of bed in the morning. Her family had stepped in to take over breakfast duties with the guests. She shouldn't let them, but she couldn't find the energy to argue or the motivation to do it herself. The numbness had settled deep into her bones. The familiar dark cloud blocked out the sun. A depressive episode, as Belle called it.

All she knew was that she felt empty inside. She didn't want to be alive, craved the thought of walking out into the waves and never coming back up. But at the same time, those same thoughts terrified her. Because she could never leave her daughter. Jasmine had promised Zoey as she still grew inside her womb that she would be nothing like her own mother.

Zoey curled up next to her, sleeping in her arms. Jasmine traced her finger around her small, round face, over her eyebrows, down her button nose. Jasmine's eyes burned with tears. Her precious, innocent daughter didn't deserve any of this. Zoey was her reason to keep going. *I'll make it through this for you. I'll be better.* For Zoey, she'd do anything.

A soft knock rapped against her door. She slid out of the bed before tucking the pillows around Zoey so she wouldn't roll off the mattress. She crept on bare feet to the entrance and opened it. Bently towered over her from the other side. His gaze flicked to Zoey.

"Let's talk downstairs."

She grabbed the portable baby monitor and closed the

door behind her before following him to the shared living room. She only had one room booked, and those guests had gone out. It was just her and Bently, and the weight of his oppressive big-brother stare. She sat on the couch, hugging a grey pillow in front of her. Bently handed her a folder.

"What's this?"

"Background check on Atlas and Oliver Remington. I had my PI friend in the city dig up what he could."

She cringed. It felt like a violation to look. But did she owe them anything? Atlas had made it clear he'd come there to use her all along. Just like Oliver had, apparently. Her loyalty was to her daughter. So, she flipped the file open.

"They are loaded. They both work for their family's company, Remington Empire. Oliver is married, going on seven years."

She nodded.

"And his wife is newly pregnant."

She sucked in a breath. Zoey was going to have a half-sibling.

"Do you want to file for custody? You can get back child support, and—"

She waved her hand in the air, halting her brother's speech. "I just want to be left alone. I don't want anything from them."

"But, Jaz, you're barely surviving here. You deserve some help," Bently argued, sitting close to her.

"I want Zoey to have a father in her life who will cherish her the way she deserves. I don't care about who he is or his money. I can take care of my daughter."

He shook his head.

That's right. I can be as stubborn as you.

Her phone chimed and the front door opened a moment later. A woman walked in, looking around.

Jasmine stood. "Can I help you?"

"Are you Jasmine Evans?"

"Yes."

She handed her over an envelope. "You've been served."

Jasmine took the note from her as Bently got to his feet. The woman disappeared out the way she came.

Jasmine's heart pounded.

"What is it?" Bently asked.

She broke open the seal and slipped the paper out. Reading over the words, her hands began to tremble.

"Oliver has a court-ordered paternity test. I have thirty days to comply."

"Fuck," Bently swore.

The paper shook in her hand.

Bently pulled her against his chest. "I'm gonna get you a lawyer."

She nodded. "What if he tries to take her away from me?"

"I promise we won't let that happen."

Bently's promises carried weight. But would they match up against the Remingtons' money? She couldn't afford an attorney. She'd have to rely on her brothers again. But it didn't matter because she'd do whatever was necessary to keep Zoey safe. Even if she had to give up everything that meant the most to her.

"Jaz?" A familiar voice broke through her thoughts.

Bently released her. She turned around as Emma walked over to her, arms wide open. Emma set down the motorcycle helmet on the coffee table before sweeping Jasmine up into a hug.

"What are you doing here?" Jasmine asked.

"I have forty-eight hours before I need to be on a plane to Japan. I couldn't leave you hanging when you needed me most." Emma squeezed her tighter.

"I'm gonna go do what we talked about," Bently said. "Nice seeing you, Em."

Emma released Jasmine. "You too. Say hi to your wife for me."

"Will do." Bently gave Jasmine a kiss on her forehead before he left.

"I still can't believe that playboy Bently is married and settled down." Emma shook her head.

"He deserves a happily ever after."

Emma tucked a strand of her blond hair behind her ear. "So do you, babe."

Jasmine shook her head, sitting back on the couch.

Emma slipped the backpack off her shoulder. She unzipped it and pulled out three bottles of wine.

"You came prepared."

"Almost. I'm gonna go grab some cups." Emma disappeared into the kitchen before returning with two glasses. "Just like old times."

Jasmine smiled. "Except these are a step up from Solo cups and stolen liquor."

Emma laughed. "We had some good experiences. Remember how Remy would be terrified the whole time that we would get caught?"

"Yes. She was always such a good girl."

"Who would have thought she'd end up with the baddest boy in Shattered Cove?" Emma poured them each a half glass of wine before handing Jasmine one.

Jasmine sipped it.

"And before you tell me they deserve their happy lives, know that I don't disagree. And someday, you'll find that too."

Jasmine took another drink. "I thought maybe I'd found it with . . . him." She couldn't say his name. It hurt too much. "I told him I loved him."

Emma's eyes widened. "What did he say?"

"He said it first. He said he'd be there. And then . . . everything fell apart."

"Do you think he meant it?"

"I'd thought so. But then after it all went to shit, he said it wasn't real."

Emma sat forward. "Do you think he could have been lashing out because he was hurt about the his-twin-brother-being-your-baby-daddy thing?"

Emma—always straight to the point without sugarcoating. "It's possible. But it doesn't matter anymore. It's over. For good. He hurt me so bad."

"I don't care what that man had going on, you don't deserve what he said to you."

Don't I?

Everything he'd accused her of was untrue or she'd had good reason for. Reasons she'd defend with her dying breath. She'd made mistakes. She'd fucked countless strangers. She'd been the other woman before. But she'd learned and grown. She'd turned her life around and worked hard to become the person she was today. Sure, she had a long way to go. But she was proud of her progress. Not many people could live through the hell she had and break the cycle. She'd done that. Alone. Fought demons in the dark, wounded and blind. All for the little light she'd birthed into the world. She'd sworn that darkness would never touch her child.

Emma set her glass on the table and put her arm around Jasmine. "I'm so sorry. We can't choose who we fall in love with. I wish we could. It would save us all some heartache."

"I guess we both have a thing for brothers, huh?" Jasmine joked.

Emma slapped her arm playfully. "Bitch."

"Did you stop and see Link?"

Emma took a gulp of her wine. "Nope. Came straight here from the airport. I'll go see Dad at the garage before I head back. Maybe Lincoln will be there."

"You ever gonna make a move and take a chance on that?"

Emma rolled her eyes. "So things can be even more awkward and strained between him and I? No, thanks."

"Maybe you'll meet the man or woman for you on this tour," Jasmine joked.

Emma smirked. "Or maybe the woman for me is sitting on this couch." Her eyebrows moved up and down suggestively.

Jasmine giggled. "I wish it were as easy as that."

"I know. Too bad that one time we kissed it felt like I was smooching my sister." Emma shrugged.

"You're strictly a stepbrother kind of woman. Got it."

"See if I bring you wine ever again." Emma scoffed.

Jasmine took another sip, the alcohol easing into her system. A few moments of silence passed.

"So, what are you gonna do?" Emma asked.

Jasmine drained the last of her glass and looked her dead in the eye. "Prepare for fucking battle. If this guy thinks he can take my child away from me without a fight, he's got another thing coming."

"Yes! That's the boss I wanted to see. You got this." Emma cheered.

Jasmine was done being used. Done letting herself take responsibility for others' mistakes. She was finished with punishing herself. She wouldn't hold back. Zoey deserved better. *I deserve better.*

30

ATLAS

tlas stared at the grey ceiling. Sleep had evaded him since he'd gotten back to his penthouse almost three weeks ago. He sat up, pulling the covers away. His feet touched the cold marble floor, jolting him. Rubbing a hand over his face, Atlas sighed. This was more than exhaustion. He had zero motivation to get out of bed and go to work. He'd been moving through the motions. His house was too damn quiet. There were no creaking floors as he walked to the bathroom. No view of the ocean from his windows. He missed the salty sea breeze that had greeted him each morning.

And the two faces that had sat across from him at the breakfast table almost every day. Zoey's questions and love for ice cream. *She's my niece.* Sure, the paternity test hadn't come in yet, but it explained why he'd felt attached to her in some way. She had Oliver's eyes. *My eyes.*

Atlas relieved himself and then went to the kitchen before starting the cappuccino machine. The earthy scent of coffee wafted up a few moments later. It was nothing like the bitter stuff Jasmine had made. His stomach soured. *Christ, did she have to ruin everything for me?* He dumped the cup into the sink as his phone buzzed.

He unplugged it from the charger and lifted it as his dad's name flashed.

Father: *Meeting in the conference room at 8. Results are in.*

A weight settled in his chest, slinking into his belly. Atlas fisted his hands, anger burning through his veins. Rage at himself for letting his guard down, for trusting Jasmine. For thinking he could have something good just for him, untouched by his family. His brother had been his best friend his whole life, but now . . . he didn't know how to feel.

He closed his eyes, her vulnerable green gaze flashing in his mind. The last things he'd said to her repeated in his mind. Guilt and pain shredded his heart into ribbons. "How could I be so stupid?" he asked the empty kitchen. "Everybody fucking wants something from me." *And I'm always second best. She thought I was Oliver, the father of her child.* Had those moments between them meant nothing? Was it all a ploy to manipulate him? The memory of her shaking and sobbing in his arms rocked through him. *No. That was real.* Wasn't it? How could he know what to trust anymore? Atlas picked up the crystal bowl from the counter and flung it against the wall, shattering it into countless broken pieces. Much like him.

* * *

Two hours later, Atlas pulled open the door to the conference room. His mother and father were seated on one side of the table with the family lawyers on the other. Oliver paced at the far end, his suit crumpled and his hair wild.

His brother's eyes darted to his, relief flashing when they

made eye contact. Atlas diverted his attention to the empty chair at the end of the long table before he sat.

"Okay, everyone's here. Let's get this over with," his father commanded.

"Sit down, Oliver," his mother snapped. She never talked that way to her favorite son.

Oliver took a seat next to his father.

"I can't believe you'd be so stupid," she continued.

"It wasn't my fault. I used a condom. How is this possible?" He shook his head.

"Did you check if it broke?" his mother asked.

"I—fuck." He shook his head.

"You could lose your shares in the company. You know how your grandfather is. Your brother hasn't had this problem and he's not even married," their father grated.

Oliver's head dipped; his shoulders slumped. This was the moment when his parents saw Oliver as a failure, and for once, Atlas was the son in favor. Why didn't it feel better?

"Where's Christina?" Atlas asked.

Everyone's head snapped towards him.

"Why would I tell her if the bastard's not mine?"

Atlas shook his head, disgust bubbling up. "She's your fucking kid, Olli. You and I both know it."

The first lawyer cleared his throat. His grey hair reflected the light overhead. "I have the results right here."

"Well, get on with it. Is Oliver the father?" his mother asked.

The lawyer slid out the paperwork and opened a file. His bushy eyebrows drew together. "Yes. Oliver Remington is a match. He's the father."

Their father's hand slammed onto the table at the same time his mother shot out of the chair, arms crossed, eyes blazing.

Oliver's face paled. "What do I have to do to make this go away?"

His question felt like a slap in the face. Atlas narrowed his gaze on his brother, perhaps truly seeing for the first time who Oliver was.

"How many times have you cheated on Christina?" Atlas asked.

Oliver jerked his attention back to him. "Why the fuck does that matter?"

Atlas let out a breath. That answered that question.

"That is not the problem here. The problem is she had the baby and now that child is entitled to *our* money," his father argued.

Atlas shook his head, disgust roiling in his gut.

"Maybe you can say it's yours." Oliver turned towards him; his eyes brightened.

"We have to pay her off. Keep her quiet so your grandfather and the tabloids don't get wind of this," their mother interjected.

If Oliver had any hope of staying a part of this company and being in their old-fashioned grandfather's good graces, he had to make this disappear—make Zoey disappear.

"And if she doesn't take the deal?" Atlas asked.

Jasmine didn't seem like the type, but he'd been wrong about so many things when it came to her. Did he even know her at all? She'd known the moment he walked into the inn who he was. *But she tried to tell me before we slept together.* Hadn't she? It didn't matter. Trying and doing were separate things. In the end, she'd been like every other person in his life, manipulating him for their benefit. *Just like I did to her.*

"Then we threaten to take full custody of the child and ruin her. We'll go after her business, her family. We'll ship the child to a boarding school in Switzerland or something," his mother said, her voice monotone.

Atlas shot to his feet. "Zoey!"

All attention diverted to him.

"What?" his father asked.

"Your granddaughter's name is Zoey. But I guess that doesn't matter to you since you're going to ship her off to another continent anyways," he growled, heading towards the door.

"What has gotten into you?" his mother asked.

"Fucked if I know!" He left.

But the truth was, he couldn't stand another moment listening to his family dehumanize that little girl. She was nothing but a victim of her parentage. And despite the turmoil with Jasmine, he loved Zoey. He wouldn't let his family hurt her.

31

JASMINE

Jasmine set the phone down, her hand shaking. Her chest squeezed tight. She forced a breath in.

"Was that the results?" Mikel asked, sitting next to her on the porch. The sun hung low in the sky. Seagulls cawed as they dove for their dinner. The salty breeze tickled her skin.

She nodded, unable to speak. Tears blurred her vision.

Her brother's strong arm wrapped around her and pulled her close. She wiped the tears before they could fall as she turned away.

"Do they want a meeting?" Mikel asked.

Jasmine nodded.

"We'll call the lawyer and go with you," Bently said, taking the empty spot on her other side.

Jasmine's gaze flicked to the beach where Zoey was happily playing with her cousins. "I got this. I made the decisions that I did. I should be the one to deal with the consequences."

"We're gonna come anyways. You shouldn't do this alone," Bently said.

"You think I'm incapable? Just because I made a lot of bad choices in the past, it doesn't mean I can't take care of myself now," she snapped.

Bently turned to face her. "I don't know where you get off thinking I believe you're incapable of anything. Damn, woman. Have you looked in the mirror? You are raising a child by yourself. You bought a run-down house that's old as shit and turned it into a destination on the seacoast. You work harder than anyone I know, and you still manage to be the best mother Zoey could ever ask for."

Tears streamed down her face. Bently wiped them away with his thumbs. "You are a fucking warrior. I'm just happy to fight by your side."

"We got your back, Jaz," Mikel added.

She looked between her brothers, emotion bubbling up: gratitude and joy. She had a family who loved and supported her. Brothers who would be there for her no matter what. "You two are the best brothers in the world. Do you know that?"

Mikel shrugged. Bently flinched. A dark shadow passed over his face.

"What is it?" she asked.

He shook his head. "Nothing."

"Bently—"

"I wasn't there for you when you needed me most." Bently's voice was hoarse. His shoulders slumped like he'd been carrying this secret for a lifetime.

She sucked in a breath. There was no doubt in her mind what he was referring to. *No.* Jasmine shook her head. This conversation was long overdue. "Don't do that. Don't carry your father's sins. The fault lies with your father and only him."

"I should have seen it sooner. I should have been the one to take care of it," Bently whispered.

Jasmine's stomach dropped. She looked to Mikel, the confession in his dark eyes. His gaze shifted to the floor. She slapped a hand over her mouth. The brother she'd given such a hard time to for abandoning her. The one who'd struggled for so long with his addiction, only to return and have her be so hard on him. "But he died of an overdose. I thought he killed himself like Mom."

Mikel shook his head. "I couldn't let him touch you again, Jaz."

Her mind was reeling. Her brother had protected her. He'd risked everything to make sure she was safe from a monster and then carried that guilt in silence. She turned to Bently. "You knew?"

He nodded darkly. "I went there to do it myself, but he'd beaten me to it."

She wrapped one arm around each brother and pulled them close. "We might be the most fucked-up family, with literal skeletons in our closets, but you guys . . . I just can't even express how much I fucking love you."

"This is so fucked up," Mikel said as she released them.

She licked her lips, pressure in her chest expanding. The words stuck in her throat. She sucked in a haggard breath, gaining courage. They needed this. But so did she. And she was strong enough to survive the telling, capturing back just a little more of her power. "It started when I was five."

Both of them tensed by her side. "He was good at hiding it when it happened. He threatened me if I told, no one would believe me. And that he'd hurt you all. It escalated over the years. Then . . . Mom found us . . . She walked away. She left me with him and killed herself. I felt like it was my fault that she died. I never said anything because I thought I deserved it." The words rushed out of her. Her brothers needed to hear this, if only to clear their consciences.

"I'm sorry I didn't see it sooner," Bently said defeatedly.

"You were a kid. You had enough to worry about. I remember how many times you stepped in to save me or Mikel from his fists. So I know there were countless times I can't remember because I was so young. You kept me safe when I needed it most. You saved me. Both of you."

Bently wiped a tear from his eye, sniffling. Mikel cleared his throat and pinched his nose.

"Do you regret it?" Jasmine asked Mikel.

"Not for one second."

"We made it through a horrible situation. We all survived the way we could. And we beat the system. We broke the cycle. We won't be anything like them. We'll make sure our kids have the best lives, filled with love and laughter. You both inspire me," she said.

"You too, sis." Mikel kissed her forehead.

"To the reconstruction of us. We broke the cycle so our kids don't have to," Bently agreed.

"I'm sorry I took so much of my anger out on you." She shifted to face Mikel.

He shook his head. "I should have told you all what was going on with me."

"We all should have talked more instead of bottling it up and pretending we were okay," Bently added.

"Let's make a promise that we'll be honest with each other from here on in. When one of us is struggling, we can reach out," Jasmine proposed.

"Okay," Mikel agreed.

Bently hesitated and sighed. "I'll try."

She smiled, her broken, tattered heart stuttering to life.

"When are we leaving for New York?" Bently asked.

"Tuesday."

"Let's go up Monday, rent some rooms, take the kids to a museum or something," Mikel suggested.

"You'd do that?" Jasmine asked.

"We got your back. Always. I know you want to go in alone, but we'll be outside waiting," Bently said.

The well of gratitude in her rib cage overflowed. "I don't know what I did to deserve such a great family."

"You're you. That's more than enough. Don't ever doubt yourself, Jaz," Mikel said.

"What do you hope will happen with Oliver?" Bently asked.

Jasmine ran a hand through her hair. "I want Zoey to have a father in her life who loves her and treats her right. If he isn't willing to do that, I just want him to leave us alone. He didn't seem anything like Atlas. The way he spoke to me and looked at me." She shivered.

"You could still get some financial support," Bently suggested.

She shook her head. "If he doesn't want to be a dad, I don't want anything from him."

"No matter what you decide or what happens in there, we got your back," Bently promised.

"Thank you. I love you guys so much." She stood, reaching out a hand to each brother. They took them and got to their feet. Jasmine wrapped them both in a group hug.

Two men who'd loved her since birth, even though she only shared half their DNA. Two brothers who'd risked everything to protect her. Two men who'd walked through hell with her, and showed her what it was to be a man, a husband, and a father. She wouldn't settle for any less for herself or Zoey.

Jasmine was going to face her fears and do it with the confidence that she'd fought so hard to gain. Bently was right; she was a fucking warrior. And it was time she believed it too.

32

ATLAS

Atlas's leg bounced under the table of the conference room. He hadn't been able to sleep the night before knowing he was going to face Jasmine today. The family lawyers were having low discussions with his parents. Oliver sat next to Christina, stone-faced. Christina leaned away, wearing the mask of indifference that so many in their social group had mastered. But even the makeup she wore couldn't hide the dark circles under her eyes.

Knock. Knock.

His heart jumped. His stomach knotted and flipped.

"Come in," his father instructed.

The door opened and a redheaded woman in a pants suit walked in, file in hand. Jasmine trailed behind, her head held high. The simple floral dress she wore hugged her figure. Her green eyes met his, her mouth parting. The tension in the room wound around him, pulling tighter, making it hard to breathe. She darted her gaze away, focusing on Oliver. *Right. The whole reason we are even here.* He'd been a fool to think she ever wanted him.

"Good morning. I'm Bridget Stevens. I'll be acting as Jasmine Evans's attorney." Bridget motioned towards Jasmine before they took a seat.

"Andy Graham, Mike Fabricco, and Terry Buldoc. We're the family lawyers for the Remingtons." Andy introduced three of the ten lawyers their family employed for various needs.

Bridget scanned the room, looking between Atlas and his twin brother. "Which one of you is Oliver?"

"I am," Oliver said.

The lawyers started the conversation, but their voices droned into the background. Atlas couldn't take his eyes off Jasmine. She looked so small and alone. His family had hired sharks for lawyers, and hers appeared to be fresh out of law school. Jasmine sat straight, not glancing his way again. And it fucking tore him up inside. He knew he'd hurt her. But how could he ever make things right with so much unknown between them? She'd been with his brother. She'd lied to him. How could he trust her again? *I lied to her too.*

"I'd just like to know what you planned on getting out of blackmailing my son?" his mother asked bluntly.

Jasmine flinched. "I had no idea who your son was when I met him, so how could I be trying to blackmail him?"

"Oh, that's right, you were just some floozy in a bar bathroom." His mother dismissed her.

Atlas clenched his fists, his jaw ticcing.

"Excuse me—" Bridget started to say.

Jasmine sat forward. "I will not let you hold my past choices over my head. Not when Zoey's father made the same decision as I did—only he was married. I'd say infidelity is far more immoral than a young woman choosing what she does with her own body. I regret nothing because I got my beautiful daughter from it."

His heart lurched. He was proud of her for standing up for herself, but the truth of their union was a painful reminder that he had no place harboring any lingering feelings for her.

His mother's face turned beet red. "Why, you little—"

"Stop!" his father interjected, annoyed. "What do you want to make this disappear?"

Jasmine swallowed, blinking rapidly. She stood up, pulling out several photos and sliding them on the table towards Oliver. "Zoey Jane Evans is your daughter's name. I named her Zoey, meaning life, because as I grew her, she gave me a new life." She pointed to the first image: a shot of Zoey proudly beaming next to a sandcastle covered in shells. "She's three years old. She loves playing on the beach and with her cousins." She motioned to the next. "Zoey is kind, and beautiful, and strong. She's your daughter."

Atlas's eyes flicked over the photos. *She gets her strength from you.*

"We don't need the dramatics or to have my son's indiscretions flaunted in his pregnant wife's face. Have some class." His mother shoved the pictures away.

"She's your daughter," Jasmine pleaded with Oliver, who wouldn't even look her in the eye.

"She's a bastard!" Christina shouted, erupting into sobs.

Oliver put his arm around her.

Jasmine gathered the pictures together and sat back down, resignation steeling her features.

"Why should we care?" his mother asked coldly.

"Because she's a part of your family," Jasmine answered.

The silence was deafening. Atlas could read the realization written across his parents' faces because the same one popped into his mind. Being part of their family meant being a part of the Remington empire. Did she mean Zoey was entitled to a portion of the shares of the company? She was here for her cut.

His mother shook her head. His father's sharp gaze was unflinching towards the mother of their grandchild and the rightful heir to a small fortune because of her bloodline. Their grandfather was old-fashioned and ruthless. If he found out, Oliver would be kicked out of the company and lose his shares.

"What do you want?" Atlas asked, his voice hoarse, afraid of the confirmation.

Jasmine turned towards him, her expression softening. Her gaze wavered, the pain in her eyes still fresh. "If Oliver doesn't want to be a part of Zoey's life, if he can't accept her as his daughter and treat her how she deserves to be treated, I want him to sign over his parental rights to her. I want assurances you will leave my inn alone and never reach out to us again."

"And . . . how much?" Atlas pressed.

"I don't want your money. If my daughter needs something, I'll provide for her." Jasmine lifted her chin. She slid the pictures in the file and motioned to the lawyer.

"You have until Friday to give us an answer." Bridget stood.

The room tilted. Jasmine didn't want their money? She was truly walking away from potentially millions of dollars.

The door burst open and Joseph Remington himself walked in. Atlas's grandfather stood tall in an expensive, tailored suit. His very presence was still so commanding at eighty years old. His white hair was neatly combed to the side as always.

"Dad! What are you doing here?" Atlas's father gasped.

His grandfather shook his head, tucking his hands into the pockets of his suit. "You think I don't know what the hell is going on in my own company? These lawyers work for me as long as I have breath in my lungs. I got the paternity results before you did, you baboon." He walked towards Jasmine, eyeing her up and down critically.

Atlas stood, wanting to get between Jasmine and his grandfather. She'd been through enough. *I've put her though too much.* All this time, she'd meant everything. She'd loved him. Jasmine had laid it all on the line and he'd thrown it in her face and walked away. He'd left her when she needed him most. Shame coated him, weighing heavily on his shoulders.

His parents exchanged worried glances. Oliver was white as a ghost, holding on to his wife as she wiped her running mascara.

"Tell me, Miss Evans, are you good at math?" Grandfather asked.

Jasmine's brows formed a triangle. "Are you asking me that because I'm Asian?"

Joseph chuckled. "Oh dear, you are a feisty one. No, that's not what I meant. See, I'm trying to understand why you would let go of a multimillion-dollar inheritance for your daughter. That doesn't sound so smart."

"That depends on how much I value my daughter and her safe and loving upbringing, Mr. Remington," Jasmine replied.

He nodded towards Jasmine. "I like her."

"Dad—" Atlas's father tried to speak.

"You and your wife are not needed here. Get out," Joseph growled.

"But, Dad—"

"Out!" his grandfather shouted.

His parents stood and stalked out with one hate-filled glance towards Jasmine before they exited.

"You too." Joseph nodded to Oliver and Christina, and the lawyers.

"Yes, sir," Oliver agreed, quickly obeying, no doubt trying to hang on to the thread of hope he wouldn't lose everything.

"Stay." His grandfather motioned to Atlas before turning back to Jasmine and her lawyer. "I'll have the papers drawn up this week. Zoey will have a trust in her name that she can access when she turns thirty. Until then, if she needs anything for education or her care, let me know directly. I'll send you a check to keep her taken care of for a while. Think of it as back child support."

Jasmine waved away the card he offered her. "I can't—"

His grandfather shook his head. "No strings attached. She doesn't have to be a part of this life and our family if she doesn't want to. But I would love to get to know her, see her a couple of times a year. Maybe an invite to her next birthday party."

Jasmine nodded, her eyes brimming with tears. Atlas wanted to wrap her up in his arms and tell her it would all be okay. But he'd lost that right.

"Is there anything she needs right now?" Joseph asked.

"No." She shook her head.

"She needs a decent car," Atlas spoke, drawing her attention.

"It will be delivered tomorrow."

Jasmine whipped her attention back to his grandfather. "I'll pay you back. I promise."

He shook his head. "Being a part of my great-granddaughter's life will be enough payment. You haven't seen a very good representation of my family. But for as long as I'm alive, the Remingtons will never shirk their responsibility and they will always take care of what's theirs."

Jasmine glanced back to Atlas as if she needed his assurance. The realization was like a sucker punch to his stomach. Some part of her still trusted him—at least more than she trusted his family. "My grandfather has many faults, but he's true to his word." *Unlike me.*

She smiled, eyes shiny with tears. "Thank you so much, Mr. Remington."

"Call me Great-Grandpa Remington." He chuckled.

Jasmine nodded towards the door, and spoke to Bridget. "Can you give me a minute?"

Her lawyer said, "Of course."

After she'd exited the room, Jasmine walked over to Atlas. He stood, holding his breath. This woman had every right to hate him. He'd promised her he'd face anything with her and then at the first sign of difficulty he'd left her alone to weather the storm herself. He'd succumbed to his own insecurities rather than trusting in the love between them. But they were still living in two different worlds. He was a part of the Remington empire and she lived in a small town running an inn that she'd never give up.

"Atlas?" Jasmine's voice trembled slightly.

"Yeah?" *I'm sorry, my love.*

"Thank you."

Of all the things he'd expected her to say, that wasn't one of them. She must have read the confusion on his face because she continued, "You gave me and Zoey an amazing couple of weeks. And I wanted you to know I'm sorry for any pain I caused you."

His heart broke all over again. Regret over the hurtful words he'd muttered to her at their last encounter burned his neck with shame. "You don't have anything to be sorry about. I'm the one who owes you an apology." He wanted to reach out and hold her. But they had an audience.

"I'd better go." She gave him one last lingering glance before she nodded to his grandfather and walked out the door.

"That one's got gumption. Don't see that much these days. She's a fierce protector of that little girl," his grandfather said.

Atlas nodded. "She's doing the right thing keeping Zoey away from all of this."

"You don't meet a woman like that every day, son. Believe me, I've spent a lifetime trying."

"She's the most genuine person I've ever known," Atlas agreed. *And I love her.*

"Too bad she isn't Remington-marriage material." His grandfather shook his head.

Atlas tensed. "What's that supposed to mean?"

"She's not from our social status. She's an innkeeper for Christ's sake. She isn't Remington material, but she's the mother of that child and there isn't anything we can do about it now."

Rage burned hot, slicking over his skin. Atlas shook his head. "I quit."

Joseph's mouth dropped open. "No, you don't. You're the only one in this family I can trust."

"I can't do this anymore. I don't want it." He pulled out his tie as he stalked towards the door. If he hurried, he could still catch her.

"Ha! Since when is business about what you want? You weren't complaining when it paid for that penthouse or the jets that flew you and your friends all around the world. You sound like a whiny, ungrateful child."

Atlas opened the door and turned. "I quit, effective immediately."

"You won't get another dime from me! You really want to forfeit shares in a billion-dollar company? All for a woman?" His grandfather was fuming. He'd never seen him so angry.

"You said yourself—a woman like that doesn't come

around every day. She's worth more than my inheritance. She's worth . . . everything."

"Atlas, don't be rash. Let's think this through—Atlas!" His grandfather's shout echoed as he slammed the door shut on his past and sprinted to the stairwell towards his future.

He was done letting others decide what was best for him while he tried to live up to everyone else's expectations except his own. He needed to find the woman he loved, beg her forgiveness, and hope by some miracle she'd give him a chance to make things right.

33

ATLAS

Atlas pushed open the heavy metal doors and rushed into the lobby. Sweat beaded down his forehead as he searched for the one face he needed to see.

Jasmine. There she was, wrapped in a group hug from her family. They'd been here all along. She wasn't alone.

Bently seemed to notice him first, his shoulders bunching as he stepped in front of Jasmine protectively. Mikel and Andre were soon to follow as all eyes pointed at him. The conversation was swallowed up by stunned silence. Even the kids seemed aware of the tension.

"What do you want?" Bently asked.

Jasmine peeked her head out from behind the giants standing guard before she stepped beside them.

"Can we talk?"

Her chest rose and fell before she nodded.

"Mr. Atlas! You didn't say goodbye." Zoey pushed forward, her big grey eyes saddened.

"I—"

Jasmine spun around, crouching to face Zoey. "Sweet-

248

heart, can you go with Uncle Bently to the car? I think he needs someone to hold his hand."

Zoey's eyebrows scrunched together as she looked critically between her mother and uncle. "I guess so."

Bently held out his palm. "Come on. We'll find somewhere to get lunch after this with ice cream."

"Ice cream!" Her face lit up.

Lyra and Phoenix cheered with her as the group filed away. All adult sets of eyes cut him a warning glare, the equivalent to *hurt her anymore and die a slow, painful death.*

He nodded. Message received.

Jasmine turned to him, looking over at the lone receptionist pretending not to listen in. Atlas motioned across the other end of the room by the trickling water fountain. They walked side by side in silence until they were farther away.

He blew out a breath, searching for the right words to say. But there were none. "*I'm sorry* doesn't feel adequate."

She met his eyes, a newfound confidence glowing from her. "I really try not to care what people think of me, but I need you to know nothing between us was a lie. I meant *everything.*"

"I did too."

Her expression softened as she looked down, like she wasn't sure what to believe. He deserved that.

"I was in a really bad place when I met Oliver."

His muscles tensed and his chest squeezed. He didn't want to hear about his brother, but if she needed to get this out, he'd let her.

"Random sex with strangers was my way of hurting myself because I thought I deserved the punishment. But Zoey came along and changed my whole world. She showed me how to love myself . . . But you, you were never a punishment for me. Being with you was something I've never experienced before. So, thank you for showing me I'm not as broken as I think sometimes."

His hands reached out to cup her face. His self-control snapped. Pain lanced through him at the thought of this beautiful woman hurting so much. *And I made it worse.* "You're not broken. You're the strongest woman I've ever had the privilege of knowing. Baby, you're so beautiful and genuine. Zoey is every bit of the amazing girl she is because of you, and only you. I'm so fucking sorry I ever did anything that would make you doubt that."

She closed her eyes, her body trembling against his.

"I can't begin to apologize for what I said to you that day at the inn. I lied. What we had between us was everything and more. I originally came there to buy the inn, but I gave up on that before we were together."

Her eyes opened—green orbs piercing to the depths of his soul. "You said you were in this regardless of what that meant. And then . . ." Tears welled in her eyes, a direct hit to his ragged heart.

"And then I left you when you needed me most. I walked away." His voice broke.

She nodded. "For a long time, I settled for a lot less. But I won't do that anymore. Zoey deserves a man in her life who won't run when things get tough. And so do I. We deserve someone who will love us through the storms because trust me, I've got plenty of ghosts in my past."

"You deserve the world," he agreed.

"Atlas?" Her gaze searched his. The question hung in the air between them. Could he give her that? *Yes.* But he'd already gone back on his word. She deserved to be shown through his actions. He'd make this right.

"Can I say goodbye to Zoey?" he asked.

Jasmine stepped back, cringing away in rejection. Her eyes darted to the floor before she nodded.

Shit. He reached out his hand to her shoulder. "If you think for one goddamn second I don't want you, you're wrong."

Her attention focused back on his face.

"I'm coming for you, Jasmine. I'm gonna prove just how much I'm in this. I'm gonna earn your forgiveness, and a place in your and Zoey's life. Then I'm going to spend my days making sure the both of you know just how important and worthy and amazing you truly are."

She blinked, tears falling. Fear and disbelief were painted across the curves and contours of her face.

It's okay, sweetheart. I'll show you.

"Now, let me give that girl a proper goodbye *for now*."

She turned and walked towards the elevator. He followed her in before riding it down to the parking garage. He stayed by her side as she led him to the two SUVs parked side by side. Jasmine opened the door of the one closest to them, children's laughter pouring out.

"Zoey? Atlas wanted to say bye."

A moment later, a dark-haired angel climbed out of the vehicle, holding her mother's hand. She looked up at him with a soft smile. "Goodbye, Mr. Atlas."

He crouched down to her level. "You can call me Atlas if you want."

She tipped her head to the side.

"I'll see you again sometime soon, okay?"

"Otay."

"Until then, can you do me a favor?" he asked.

"What?"

"Give your mommy an extra hug and kiss every night for me."

Zoey giggled, looking at her mother. "I fink I can do dat."

"Have a good trip home, princess."

Zoey surged forward, wrapping her tiny arms around his neck and squeezing hard. Atlas's eyes widened in shock. *She's hugging me.* He smoothed his hand over her back, cherishing the connection. His eyes darted up to Jasmine's as she wiped her eyes.

"Okay, sweetheart. We need to get going," Jasmine said.

Zoey released his neck and pecked him on the cheek.

Jasmine picked her up and put her back in the SUV. "Buckle up." She shut the door.

"Jasmine, I—"

"Atlas?" Veronica's voice echoed in the garage, grating on his nerves. He closed his eyes, wishing her away.

"Oh, aren't you that innkeeper? What are you doing in New York City of all places?" Veronica eyed Jasmine up and down.

"What are you doing here, Veronica?" Atlas snapped, stepping in between the women.

Veronica rubbed her glossy lips together. "I have an appointment with your mother in fifteen minutes to discuss the engagement dinner for us, silly."

Jasmine's gasp pushed him over the edge into rage. He spun around, palms up. "It's not true."

"I have the confirmation right here, and a few sample invitations in my bag if you want to see," Veronica pushed.

"Don't you think I'd know if I was engaged?" he snapped.

Veronica rolled her eyes and held up the paper. "I know you'll have your mistresses from time to time, but come on, Atlas. You can do better than her."

His fists clenched. Seething with anger, he grabbed the invitation and ripped it down the middle. "There. Will. Be.

No. Fucking. Engagement. Between. Me. And. You. I don't know how many fucking ways I can say it."

"What the fuck is going on?" Bently asked, coming around the front of the car.

"We need to go," Jasmine said.

"Wait, please," he begged.

Bently wrapped an arm around Jasmine protectively.

Jasmine shook her head and opened the door, climbing inside.

He wanted to reach out and stop her. Everything had gone to hell. Bently shut the door behind her, folding his arms over his chest. "Leave my sister alone."

"I love her."

Veronica gasped.

Bently's gaze turned to Veronica and then back to him. "I want to believe you, man, but nothing you've done proves your words true. If you ever bother my sister again and hurt her . . . Let's just say, you've been warned." He walked back to the driver's side and got in, then backed the car out before disappearing from the garage.

"Our parents have planned this since we were kids. Why would you risk everything for some small-town bitch?" Veronica snarled.

He whipped around, stepping into her space. She winced.

"I don't give a fuck what my family wants. I wouldn't marry you if my life depended on it."

"You'll lose everything," she threatened.

He scoffed. "I already walked away. I just quit the company before I came down here. Guess you won't want that engagement party now either since all you really cared about was my money and connections."

"You're lying. You don't have the balls."

He threw his hands up. "I don't care what you believe. It's the truth."

She looked frantically around the garage and then back to him. "That woman won't want you now either. What do you have to offer her if your hands are empty?" She huffed and stormed off to the elevator.

Atlas ran a hand over his face. *Fuck.* How was he going to fix this? How would Jasmine be able to trust him again? This was the exact drama he'd wanted to keep her out of. But Veronica had a point. Who was he without his money and power? Was Jasmine better off without him? He glanced at the elevator. There was no way he was going back there. What was he going to do?

34

JASMINE

Jasmine shuffled around the papers on her desk. She'd reread them three times because she was so distracted. It was Friday—three days with no word from Atlas. But today was the day she was supposed to hear back from the Remingtons about their decision. Would Oliver terminate his parental rights without issue?

Would she ever see Atlas again? His apology had seemed so sincere. He'd promised to earn her forgiveness. But then that woman had shown up. Was Atlas like his brother? Married to one woman and having mistresses?

Her phone chirped and the front door opened a moment later. A tall man in a dress suit walked in, a large envelope in hand. "Miss Evans?"

"Yes?" She stood. Her body trembled, her knees knocking together. Nerves bound and twisted her insides.

"I have a delivery for you." He slid the white paper into her hands. She stared down at the return address. *Joseph Remington.*

She took a deep breath and glanced towards Zoey playing

happily on the rug nearby and back up to thank the courier, but he'd already gone. She ripped open the tab and pulled out the documents.

The form for relinquishing parental rights was signed by Oliver. This was it. She was free. He wouldn't come and try to take her baby from her. She turned the page. A check written out to her in the amount of one hundred thousand dollars was attached to a note.

This is the first payout of Zoey's trust. If you need anything else, please don't hesitate to contact my office. Signed, Joseph Remington.

She blinked away the emotion that welled up. A weight lifted off her shoulders. Zoey wouldn't have to do without. But sadness for her baby finding out someday that her biological father didn't want her dulled the elation. She walked towards the couch and sat by her little girl. Zoey would discover that Oliver had abandoned her, a pain Jasmine knew all too well herself. But Zoey had an entire family who surrounded her with affection and support. Their tribe was comprised of unique individuals, bonded together with affection strong enough to fight the deepest, darkest adversaries. Love was thicker than blood.

She placed the paperwork back in the envelope and called Bently. He picked up on the second ring.

"Did they get back to you?" he asked.

"He signed the paperwork. It's over."

"We'll all come. Let's fire up the grill and celebrate," he suggested.

Gratitude glowed in her chest. "Sounds like a good idea. See you soon."

"Did Atlas contact you?" he asked.

She shook her head, even though he couldn't see. "No." She'd hoped that he would be the one to bring her the news. But it seemed he hadn't meant what he said after all.

"See you in an hour," Bently said.

Jasmine hung up her phone, eyes flicking to the photo icon. She clicked it, finding the pictures of Atlas and Zoey together. Her heart ached. Someday, Jasmine would find someone who would love her the way she deserved to be loved and accept Zoey as their own. She wouldn't ever settle for less.

Zoey walked over to her.

Jasmine set the phone down. "Your cousins are coming over for a cookout."

The little girl's face lit up with a big smile. "Right now?"

Jasmine nodded. "In an hour."

"Yay!" Zoey squealed and hugged her neck, choking her. Jasmine closed her eyes and pulled her daughter into her arms. She didn't need anyone else. It was going to be her and Zoey against the world, with their family by their side. And if a man worthy of them did ever come along, he'd have a lot to live up to.

35

JASMINE

TWO WEEKS LATER

The ocean waves crashed against the rocky shore. Jasmine inhaled the salty sea breeze, closing her eyes to the warm summer sunshine. It was a great day for a wedding.

Zoey's giggles bubbled up, carried by the wind. Jasmine opened her eyes, searching the sand ahead. Her daughter ran around in bare feet, her white lace tutu dress billowing in the wind as she darted away from Mikel. Bently carried Phoenix on his shoulders, dodging and weaving through the girls as he laughed hard.

Jasmine pulled out her phone and snapped a picture. Her heart warmed at the sight. She might not be able to give Zoey her dad, but her little girl was more than lucky to have two uncles and their best friend who loved her like their own. Jasmine didn't look like them, but they were all unique, and that was what made them each so special.

She turned back towards the inn, taking in the white paint her family had all pitched in and helped with. The windows she'd scraped and washed herself. All her hard work had paid off. She didn't need anyone else to realize her dreams and create the life she wanted for Zoey.

Her heart was still broken, her mind still scarred. But she could now look in the mirror and see someone worthy of her love. It continued to be a daily battle, the dark cloud of her depression hovering on the horizon. But she'd been vigilant. She'd never stop healing. For Zoey and herself. Because Jasmine finally believed *she* was worth it.

"Miss Evans?" Rae, one of the kids from Aaron's facility she'd hired recently, asked.

"Yes?"

"The caterer is here, and the delivery of chairs for the wedding. And there is someone at the front desk asking for you," Rae said, ticking off her fingers one by one.

Jasmine's heart fluttered. *When will this stop?* He wasn't coming back. Why would he? His life was there, and hers was here, no matter how beautiful his promises.

"Thanks." She walked to the inn. "Did you get the suite all set for the happy couple?"

"All done except for the bouquet of flowers. Just waiting on the delivery from the florist."

"Awesome," Jasmine said, opening the back door for her employee. The young woman reminded Jasmine a lot of herself. She was a hard worker, but something weighed heavily on her shoulders. It was part of the reason she'd hired her. One kindred spirit recognizing the other.

Rae settled in at the front desk. "They're in the living room."

Jasmine turned the corner and came face to face with a man she hadn't seen in too long. "Cory!"

The man's eyes lit up, turning from his blushing bride-to-be. "Jaz. Been too long. The inn is gorgeous." He welcomed her into a hug.

She broke away only to end up in another set of arms. "Brittany, what are you doing here? And Cory, aren't you supposed to avoid seeing the bride on the wedding day?" Jasmine asked.

Brittany laughed. "You know we don't believe in those old superstitions."

"Well, I don't know; we've had a rough go of things. Maybe we are tempting fate." Cory chuckled.

Brittany turned to face the man she was going to marry in less than seven hours. Her love for him was written in her expression. "Whatever happens, I'll stay by your side through it all."

He leaned down and kissed her nose. The moment was too precious. Longing rose within Jasmine. *I want a man to look at me like that someday too.*

"Okay, you two lovebirds. Save something for the wedding night. I'll make sure to keep the sound machine on extra loud tonight." Jasmine laughed.

Cory waggled his eyebrows up and down as Brittany's fair cheeks blushed.

"Are Aunt Tilda and Uncle Matt here yet?" Cory asked.

"No, but your favorite cousin is," Remy said, walking into the room with a big smile on her face.

They greeted each other with more hugs.

"Where are the kids?" Brittany asked, looking between Remy and Jasmine.

"Outside with the guys. Andre and Mia should be here soon," Jasmine answered.

"Oh, and the cake is in the van. I need to get the guys to help me bring it in before it melts," Remy said, darting towards the kitchen.

"Your Lighthouse suite is all set, and, Cory, you can use the Anchor suite for you and the guys to get ready. Rae has your keys." Jasmine motioned towards the front desk—her heart sputtered. Two grey eyes stared back at her. *Atlas.*

Cory and Brittany walked past her towards the kitchen, oblivious to the whirlwind of panic, hope, and heartache that spun her up inside. Her knees trembled, knocking together. The man's presence shook her like an earthquake.

He stepped forward until he was only inches from her. His clean, soapy smell triggered sensory memories. The way he'd felt when he'd rocked inside her. The taste of his kiss. The warmth of his body curled around hers as he'd held her.

She blinked, unsure and apprehensive.

"I missed you," he said, his voice unsteady.

"What are you doing here?" she asked.

His eyes crinkled at the edges. "I'm here for you." He pulled out a bouquet of yellow sunflowers from behind his back and handed it to her.

She accepted it with a trembling hand. Her gaze took in the jeans and black shirt that fit him so well. "Atlas—"

"I did a lot of thinking. I know I haven't given you a reason to trust me. I know I hurt you . . . deeply." He ran a hand over the back of his head, a surprisingly self-conscious gesture. "But I was hoping you'd be willing to have dinner with me and give us a chance to talk."

Her heart tugged at his words. She wanted to say yes, but this man had indeed caused her pain. He'd said he would be there for her and then run away at the first sign of trouble instead of giving her the benefit of the doubt. He'd lashed out at her. She had a lot of baggage, and she needed a man who could handle all of her, not just the pretty parts. Someone who'd be straight with her—honest about all aspects of his past, too.

"Is your fiancée joining us for this dinner?"

He winced. "I was never engaged. I never intended to

marry her. I told you that my parents had expectations for every part of our lives. But I wouldn't have gone through with it even if I'd never met you."

She believed him. But all her emotions muddled together. How could she trust this man again? It wasn't just her heart she would be risking, but Zoey's.

"Just dinner. I'm not the type of man to beg, but if you need me to get on my knees and plead, I will. I'll do anything for you, and that's what I'm here to show you." His eyes flashed with determination.

"My cousin is getting married today. I can't get away."

"Bently said he'd watch Zoey tonight. And everyone else said they could handle the cleanup so I could pick you up at eight?" Atlas asked.

She tilted her head. "You talked to my family? *Bently* said he'd watch Z so *you* could take me out?" Was she dreaming?

He stuck his hands in his pockets and shrugged. "I came to talk to them first. I wanted them to know my intentions."

Say what? "And what are they?" she asked, still trying to wrap her head around all of this.

His gaze locked on to hers, intense and full of promise. "To show you every day just how beautiful you are, inside and out. To be there for you through the good and the bad. And to be a part of your and Zoey's life. I'm gonna make you mine, Jasmine. In every sense of the word. Because life without you isn't truly living."

She swallowed. "I'll see you at eight."

36

JASMINE

The wedding was beautiful, but Jasmine had a hard time staying focused. Her mind kept wandering towards Atlas. She kissed her daughter goodbye before Belle carried Zoey to their truck. Bently pulled Jasmine in for a hug.

"I can't believe you are doing this for Atlas," she said.

He let her go and looked her in the eyes. "I'm doing this for *you*."

He must have seen the question in her expression because he continued, "Hear him out. And if you don't think he's the one for you, I'll make sure he doesn't bother you again. But don't make the same mistake I did and push everything good away because you think you don't deserve it."

She nodded.

"But don't let him off easy either. Make that man earn your forgiveness. Because you're worth it." He leaned down and kissed her forehead.

"I will." She chuckled.

His phone chimed in his pocket. He pulled it out and

answered. "Hey, Charli—" His face transformed to worry. "Slow down. What happened? . . . Is he okay? . . . I'm on my way. Sit tight."

He hung up the phone.

"Did something happen to the baby?" Jasmine asked, fear streaking through her.

He shook his head. "No, Finn was in an accident. He's being airlifted to the hospital in Washington."

"Oh my God." Jasmine gasped, covering her mouth. *Poor Charli.*

"I'm gonna head over there now, and Belle will take Zoey to our house."

"I can just keep her."

He shook his head. "No, Belle has her. You enjoy your night."

He waved, walking around the car. "Give him hell."

"Tell Charli to text me if she needs anything," she called after him.

"I will." He got in the vehicle and drove off. She checked her phone. Only thirty minutes before Atlas would be there. Jasmine slipped inside to her room. She freshened up her eyeliner and slid on some ChapStick. She pulled at the fabric of her dress. She wouldn't change. This was the nicest dress she owned.

Knock. Knock.

She jumped, her nerves making her feel on edge. She checked her phone. *7:45.* It was probably someone else. She reached out and turned the knob, her stomach twisting with it.

Atlas stood outside her door. His black dress shirt was unbuttoned at the top, and the sleeves were rolled up, showing off his sinewy forearms. "I know I'm early. So, if you're not ready, I can wait."

His deep voice vibrated through her. His eyes lit with need as his gaze caressed every inch of her exposed skin.

"I'm ready." *Not really.*

The corner of his mouth turned up. He held out his hand to her. "I have a surprise for you."

She slipped her palm into his and allowed him to lead her down the stairs to his black Mercedes. He opened the door for her and she sat inside, slipping her phone in her pocket.

He turned the radio on low while they drove the few miles towards town in silence. The tension and anticipation in the car were too thick for conversation. Her body sparked like a live wire. The man was pure temptation. But she needed more than sexual attraction. She needed a man who'd be strong enough to weather the tumultuous seas with her.

He parked the car in front of the run-down building she'd passed countless times on the way to town. She turned towards him. "What are we doing at the old fish market?"

He unbuckled his seat belt, a nervous smile painting his lips. "Come on in and see."

She got out and shut her door before following him to the front. He pulled out a set of keys and unlocked the entrance.

The smell of stale air tinged with fish still lingered even after all the years this place had been left empty. She wrinkled her nose. He switched on the light, illuminating the large open room. It had been gutted out and cleaned. A blanket was laid out in the middle with a picnic basket, a bottle of wine, and two glasses.

"What's this?" she asked.

He took a seat on the floor and patted the spot next to him. She joined him, still trying to understand what all this meant.

"This is Atlantis—or it will be. I bought it. I'm gonna build a wraparound deck outside so guests can dine overlooking the harbor. And I'll renovate the whole place." He looked around, his eyes sparkling with vision.

"Your restaurant?"

His gaze met hers. "I'm moving here. I'm building a business in Shattered Cove. And, I hope, a life with you."

She shook her head. He was really doing this? *Amazing.* "What about New York? Your family? The job you wanted so badly?"

He took a deep breath. "I didn't really want that life. I did it because it was what was expected of me. But it never made me happy. I was too scared to do my own thing. I wanted them to . . . see me as worthy. But you made me question things."

She nodded.

"They offered me the position I wanted so bad, and for once I was the son they admired. But it felt like . . . nothing. Worse than nothing. I realized the only thing I truly wanted was you."

She chuckled with sardonic humor. "I bet they loved that."

He dipped his head. "I had to walk away from everything. My job, my family, my income. It's all gone. I don't have much to offer you, except me."

She sucked in a breath. "What do you mean you walked away from your family?"

"If you don't follow their rules, you get disowned. I chose to leave for myself because I deserve more than being a pawn in their power game. I want to be a chef, run my own restaurant, and bring people together to enjoy great food. But more than anything, I want to be there for you and Zoey in any capacity if you'll let me. I'd like to date you without any pretenses or secrets. Just the two of us getting to know each other and building a life with Zoey."

She swallowed, digesting what he'd said. "Why did you say

what we'd had meant nothing? Why would you try to hurt me?"

He looked down, his shoulders slumped in shame. "My whole life, Oliver had been chosen over me. I thought I'd finally found one good thing that wasn't touched by him. Finding out you'd thought I was him the whole time, I assumed you'd do the same. I thought you'd want Olli instead of me."

She winced. "I didn't fall in love with Oliver. I fell for you."

His gaze met hers, hopeful. "I was too stubborn and insecure to see that. I wanted to believe I wasn't good enough, so that's how I filtered the situation. I won't ever make the same mistake. I thought you played me. Like Veronica and several other women have in the past. That's still no excuse for how I treated you."

"You said you wanted something untouched by your brother. But, Atlas, Zoey is his. I can't be with someone who wouldn't give her the love she deserves simply because of who her father is."

He shook his head, reaching out and cupping her face in his palms. His eyes bored into hers. "I swear, I can't explain it, but that little girl stole a piece of my heart the moment I met her. I'd never think less of her—or you—because of Oliver. He's the one who's missing out on two incredible ladies. The only thing she got from him is his eyes, which happen to be the same as mine." Nothing but honesty was reflected back in those grey orbs.

"I'm not an easy person to love. I've got a lot of baggage —things I've never told anyone about. I can't afford to let you in and have you walk out so easily another time."

He shook his head. "Never again."

"You can't say that without knowing it all."

His hands dropped to hers, waiting patiently. She inhaled a shaky breath. Was she going to do this? Tell him just how fucked up she was and see if he ran for the hills? No, she'd tell him because each time she did, she reclaimed power over the trauma. Because he did need to understand there were things she may never be able to do sexually. That depression was a struggle for her that came and went.

"My stepfather started molesting me when I was five."

His hands tensed in hers. His jaw ticced, anger and deep sadness roiling in his gaze.

"It escalated over the years. He made me . . . that's why I couldn't give you a blow job."

He pulled her into his arms, holding on to her tightly. His chest rose and fell with steady breaths. Atlas's heartbeat thumped wildly.

"I don't know if I'll ever be able to . . . I can't tell you how many men I've had sex with because the truth is, I don't know. I lost count." Shame swirled inside her.

Dirty slut.

You're nothing but a whore.

This is all you're good for.

No. She took a deep breath. That wasn't true—it never was.

I am beautiful.

I am strong.

I'm a survivor.

"But when I found out I was pregnant with Zoey, everything changed. I was terrified and alone. But she altered my life. She made me learn to re-parent myself. To see the child I was when I was victimized, and forgive myself for not being able to protect me. Zoey's been my reason for breaking the cycle. She's my little North Star, my lighthouse in the darkness."

Atlas kissed her forehead. "I'm so sorry that you had to go through that. I can't fucking imagine."

Her heart warmed. Hearing him validate the severity of her trauma brought her a sense of comfort.

"I want to kill the man with my bare hands."

Her eyes widened. "He's already gone."

"Thank you for sharing this with me. I know it can't be easy."

She nodded. "But you need to see how broken I am. I need you to know I have scars that have scars. Sometimes I get so sad I can't get out of bed. And sometimes I lose my way."

Atlas tipped her chin up to look at him. "Then I guess I'll have to be your lighthouse too so you can find your way back."

Love in its purest form burst from her chest. This gorgeous man looked at her like she was the most precious being in the world. She wasn't her past. Or her shame. With Atlas, she was beautiful. He saw past her scars and saw beauty. Beyond her trauma and recognized her strength.

"Atlas?"

"Yeah, sweetheart?"

"I'd like that."

He leaned down, melding his lips with hers. The kiss was soft and gentle, life-giving. His hand came to the back of her head. His forehead touched against hers and they both fought to catch their breath.

"Are you hungry?" he asked.

"Yes," she answered breathily. She was starving for him.

He reached into the basket and pulled out several bins of Tupperware.

She slid off his lap a little deflated. "Oh, you meant for actual food."

He chuckled. "I had a friend in New York show me how to make some of his favorite Korean dishes."

Her heart fluttered. "You did this for me?"

"I'd do anything for you." His tone was serious.

She smiled, fighting the happy tears that blurred her vision.

His mouth slanted over hers, kissing her cheek next, and then her forehead, and her other cheek in a circle. "And we're gonna take this as slow as you need. I'll wait until you're ready to let me back in fully. There's no rush when we have forever."

Atlas lifted his fork to her lips. She opened her mouth and took a bite of the delicious cold noodles he fed her. Sweet, tangy, and a bit spicy, the food burst with flavor.

"It's so good." She smiled. "Please give the chef my compliments."

He chuckled. "Watching you enjoy my food is all the reward I need." Atlas traced a finger over her cheek and down her jaw. His grey eyes darkened.

"What else did you make?" she asked.

He opened the other containers before feeding her each and every bite as they shared the feast he'd prepared for them. The wine relaxed her, the conversation excited her, and the company made her body buzz alive with awareness.

"I'd better get you home." Atlas cleared the empty containers and put them back in the basket. She helped him fold up the blanket and waited outside while he locked up the building that would soon be his restaurant. His hand pressed on her lower back, guiding her to the car. That little touch sent a zing through her body. Energy crackled between them. She buckled up as he loaded their dinner things into the trunk before joining her.

The tension in the car was thick on the drive back to the

inn. Was she ready to open up to him completely again? Her body wanted him, but her heart was still hesitant.

They arrived home, and he walked her to her room. She opened the door and turned to him.

Atlas reached out his hand and cupped her face. "I'm not expecting anything from you. I know I still have a lot to prove to you, and I will start tonight. Would you just let me hold you?"

She swallowed, emotion welling up in her throat. Jasmine nodded. "Yes."

He shrugged off his shirt as she slipped into the bathroom, pajamas in hand. Something about changing in front of him felt too vulnerable. She brushed her teeth and relieved herself, then pulled out an extra toothbrush from under the sink before she set it on the counter. She took a deep breath and walked back into the room to find him sitting on the edge of the bed in nothing but low-hung jeans showing off the defined V of his hips.

"I-I have an extra toothbrush if you want it."

Half his smile turned up as he stood, trading places with her. "Thank you."

She climbed into bed. The water in the bathroom turned on. Her nerves melded with her arousal, creating a hurricane of emotions tumbling through her.

A few minutes later, the bed dipped and his warm body pressed against her back. Atlas's arms wrapped around her, pulling her close to him. "Is this okay?" he asked.

"Yeah." She turned to lay her head on his chest, running her hand over his soft, olive skin. *Is this real?* Was this really her life now?

His palm gently rubbed up and down her arm. She closed her eyes, fighting the tears of contentment and joy that lapped the edges of her lashes.

"What are you thinking about?" his deep voice rumbled against her ear.

"I'm just . . . still trying to believe this is real, that you're here."

His finger traced over her hand against his chest. "I'm sorry I ever gave you reason to doubt me. I'll never keep anything from you again, unless it's to surprise you with something good." He chuckled, tilting her head to look at him. "I promise to believe you always have the best intentions in mind. I swear to you that if I feel like running again, I'll stay."

She rolled over to his arm to get a better view of him.

"I'm more than in this, baby. You've taken residence in here." He pointed to his chest. "You've become part of me." He pressed his hand over her rapidly beating heart. "And you've stolen a piece of me I'll never get back. You've captured my heart. And I give it to you freely because I know there is no person on this planet more worthy. I trust you. And I'm gonna remind you every single day just how much you mean to me until you believe it—and then, I'm gonna keep doing it."

He wiped the moisture from her eyes.

"Loving you is my dream—my passion. *You* are everything to me."

She sniffled, her heart bursting with happiness. Joy bounded out, bouncing off the walls and engulfing her in a warm glow of pure love. "You're too much," she laughed.

He smirked and kissed her forehead. "I'm just getting started."

37

ATLAS

Atlas wiped the sweat beading on his brow. His back ached. He'd spent the majority of the day doing grunt work at his future restaurant. This was a far cry from his office job, but he wouldn't change a thing.

"Atlas?" Mikel called from the open door. It led to the deck they were constructing around the building that would overlook the bay.

"Yeah?" He set the paintbrush down and straightened.

"Can you go get the board stretcher from the back of the truck?" Mikel asked.

Andre's bark of laughter followed the request.

"Sure. What's it look like?"

"It's a board with two nails and a rubber band," Mikel answered, turning his head away as his shoulders shook.

Atlas dusted off his hands on his pants and walked out the front door into the gorgeous summer sunshine. He inhaled a deep breath, taking in the green trees swaying in the breeze, the blue sky, and the lingering scent of the sea. *This is my life now.* And what a beautiful life it was.

He opened the back of the truck and moved some machinery and tools which he didn't recognize. He searched to no avail. His frustration grew. There were boards, but none with nails and a rubber band.

Crunching gravel drew his attention to the right. Bently pulled in next to him and got out of his sheriff's truck. "Hey." Bently nodded.

Atlas waved. "Stopping by to see the progress?"

Bently eyed the truck bed. "Yeah. What are you lookin' for?"

"A board stretcher. Mikel said it was—"

Bently shook his head and burst out laughing.

"What?" Atlas looked down at his shirt.

"You make it too easy for them." Bently chuckled. "There's no such thing as a board stretcher. You can't stretch wood."

"So this is a joke?"

Bently nodded towards the restaurant. Atlas turned to find Mikel and Andre doubling over in laughter.

They'd been constantly razzing him about his lack of experience with physical labor the last few weeks. How was he supposed to know the difference between a Phillips-head and a flat-head screwdriver? His family had always had people for those sorts of things. *Not anymore.* He still had a lot to prove when it came to Jasmine and her loved ones.

"You should have left him another ten minutes," Andre said.

Atlas shook his head.

"I thought you'd learned your lesson the last time you harassed a client," Bently retorted.

Is he sticking up for me?

Andre's laughter died down, his eyes narrowing.

Bently slapped his hand over Atlas's back, ushering him

forward. "Come on. Show me what you guys got done. I think Belle and the ladies are gonna come over Saturday to do some painting while we finish the back deck."

Atlas turned to face Jasmine's oldest brother. Her family was so different to his. These guys were going to take the day off to help make his dream come true that much quicker. The affection and loyalty hit him square in the chest. "Thank you, guys. For everything. I just . . . I don't know how I'm going to repay you."

Mikel bumped his shoulder with his own. "Take care of Jasmine and Zoey—that's all we ask."

Atlas nodded. "Of course."

"And obviously, we'll be sending you a bill." Andre added with a smirk.

"What are you guys doing standing around, doing noth-ing? Is this what y'all are being paid for? To gossip?" Jasmine's voice had him turning around. Her beautiful smirk lit up the room like the sun breaking through the clouds.

"Hey, sweetheart." He opened his arms to give her a hug and then thought better of it. "Sorry, I'm all sweaty."

"That's okay. I like you all sweaty and dirty." She winked playfully as she wrapped her arms around his waist.

The three other men in the room groaned in unison.

"That's too much information." Mikel cringed.

Jasmine's throaty laughter spilled out. "Payback's a bitch."

Mikel waved her off. "I'm going to go do some real work." He and Andre left out the rear exit.

Jasmine turned to her remaining brother. "Hey, Bent, I wondered if you could watch Zoey two Saturdays from now? I've got a wedding event at the inn."

"I can do it," Atlas offered.

Bently and Jasmine turned to him.

He shrugged. "I mean, if you're comfortable with that. I

can take her for lunch and ice cream. Maybe to the park after that?"

"You would do that? Alone?"

Atlas reached out before brushing a lock of hair away from her face. "Of course. You don't have to do this on your own anymore. I'm here. I've got your back."

Jasmine nodded. "I guess I just keep forgetting."

"Well then, I'll keep reminding you." He kissed her nose.

Her smile widened.

His body heated. It had been so long since they'd been together. He was giving her space like he'd promised, going slow. She set the pace, and he'd be patient for as long as she needed to feel safe enough to take this next step. He'd done a lot of damage leaving her the way he did. Trust took time to build. Jasmine was worth the wait.

"Okay, well, since that's settled, I'm gonna see myself out. I'll be back Saturday, with beer." Bently excused himself.

Atlas didn't take his eyes off Jasmine as he said, "Yeah, thanks again."

Jasmine took a step forward, leaning into him. His lips melded with hers, softly and sweetly.

"Have they been giving you a hard time?" she asked.

"They've been great—highly entertaining." They were treating him like one of their own. And it meant the world to him after losing his own family for pursuing his own desires. He hadn't heard a word from his brother or parents since he left the city to set up shop in Shattered Cove. He was just grateful his grandfather hadn't cut off his access to his trust. The biggest loss had been Oliver. But his twin's true colors had come out, and he was ashamed he hadn't seen them sooner. Atlas would be a better man. He'd choose his family from here on out.

"Hey, while you're here, I wanted to see which tables you

thought I should order." Atlas walked over to the counter and picked up a magazine. Jasmine joined him as he pointed out his top three choices.

"The reclaimed wood ones would be perfect. But I know my brothers could probably hook you up with them for cheaper or refer you to someone local to make them."

"Really?"

"Yeah. It should help with your budget."

"I'll ask them." Atlas looped his arms around Jasmine, pulling her against him once more. "I think I love you more every day."

She giggled. "I think it's my family."

"Them too. I don't know what I did to deserve you all."

Her expression grew serious. "You were you, Atlas. You just needed to find someone who accepted you for who you truly are. And that's why we work so well together. Because you accept me too. You haven't tried to change me, and I won't ask you to be someone you're not either."

His lips coasted over her forehead, brushing softly against her skin. "That's one of the million reasons I fucking love you."

"A million, huh?" she teased.

"Want to hear them all?"

"Of course."

"Let me cook you and Zoey dinner tonight. And after she goes to bed, we'll sit on the couch with a glass of your favorite wine and I'll tell you all about them."

She grinned. "It's a date."

38

JASMINE
ONE MONTH LATER

Jasmine walked into the restaurant, searching for Atlas. The walls had been painted with a soft grey. Pendant lighting hung over the newly refinished bar and the spaces where tables would be. A few stunning blown-up photos of local farmers harvesting their crops and fishermen with their catches adorned the walls. Atlas had secured agreements with all of them. True to his vision, he'd tried to source his ingredients locally.

"Is he in the office?" Zoey asked, tugging Jasmine's hand towards the back room.

She shifted the cup of coffee in her hand so it wouldn't spill as she took in the rest of the room as they walked. Faux, dark cherry wooden beams covered what used to be exposed pipes through the center of the room. Several boxes were stacked, unopen on top of the bar.

They walked down the hallway, past the new bathroom, and stopped in front of a frosted-glass door.

Atlas's light snores drifted out. Jasmine turned to Zoey,

putting a finger to her lips. "Be really quiet. Atlas is still sleeping."

Zoey nodded and mirrored the action, whispering, "Otay, Mommy."

Jasmine opened the door to find Atlas stretched out over the brown leather couch that barely contained him. His feet hung off the end, paint-stained work boots still on, like he'd crashed here after yet another long day of hard manual labor. He'd stopped by the inn last night for dinner and to help put Zoey to bed, which had become their nightly routine. He'd also tested out some dishes for the restaurant and got their opinions. Zoey thought she was a food critic now.

Jasmine's rooms had been booked solid all summer, but wedding season was winding down now that it was September. She and Zoey were still sharing a room, so that meant Atlas had had to find other accommodations. Bently had offered him a room, but he'd insisted he was fine on his own and had been sleeping in his restaurant.

Jasmine sat on the edge of the couch, running her free hand over his chest. Zoey walked over and planted a kiss on his cheek.

His eyes fluttered open before he smiled. "This is definitely my second favorite way to wake up." Atlas stretched and sat, swinging his legs onto the ground. He rubbed the sleep from his eyes. His hair was a wild mess, making her want to run her fingers through it.

"What's your favorite?" Zoey asked.

Atlas chuckled, his voice still hoarse with sleep. "That's a secret." He winked at Jasmine.

"We brought you coffee." Jasmine offered the still-warm cup to him.

He studied it suspiciously as he took it from her. "You made it?"

She rolled her eyes. "Just try it."

He took a tentative sip, his eyes widening. "This is good."

Jasmine smiled. "I got some tips from Remy."

Atlas took another sip and grinned. "It's perfect. Z, I've got some of the juice boxes you like in the fridge in the kitchen if you want to go grab one."

"Yay!" Zoey clapped and wandered out of the room.

"Can she get it by herself?" Jasmine asked.

Atlas placed his hand on her thigh. "I put it on the lowest shelf." He leaned into her neck and breathed her in. "I missed you."

"You saw me last night." She giggled as the scruff of his beard tickled her tender skin.

He set the coffee down on the desk to his right before wrapping both arms around her. "It's never enough."

"Well, I do happen to have a room opening up today."

He perked up. "Oh, yeah?"

"I think it's time you moved in. I mean, if you want to."

"Fuck yes I do."

She laughed. "Once the guys are done with your tables, they're going to start on the addition to the inn. That way we can all be together, but separate from the inn rooms I need to rent."

"Sounds perfect."

Zoey walked in, holding her straw and juice box out to Atlas. "Help?"

Jasmine reached for it.

"No, Daddy do it."

Jasmine blinked. She looked towards Atlas, who seemed just as stunned.

He reached out and took the items from her with a glowing smile. "Sure thing, baby girl." He handed her back the juice once the straw had been inserted.

Atlas glanced over to Jasmine, as if checking if she was okay with this.

"I asked Zoey what she thought of you moving in with us." She attempted to give him an explanation.

"How do you feel about that, Z?" Atlas asked her daughter.

"Happy."

"She asked if that meant you were going to be her daddy. So, I think that might be where she got that from."

His gaze landed on hers. "And what did you say about that?"

She shrugged, brushing an invisible strand of hair behind her ear. "I told her that's something she'd have to ask you about."

"I'd love for you to call me that if you both want it." Atlas grinned, his eyes sparkling with joy.

"You really don't care? I mean, I know it's a lot—"

Atlas placed one arm around Jasmine and the other around Zoey before pulling them close. "I promise to do my best every day to earn that title. I love you both. I'd love to be Zoey's daddy." He kissed the top of Zoey's head.

Jasmine's heart burst with the cuteness. This man was everything.

EPILOGUE - JASMINE
ONE YEAR LATER

Jasmine scanned the faces around the rustic, farmhouse-style table at what had become a monthly tradition of dinner at Atlantis with their family and friends. Remy snuggled up next to Mikel, laughing at something Mia had said. Andre held their new baby girl, Ana, sleeping against his chest. Bently's arm wrapped around Belle's as he gave her a kiss on her temple. Atlas slipped his hand over Jasmine's thigh, rubbing his thumb tenderly over her bare skin.

Fire zinged from his touch. Need and longing twirled within her. The pregnancy hormones had sent her libido skyrocketing. She ran a hand over the small bump forming in her belly. Zoey had been elated when they'd told her.

She turned to look at the man sitting next to her. He'd fulfilled his promises. Every single one. He'd used what was left of his nest egg to renovate the inn. He'd been welcomed into their fold. Of course, her brothers still had to give him a hard time now and then. But from the light in his eyes, she could tell he enjoyed their ribbing just as much as they did.

His restaurant was everything he'd described to her and more. People came flocking from the city to eat his fresh, seasonal cuisine. He'd invested almost everything he'd had left into his business—their business. He'd put her name on the deed as a surprise. Just one more way he'd proved he was in this with her. A true life partner.

"How are the kids adjusting?" Atlas asked Bently as the servers cleared the plates away.

Belle and Bently had added another teen to their home through fostering. It seemed everyone wanted a baby, but not many wanted the struggle that came with an older foster child. But Bently and Belle saw the need and opened their home and hearts.

"It's going." Bently chuckled.

"Amara is aging out of the system next month, but we're gonna let her know she's welcome to stay as long as she needs," Belle added.

Jasmine yawned. Atlas tucked his arm around her and whispered in her ear, "Wanna get going?"

She nodded.

"Well, it's been nice having you all here eating my food." Atlas chuckled. "But I need to get this one home before she falls asleep at the table."

They said their goodbyes.

"Oh, don't forget your cake," Remy said, a mischievous grin on her face.

"Cake?" Jasmine asked.

"I know you've been craving chocolate. I asked Remy to bring one for you." Atlas winked.

"You're the best boyfriend. Have I told you that today yet?"

He smiled and held her hand, leading her to the kitchen where his staff were busy feeding the few diners left this late.

"Once or twice." He lifted the small cake box from the counter.

"Have a good night, everyone." Jasmine waved.

"You too," Amanda, the other chef Atlas had hired to fill in part-time, said.

Atlas led Jasmine out the back to the Range Rover good ol' Grandpa Remington had sent after Oliver signed over his rights. He'd been cordial with Atlas at Zoey's birthday party. Eventually, he'd warmed up to his grandson, respect gleaming in his blue eyes.

Atlas drove them back to the inn—their home. She checked in with Rae, who'd been kind enough to watch Zoey for the night. After settling up with Rae, Jasmine opened the door to their section of the inn. They now had three separate rooms and a living space to themselves, but they still shared the kitchen with the inn.

She walked into their bedroom, taking off her earrings and slipping out of her shoes. She opened the top drawer of the dresser and grabbed the oversized sleep shirt before closing it seamlessly. She paused, her hands tracing over the old, wooden dresser, brows furrowed.

"I fixed it," Atlas said, closing the door behind him.

"My dresser?"

He nodded and slipped his shirt off, exposing his muscular chest. "Yeah. All it needed was a little love." He chuckled.

Truer words have never been spoken.

"And Zoey's sound asleep," he added.

She smiled as he wrapped his arms around her from behind. He tucked his chin into her neck, and his scruff tickled the sensitive skin, sending tingles skittering over her and congregating in her core. He kissed the sensitive flesh behind her ear. Her desire sparked with the tender touch.

"I want you," she whispered.

"Let's have dessert first."

"How about you have me for dessert?" she teased.

He laughed. "Just one bite of the cake and then I'm all yours."

Atlas lifted the lid and handed her a fork from his pocket before he sat on their bed against the headboard. She climbed in next to him, grabbing the fork and cutting down the edge of the extra-large cupcake. Jasmine pushed the bite into her mouth, tasting the moist, chocolatey goodness. She moaned. "This is heaven."

Atlas licked the top of her mouth. "Delicious." His eyes blazed with want.

Her heart skipped. This never got old—seeing his desire for her. She'd thought for sure it would wane over time, but it only seemed to grow the longer they were together, and the more intimate and vulnerable they were with one another.

"Feed me one," he commanded.

She cut another bite and fed it to him.

"Try the middle; it's the best part." He smirked.

She cut down the center, giggling. "Okay, chef, whatever you say. Weirdo."

The fork snagged on something. She narrowed her eyes and leaned in. A dark chunk of something hard had settled in the middle. She cut around it. "What the hell?"

Atlas reached in and picked what looked like a small ring box up, wiping the cake crumbs into the container.

Jasmine's eyes darted to his. Disbelief and hope swirled in her belly.

"Jasmine Evans—"

She slapped her hand to her mouth, dropping the fork in the box. "Yes."

He chuckled. "I didn't even ask you yet. I have a whole speech planned."

"Okay, go ahead," she said, her heart racing. *Oh-my-god! This is really happening!*

"You're the love of my life. You and Zoey deserve the world, and I want to be the man who gives it to you. Marry me and let me spend the rest of my days next to you as your husband and Zoey's father. I know she already calls me daddy, but I want to legally adopt her and make it official. And before you say anything, I already asked for Zoey's approval."

Tears spilled over her cheeks. "What did she say?"

He laughed. "She said she thought I already was."

Jasmine giggled. Joy poured out of her. "Yes, Atlas. I'll marry you. I'll be your partner in life and parenthood—in all things. I love you."

"I love you too." He opened the ring box. A silver band glinted back, the black pearl in the center surrounded by small diamonds. "I picked you out a pearl because like you it was forged through pain, but the difficult process turned it into something beautiful."

She wiped the tears from her face and held out her left hand. "It's perfect."

He smiled. "As are you." He slid the ring onto her finger.

She flicked her gaze between the symbol of her engagement and the man who'd stolen her heart. Grabbing his face, she slammed her mouth onto his. Her tongue darted out, tasting mint and Atlas. He groaned and pulled back.

"What?" she asked.

He moved the cake box to the bedside table. "There's one more thing."

She searched his face.

"I got tickets for Zoey, you, and me to go to Korea next month."

"What?" she asked, blinking in disbelief.

"So you can explore a part of your heritage. I've got a list of places for us to visit, and—"

She kissed him hard on the mouth, shutting him up. "I love you." She sucked his bottom lip, pushing him onto the bed. His hands reached for the zipper on her dress. He struggled for a moment, groaning with impatience. She broke the kiss and sat up, grinding against his groin before she lifted the fabric above her head.

Atlas's eyes zeroed in on her full breasts that had already begun to swell from the pregnancy. His hardness steeled beneath her sex that throbbed with emptiness for him.

"I want you so bad." He panted, and she raked her nails down his hard chest and over his chiseled abs.

"I'm all yours."

His fingers dug into her thighs. He jerked his hips forward, his cock pressing against her clit.

"God, yes." She sucked in a tortured breath.

He flipped her on to her back as he tore off his clothes until he was completely naked before her. He ripped free her panties before he climbed on top of her, settling his weight over her. His hands were everywhere at once, grazing up her thigh and over her soft belly. He sucked her nipples. His tongue twirled. His teeth scissored, sending a shot of lust barreling through her.

Her need built, greedy hunger splintering through her every nerve ending. Each breath was amplified. Every touch sent a thousand tiny prickles of hot desire burning her from the inside out. Love and lust and everything in between encompassed her in a hurricane of emotions. His kiss was life; his touch was heaven. Atlas's finger slipped inside her before swirling around her clit, sending a shock wave of icy fire bursting through her.

Close to the edge, she arched her back and moaned. He

slipped his tongue into her mouth, holding her tighter. Her hands moved of their own accord. Her fingernails dug into his back, pulling him towards her in the unspoken command. He dove inside her wet pussy in one hard thrust. She moaned, his mouth swallowing up the sounds. He rocked into her, wild and frenzied. He fucked her like the world depended on it. She wrapped her legs around him, opening herself wider so he could drive himself deeper until she didn't know where he began and she ended. She held on, bracing herself as he pounded against that magic spot and sent her flying over the cliff into her orgasm—free-falling into bliss. He moved in and out of her like a piston, keeping her weightless as the waves of pleasure crashed through her.

"Open your eyes," he commanded with a strained voice.

He kissed her jaw gently—a complete contrast to how hard he thrust. She met his gaze and he slowed his pace.

"That's it, beautiful. I want you to look at me when you fall apart this time."

He made love to her, torturously slowly, building her up to the edge and then backing away. The more he teased her, the more wanton she became.

"Please, Atlas. I need you. I want you to come."

He kissed her chest and shoulder before landing his mouth on her lips. "Whatever you need."

He sat up, leaning against the headboard. She climbed onto his lap, sinking onto his hard cock. Boneless and limp, she wasn't sure how she could ride him.

His hands gripped her hips, guiding her up his shaft and slamming her down. She should have known. Atlas always seemed to sense what she needed. His eyes locked on to hers. Jasmine wrapped her arms around his neck, throwing her head back in ecstasy as her swollen sex contracted around him. It felt too good to focus on anything else.

"Look at me," he ground out.

Her gaze snapped to his.

His neck muscles were taut like he was barely hanging on. "You're so fucking gorgeous. The way your tits bounce when you ride on top. The way your tight pussy clenches around my cock like it was made for me. I love how your skin blushes a deeper red the closer you are to your orgasm. And most of all, I love that I'm the one who gets to witness this. I'm the one taking you to fucking heaven."

Her orgasm rocketed through her as he tensed and roared her name in her ear. She held on to him, crying out from the intensity. His pupils dilated. His soul reached out to meet hers in the planes between the physical and the spirit world. They were forever connected in every way.

And later, as he held her naked body against his, when they moved through the twilight between awake and asleep, another piece of Jasmine was put back together. She was safe. Zoey was happy and healthy. A new child grew in her womb. And the most amazing man in the world loved her through her brokenness.

Atlas was true to his word. Every single day after that he proved he was there for her as a true partner. He wasn't perfect, and neither was she. But rather than running away, they'd run towards each other. Rather than lashing out in defense, they'd listen and give each other the benefit of the doubt. And when the dark clouds rained down over Jasmine, Atlas was there to hold her. Atlas, true to his namesake, was the man designed to carry her world on his shoulders when it was too much for her to bear. When the tumultuous seas rose, threatening to swallow her up, he guided her, his light giving her hope that she could survive the darkness.

She'd learned that the tattered, damaged parts of her could be beautiful. That through acknowledging her past and grieving it, she could shed the shame that came with the trauma. And her story was beautiful because she didn't let it define her. Jasmine was a warrior, turning her shame into her strength. The cracks were where the light shone through after all.

Jasmine became the embodiment of the lighthouse so that others lost in the storm would have hope that healing and redemption were possible.

She was a survivor.

The End

Thank you! We hope you enjoyed reading *The Lighthouse Inn*.

Want more of Jasmine and Atlas? Visit the website below to join our newsletter and get an exclusive bonus epilogue 14 years into their future.

WWW.AMKUSI.COM/TLIBONUS

You can also turn the page for a sneak peek of Chapter One in the next book, ***His True North*** (Book 5, featuring Charli and Finn's story).

Or visit the website below to order Book 5 in the Shattered Cove series right now.

WWW.AMKUSI.COM/HISTRUENORTH

SNEAK PEEK OF HIS TRUE NORTH
CHAPTER 1 - CHARLI

He's alive. Finn's alive.

Charli repeated it in her mind, a desperate attempt at self-soothing. She wiped the tears that hadn't seem to stop since she got the news five days and almost three thousand miles ago.

The sterile scent of the hospital stung her nose. She placed her hand on her growing belly.

"Your papa is going to be okay." She hoped it wasn't a lie.

She rested her palm on Finn's limp and clammy hand. His silver wedding ring was safely tucked in his personal effects. This was the first time she'd seen him without it since the twenty-year-old version of himself vowed to love her and cherish her until death do they part. Thick white gauze wrapped around his head. Superficial wounds peppered the side of his rich brown handsome face.

Could he hear her through the fog of the coma? *Wait and see.* That was what the doctor had said. "Come back to me." She choked.

"He will. My Finn is a fighter," Claire, Finn's mother, said, wrapping her arm around Charlie.

When did she come back? Charli tore her eyes away from the only man she'd ever loved.

Claire's warm brown eyes met hers with sympathy and shared pain. The woman's midnight complexion was a complete contrast to her own fair skin. But Claire was the closest thing Chari had ever had to a mother.

"I can't lose him, Mom."

Claire pulled her closer. Charlie rested her head against Claire's heart, the side of the uncomfortable hospital chair cutting into her ribs.

"Finn has a lot to fight for. He's got to come back to us, and meet his child. Not to mention, my son would never let anything get in the way of finding his way back to you, Charli." Claire's voice shook, as if speaking the words would will it into being.

"I don't think I can do this without him." Charli confessed, as she sat up.

"No matter what happens, you're still our daughter. We'll be here for you." Zeke, Finn's father said, as he came into the room.

He opened his arms to her, a rare showing of vulnerability and affection. She got to her feet and walked into his embrace on shaky legs. He patted her back as she released a sob.

"There. There." He said awkwardly. Zeke was a man of few words and even fewer emotions. Much like his son.

"Why don't you go get some coffee, and a hot meal? A walk will do you some good." Claire suggested.

When was the last time I ate? Charli turned towards Finn's unconscious body. Her stomach churned with anxiety. "I don't want to leave him."

Claire stood, taking her hand and ushering her to the

door. "You have to take care of yourself too, Charli, or you'll be no good to him when he does wake up. Besides, it isn't just you, you have to think about. You're carrying my grandbaby." Claire pressed her hand gently to Charli's small fifteen-week baby bump.

Charli nodded. "Yeah, okay. Call me if anything changes. I'll have my phone."

"Of course." Claire promised.

Charli put one leaden foot in front of the other. The tug to her heart to go back to the room was strong. But her mother-in-law was right. She needed to stay strong for her baby, and for Finn.

She walked through the large hallways in a daze. She found her way easily enough to the cafeteria. Her stomach grumbled, coming to life with the smell of grilled meat. She decided on a simple sandwich and a juice. She made herself sit at an empty table and dig in. Not tasting her food, she devoured it quickly in hopes of nourishing her body and getting back to Finn. Her phone rang in her pocket and she jumped. Heart racing, she pulled out her cell.

Mason.

Oh.

Her heart sank. Not Claire with news on Finn.

She clicked accept and answered. "Hello?"

"Hey, Charli. I just wanted to let you know we've got everything covered as long as you need. Turns out that temp help Bently, Andre, and Mikel offered? It's not so temporary at all. It's here for as long as you need it. Jasmine even said she'd wait tables. I guess what I mean to say is, you guys focus on everything going on with Finn, and take care of yourselves. We got your back here at the Shipwreck." Mason said, his voice full of sympathy.

"Thank you, Mason." Tears welled in her eyes again.

Stupid pregnancy hormones turned her into a water fountain. "I can't tell you how much that means to us."

"How is he?"

She swallowed. "Still waiting for him to wake up. But the swelling on his brain has gone down and the surgery was successful. The doctors are hopeful."

Mason was silent a moment, as if struggling for the right words to make her feel just a little better. But there was no such magic. "You guys are in our thoughts. The whole town is putting together a fundraiser so that the Reeds will have a cushion when you get home."

"Mason-"

Her phone beeped with an incoming call. She pulled her cell away from her ear. Claire's name flashed on the screen. *Oh god!*

"I have to go."

She didn't bother waiting for his response. She switched the call over and got to her feet, stumbling out of the cafeteria and towards her husband's room.

"Is he..." She couldn't finish the sentence. Hope and dread sparred for dominance in her chest, halting her voice.

"He's awake!" Claire said.

Awake. A surge of emotion flit in her belly. Charli ran like her life depended on it. Nerves swirled in her belly. Her pulse raced, ringing in her ears. For the first time since she got the call, hope bloomed within her.

Tears blurred her eyes once again as she burst into the room. A doctor and a nurse blocked her view. Zeke held Claire off to her right, love and gratitude pouring out of them as they stared towards the hospital bed.

"How did I get here?" Finn's deep voice rumbled through her, making her knees wobble. She covered her mouth and stepped forward, needing to see his face.

Finn's dark eyes searched the room, unfocused.

"Baby?" She stepped forward, unable to wait any longer to touch him. She reached out her hand, her fingers grazing his warm cheek.

"You're okay." Her voice cracked. She leaned in to kiss him, but he turned his head away.

"What the hell?" Finn asked. His eyes roamed over her, his confusion edging on panicked.

"Lieutenant Reed, do you know who this is?" the doctor asked.

"Of course, he knows me," Charli snapped. The notion that her husband of thirteen years could forget her was absurd.

His beard had grown in over the past several days of being unconscious, hiding his sharp jaw. Stitches marred his warm brown skin. She searched Finn's dark eyes, her usual source of peace, and the floor fell out from under her. "Finn?"

His brows knit together in concentration before relaxing. "Oh, yeah. You're Bently's friend, right?"

The room started to spin. Blood rushed to her ears. *No. No. No. This isn't real. Finn's still in a coma and I've drifted off into this nightmare. Wake up!*

"How old are you, Finn?" the doctor asked.

Finn turned to him. "I'm seventeen, obviously."

Claire gasped. Finn focused on his parents. "Mom, Dad, what happened? Why am I here?"

"You don't remember, Charli? Your wife?" Zeke asked.

Finn's gaze snapped to hers. "Is this a joke?"

The doctor stepped forward. "Lieutenant Reed, you've been in an accident. The truck you were riding in was hit and you've sustained a few injuries which include—"

Finn shook his head. "What? I'm not a lieutenant. You've

got the wrong guy. I'm a senior at Shattered Cove High School. I haven't enlisted yet."

Claire stepped forward and placed her hand on his. "Sweetheart, we're in Washington state."

Finn's gaze darted from face to face. His brows drew together, panic flashing in his eyes. "What year is it?" his voice trembled.

"Twenty-twenty-one."

He swallowed.

The doctor shone his flashlight over his pupils. "Amnesia can be common with head injuries like this. Your memories may come back to you in time." He continued explaining tests they would run, and listing Finn's other less serious injuries. But all Charli could do was stare back at the man she'd given her heart to when she was sixteen. Her husband, who looked at her as if she were a complete stranger.

She placed her hand over her belly growing a child they'd made in love. His panicked gaze followed her movement. His eyes widened.

His body trembled and he shook his head. "No. This isn't real!"

"I need you to try to calm down, Reed," the nurse said.

Finn struggled to sit up, pulling at wires. "No, this isn't-I'm not-"

"Pull yourself together, soldier!" The doctor ordered.

"Finn, sweetheart, just breathe." Claire came to his side.

"Maybe it's best if you wait outside." Charlie had no idea the nurse was talking to her until she tapped her shoulder.

"But he's my husband."

The red-haired nurse looked at her with sympathy. "This is a lot for him to take in at the moment. Just give him some time," she said, leading Charli out of the room.

Charli leaned against the wall in the hallway, refusing to

go farther. She collapsed to the cold, hard ground, pulling her knees as close to her chest as she could get. Fat tears rolled down her cheeks, soaking into the grey leggings she wore.

Finn had forgotten *sixteen years* of his life. He'd forgotten *her*. He'd promised she'd never have to be alone. He'd sworn after his last deployment, his enlistment would be up, and they'd raise a family. He'd made so many vows, and now he'd forgotten every single one.

Pain sliced through her heart. Flashes of moments shared. The life they'd built, gone in an instant.

All that was left was the unknown. For the first time since she'd married Finn, she felt alone. Stranded. Lost in a sea of shattered promises.

Will he remember me?

Would he come back to her?

Or was this the end of their fairytale?

To continue reading Charli and Finn's story, visit the website below to get your copy of *His True North* today.

WWW.AMKUSI.COM/HISTRUENORTH

JOIN OUR NEWSLETTER

The best way to get updates about new releases, sneak peeks, pre-orders, giveaways, and more is by joining our newsletter.

You'll also receive a **FREE** short novel that's not available on any retailer to read.

Visit the website below to join now.

WWW.AMKUSI.COM/NEWSLETTER

THANK YOU

Thank you for reading *The Lighthouse Inn*. We hope you are emotionally satisfied with Jasmine and Atlas's love story. If you enjoyed this novel, please consider leaving a review on your favorite retailer and sharing it with your friends and family.

Also, you can start reading the other books in *The Shattered Cove Series* right now!

Mikel and Remy in ***A Fallen Star (Book 1)***. eBook FREE on all retailers.

Andre and Mia in ***Glass Secrets (Book 2)***.

Bently and Belle in ***Defying Gravity* (Book 3)**.

Finn and Charli in ***His True North (Book 5)***.

Link and Emma in ***In The Grey (Book 6)***.

Lastly, if you haven't read our first complete series, ***The Orchard Inn Romance Series***, make sure you get your copy so you don't miss out on three wonderful love stories.

Thank you again for reading *The Lighthouse Inn!*

Cheers,

Ash & Marcus.

ABOUT A. M KUSI

A. M. Kusi is the pen name of a wife-and-husband author team, Ash and Marcus Kusi. We enjoy writing romance novels that are inspired by our experiences as an interracial/multicultural couple.

Our novels are about strong women and the sexy heroes they fall in love with, are emotionally satisfying, and always have a happy ending.

Discover more about us at:

WWW.AMKUSI.COM

To receive updates about new releases, giveaways, sneak peeks, pre-orders, and more, click the link below to join our newsletter today:

WWW.AMKUSI.COM/NEWSLETTER

After you join the newsletter, we will send you a FREE novella to read.

To contact us, use this email address amkusinovels@gmail.com.

Happy reading!

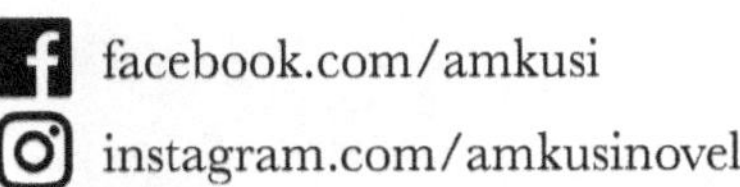

ALSO BY A. M. KUSI

A Fallen Star (eBook FREE on all retailers)

(Shattered Cove Series Book 1)

Glass Secrets

(Shattered Cove Series Book 2)

Defying Gravity

(Shattered Cove Series Book 3)

His True North

(Shattered Cove Series Book 5)

The Orchard Inn (eBook FREE on all retailers)

(Book 1 in The Orchard Inn Romance Series)

Conflict of Interest

(Book 2 in The Orchard Inn Romance Series)

Her Perfect Storm

(Book 3 in The Orchard Inn Romance Series)

For a complete list of all our books, visit:

WWW.AMKUSI.COM/BOOKS

www.ingramcontent.com/pod-product-compliance
Lightning Source LLC
Chambersburg PA
CBHW032102180726
48284CB00002B/413